The Gᴉ
to Aphrodite

Maria Savakis

To Eileen

best wishes

Maria Savakis.

Published in 2009 by Antony Rowe Publishing
48–50 Birch Close
Eastbourne
East Sussex
BN23 6PE
arp@cpi-group.co.uk

A catalogue record for this book is available from the British
Library

ISBN 9781905200900

Cover design by Temple Design and The Author

Typeset by Bookcraft Limited, Stroud, Gloucestershire

Printed and Bound in Great Britain by
CPI Antony Rowe, Chippenham and Eastbourne

With thanks to

My partner and my mum who have supported me throughout this lengthy process of writing and publishing. In addition a big thanks to Hugh, Nic and Jill for their help in the final important completion of this book.

About the author

The author's father was a Greek Cypriot and grew up in Cairo. Her mother is English. The author has travelled to America, Italy, Greece and the Island of Cyprus. She lives in Plymouth in the U.K.

PROLOGUE

I stood, surrounded by the ancient columns of the Parthenon. As if from nowhere a small girl clad in white appeared offering a gold box. 'Take this, a gift from Athena.'

Startled, I awoke, rubbing my eyes as if to erase the image. From my bedside table I selected a book, *The Psychology of Greek Gods and Myths*. As I flicked through the pages I encountered, on page 34, the goddess Athena. For a few wondrous moments I gazed at the picture, then closed the book and drifted off to sleep.

CAFÉ

As usual, the rain accompanied my journey to *Angelino's*, a small café set in the local South London community, with its play-area and internet service. I took a last, desperate drag on my cigarette which I then hastily ground out with my foot before pushing open the café door. Immediately, the aroma of strong Columbian coffee hit me. In the corner, I noticed Suzanne, my best friend and work colleague, who was hard at work cleaning tables. I'd only been in a few minutes when the door opened; it was Andrea, making her usual dramatic entrance, she was my Greek family friend and wife to Mandras, who supplied the café with continental and Columbian coffee.

'Ah, Katalina, please some of Mandras's strong coffee.' She paused to see a notice on the counter that said "25% off Greek coffee this week". Andrea's face dropped in horror. 'Katalina, what are you doing selling the coffee off like this? Oh my God Mandras will go mad.'

She looked annoyed as I noticed her immaculate red suit and matching red nails. For a second I turned to look at a black and white picture of Charlie Chaplin that hung on the wall; Suzanne had this idea that our customers would be impressed looking at a wall of photos of old film stars. I turned back to see Andrea glaring at me. 'Um, um, well it hasn't been selling that well lately … ' I began.

'Why ever not?' she demanded.

'Because the Greek coffee is a bit strong,' was my lame reply.

She stood silent for a moment, about to speak when Suzanne called across, 'Katalina hurry up!' sending me a glaring look.

Andrea turned to me again. 'Oh well never mind, I'll have some of the "25% off Greek coffee".' She paused for a second, running her fingers through her chestnut-coloured hair. She had obviously dyed it recently, as it was distinctly darker than usual. 'Anyway I didn't come in for that. Can we meet up sometime? You know, for a catch-up over things. I haven't seen you for a while.' I said that I would love to and then asked her about Mandras. He was apparently driving her mad, doing his accounts and flicking bits of rubber onto her newly-laid kitchen floor. Why he couldn't just get an accountant to do them was beyond her understanding.

When Andrea had left, I placed a cupful of beans into the grinder and pondered over what she meant by "things". The machine clattered as it ground the beans to a sand-like consistency. Suzanne called over once more telling me to hurry up as there were customers waiting. I could see only two, so I ignored her and looked out of the window at the pouring rain, thinking about the goddess Athena from my morning dream, imagining myself lying on a warm, sun-drenched beach.

Later on, more customers arrived including a young family who sat down near the play area and others who came to the counter to make purchases from our varied range of ground coffee. Then there were the internet customers. Along a shelf we had a few computers which had proved popular with local students. I also liked it, as it helped to relieve the dull moments. I sat down and checked my e-mails. There he was, Paul. We'd been communicating for several weeks. However, not having heard from him for a few days, I had begun to wonder whether he was still interested. Our messages to date had been stilted:

> **Loved the photos you sent, it looks a great place to go to. Love K**

> **Glad you liked the photos – did you see the TV programme on Channel 4? Love P**

> **Yes I did, wish I could time travel! Love K**

My messages had informed him that I was 26 and worked in a café. He, on the other hand, declined to say much about his personal life. His latest e-mails suggested that we should finally meet up.

> **Meet you at 7.30, Italian restaurant at the corner of Dower Street. Love P**

**Great, I'll see you there, but how will I
recognise you? Love K**

**Not a problem, I'll be wearing a black jacket,
look out for a gold tip pen, top right hand
pocket. Love P**

Okay, fine, look forward to seeing you. Love K.

This was it. Oh my God, I was finally going to meet him.
I was excited but apprehensive knowing that internet liaisons
don't always go to plan.

Suzanne was still busy elsewhere, so I stayed online and typed
in the word "Buddhism". Reams of text appeared describing the
second noble truth and … Suzanne called out pointing out that
more customers had arrived and needed serving. Reluctantly
I left the computer and served Mr Cotterill, a dear elderly
gentleman wearing an old tweed coat and carrying a newspaper
under his arm. He smiled at me as I served him with his usual
scone and coffee, and then muttered about a student at one of the
computers who was laughing out loud.

'He doesn't know he's got it made, does he Katalina?'

'You're right Mr Cotterill, he doesn't,' I agreed, thinking how
lucky the student was. Failing my GCSEs and being unable to go
to university, I'd had no chance. One teacher commented in my
end of year report "Slow but sure". What was that supposed to
mean – that I could take a lifetime to achieve anything? Unlike
Elvis Presley, whose photo Suzanne had placed on the counter.

The café door opened and Harry walked in with his mum. He
immediately ran over to the play area where he found a delicate
pink dress, which he slipped on over his head before admiring
himself in the mirror. Harry's mum stiffened. 'Harry please, if
your father was here … ' she exclaimed.

Her son's small but determined voice replied, 'But my father
isn't here!' Unable to argue with this logic, she shook her head
before ordering a hot chocolate and a coffee.

A lone woman sat at a window seat enjoying her coffee, when her quiet time was rudely interrupted by the arrival of two young, slim students who sat down at the table behind her and immediately launched into loud conversation. 'God you're not going to wear that are you?' one of them asked, looking at her friend in dismay.

'Yes I am, it suits me.' The dark girl raised her eyebrows and changed the subject.

Taking hold of my pad and pencil I went over to their table. Barely glancing at me, one of them ordered two cappuccinos as she brushed the rain from her suede coat. The women's laughter seemed to rise above everything else that morning.

'They're a right pair, you should see them,' I muttered to Suzanne.

'See them? I can hear them,' she said, looking back at me over her shoulder. 'It's the jet black hair and peroxide blonde; they couldn't be more opposite if they tried.' Suzanne then asked me what I was doing that evening, I told her about my new acquaintance and our date. She, of course, demanded to know how we'd met and when I mentioned the internet, she muttered crossly that I spent too much time on there when I should be serving customers. I retorted that I had a new internet phone, which seemed to appease her somewhat, but I told her that I would still need the large screen from time to time. Suzanne stood silent, regarding me for a moment before she reluctantly sighed. 'Fine okay, but take care this evening – you could be meeting the next Jack the ripper.'

It was still raining as I walked down the street and I peered up at the relentless grey clouds. I lit a cigarette, inhaling gratefully as I wondered what Paul would be like. Would he be tall, short, fat or thin?

Arriving home and in need of distraction from my thoughts, I placed a CD into the player: *Learn Greek in One Hour*. Immediately a profusion of Greek words and phrases poured out: *parakalo, kalimera, kalispera, efcharisto, ochi, nai.* I repeated the words one after another: please, good morning, good evening, thank you, no, yes; my friend Andrea would be proud.

From the table I picked up a book: *The Ancient Treasures of Athens and Olympia*. Opening it randomly, I gazed at the picture of the Parthenon: a great building and not the pile of rubble that some would call it. Watching the scenes unfold, I imagined myself lying face down on the ground, my fingers running through the stones and grit, the sunshine streaming down on my back. That Greek soil had been there for centuries, my Greek heritage, a heritage I knew little about. It made me think of my father. He had died five years ago. Since his death, I'd always felt there was a part of me missing. When I was small, he showed me a picture of the Parthenon; he was so proud as he told me how it still stood, even after the Turks had invaded.

I'd only known him for a short time, my mum having left him when I was young. A few years later he would visit me occasionally, always arriving with a brown holdall from which he produced boxes of Roses chocolates. We would go to Southampton to visit the Greek Orthodox Church. On the shelf stood a photo of us, taken when I was only four years old.

I picked up my book on the psychology of Greek gods and myths. At the back of the book I found an advertisement for an internet website which offered a personal self-help service:

"Visit Athelia.com, the unique website that introduces you to the Greek gods. Have a chat with your favourite deity," it invited.

Grabbing my new mobile I typed in the address. On the small screen appeared an image of a little girl advertising her name as Athelia. She had straight hair and grey eyes and wore a white dress – the image of the girl from my dream. Scrolling down the screen, I was urged to log on and chat with my chosen Greek deity – "We can fix anything ... " Curiosity overcoming common sense, I asked to speak to Aphrodite, goddess of love:

Dear Aphrodite I have found somebody and am meeting him for the first time

Dear Katalina	**What is your problem?**
Dear Aphrodite	**I'm not sure? Well, yes I am, I met him through the internet and …**
Dear Katalina	**You are worried that he will be an ex convict?**
Dear Aphrodite	**Yes sort of, but I'm sure he's not, he sounds great, but …**
Dear Katalina	**It's only a meal, my son Eros will send his arrow at the right time, don't worry.**
Dear Aphrodite	**I don't want his bloody arrow just some helpful advice.**
Dear Katalina	**Listen, you will be fine. Just make sure you have your phone with you. And wear something nice.**

An intriguing website, I thought as I logged off and went to get ready. In the bedroom I began pulling out clothes: some were too tight, others just looked awful. Finally I settled for a pair of clean jeans with a white vest and blue jacket.

I caught the no 22 bus which was twenty minutes overdue. Arriving late at the restaurant, I looked around anxiously. What if he's an axe murderer or just got out of jail? As I was having second thoughts and thinking about leaving, a waiter appeared, asking me if he could help. I felt embarrassed as I thought about telling him that I was looking for a man in a black jacket with a gold tipped pen. How suspicious would that look?' About to speak, I spotted a man wearing a black jacket, white shirt and jeans with a gold tipped pen in his right hand pocket. Paul, thank God. He was tall with short, dark hair and looked slightly older than I had expected.

'Hi I'm Paul and you must be Katalina,' he said smiling.

'Yes I'm Katalina,' I replied feeling my cheeks burning a little, as I took in his broad smile and bright blue eyes. 'God I feel such an idiot, I thought I was late,' I said nervously.

'No, no, not at all, I've only just got here myself.' Paul led me over to a table and courteously pulled out a chair as the waiter came up. Paul turned to him and introduced us. 'This is Luigi, my old friend.'

Luigi frowned slightly. 'Less of the old,' he said and turned towards me. 'Ah signorina, it's Katalina, I believe. Paul has spoken of you. I hope you have a pleasant evening.'

So Paul had spoken to this waiter about me already. Was that a good sign? 'Hello Luigi it's good to meet you too.' He nodded and passed us the menus.

'What you would like to eat?' Paul asked.

I quickly scanned the menu. 'Spaghetti, I think. That's what most Italians eat, don't they? God, that was stupid of me.'

'No, not at all, we do eat spaghetti, but we eat other food as well,' he stated, rather indifferently.

'Did you say "we" eat?'

'Yes, I'm half Italian, but my parents live in America,' he added as I detected a faint American accent. He went on to tell me that he worked at the university, teaching and researching ancient Greek and Roman history and worked for *The Times*, writing a column for them once a month. At that point, I felt distinctly inadequate. He was obviously intelligent, very intelligent. He asked if I'd ever seen the Elgin Marbles and I felt embarrassed to admit that I hadn't. After all, I was the Greek, not him. I used to think that they were round marbles with flecks of cream, but decided to keep that to myself. He suggested that he take me to the British museum some time to see them. Feeling the need for a cigarette, I took a packet out of my bag and asked if he minded. Although he said he didn't, he did look a little put out and pushed his chair back. So that wasn't a good move.

'Better now?' he smiled when I had finished.

'Yes thank you. I know it's a filthy habit, but … '

'Please don't apologise, my father used to smoke.' Taking another drink, he went on to tell me more about his work. The editor of *The Times* had asked him to trace the origins of an Aphrodite statue in Ostia, Rome that had been discovered by Edward Horatio in 1747. A Professor Buttlini suspected that it was Greek in origin and dated back to between 330BC and 340 BC, around the time of Alexander the Great. In addition, there was the possibility that the statue had been commissioned by Alexander himself. Paul asked me, rather patronisingly I felt, if I'd heard of him.

'Yes, he was a great Greek,' I replied politely. At present, the gold and ivory statue was housed in the Los Angeles museum under the watchful eyes of the Americans. 'That's amazing. You believe the statue could be Greek?' I asked, digging into my spaghetti.

'Yes. I thought you would be interested,' he said, noting my enthusiasm.

'So what happens next then?'

'I guess more hard work and travelling,' he replied, placing his glass back down.

'Travelling?' I enquired.

'Yes, to Greece possibly,' he said, pouring me more wine.

Paul stared at his glass for a while and I wondered what he was thinking. I had focused on the words "travel to Greece."

Luigi appeared, placing a bill on the table. We left the restaurant and Paul offered me a lift home. As I moved to get out of the car, he gently pulled me back and gave me a soft kiss on the cheek. Back in my flat I sat down and pondered. He was lovely; he wasn't an axe murderer; he was Paul and he liked ancient Greece.

The next day I told Suzanne about our date. She was all ears, wanting to hear all the details. I told her about the waiter, Luigi, and the fact that Paul had already mentioned me to him. Also that Paul was an archaeologist and liked ancient Greece and we would be meeting up again. She told me to be careful and to keep her updated.

SARIS AND SEQUINS

Over the next few weeks, Paul and I met up on several occasions, having coffee and meeting up at the restaurant. We talked about lots of things including religion. He said that he hadn't much time for it, having been brought up a Catholic, forced to go to church. However our main interests circled around the areas of ancient Greece and travel. It was fascinating as we talked into the early hours.

That evening, after returning from the restaurant, I suddenly thought of Andrea. Remembering that she had come into the cafe some time ago asking to catch up, I rang her suggesting we meet up soon. She sounded put-out that I hadn't contacted her sooner so I hastily agreed to her suggestion that we meet the next day, Tuesday, even though I had arranged to meet Paul later at the British Museum.

'Aren't you going yet?' asked Suzanne the following day, as she picked up dirty cups.

'Yes in a minute, just got to go on the internet,' I replied, listening to two students debating whether they should revise for their exams or go to see the latest "Rambo" film.

After a quick discussion, they concluded that Rambo was far better and a ten-minute revision spree would be enough.

'It's your afternoon off, anyway why can't you use your phone?' Suzanne asked in an irritated manner.

'Because I want to look at pictures of Cyprus,' I retorted, showing her my holiday brochure.

Suzanne flicked a page over. 'Um, looks great. Anyway I thought you were going to see Andrea and then this Paul.' She looked at me as if I should say more about him.

'Yes, yes, I am but I've just got to go on here first,' I stalled, pointing to the computer.

'Oh and don't forget our night out with the girls, remember, the Indian dancing,' she said turning towards the counter to admire her photo of Elvis Presley.

'As if I could … ' I muttered as Suzanne left me to it.

Typing "Cyprus" into the search engine, I glanced at the articles about the island, and in particular, Aphrodite's rock, a special place for young lovers. A recent news report caught my attention:

"A young Greek-Cypriot shot a Turkish soldier, close to the border, the Green Line, which separates North Cyprus from the South. The young Greek, named as Kostas Sokritos, had initially been involved in a peaceful demonstration. Later a mob of Greeks and Turks started fighting over a dispute involving the flying of the Turkish flag over the Greek occupied area. Greek and Turkish police Forces are co-operating in a manhunt for Sokritos."

I looked at the surname: Sokritos was my family name. 'Oh my god, Suzanne, look at this!' I gasped. 'A Sokritos has shot a Turk.'

'What are you on about,' she said as she walked across and peered at the screen. 'You haven't shot a Turk lately, have you?'

'Don't be stupid, but … '

'Just go and see Andrea, please,' Suzanne said, almost forcing me out of the door.

Had I shot a Turk? Of course I hadn't. I was still trying to dismiss the ridiculous notion when I spotted Andrea standing outside a haberdashery. Walking towards her, I noticed how smartly dressed she looked, wearing a Navy blue suit and a crisp white blouse with flouncy cuffs and collar. Her dark, shoulder-length, wavy hair revealed a soft yet strong face.

'Ah, there you are!' cried Andrea, waving at me.

'Yes, sorry, I hope you haven't been waiting too long.'

'No, it's OK. Please, we must go into this shop; there are some new, interesting materials that I want to see.' Long rolls of material lay on both sides of the shop, including silks and cottons, some plain and some patterned. One roll caught my eye, bright reds, oranges and yellows embroidered with gold. The Indian dance came to mind. Perhaps I should buy some and get Andrea to make me a special Indian dress, for tonight, but perhaps not. Andrea was staunchly Greek, and although tolerant of other cultures, somehow I didn't think she would quite approve.

I looked round to see her trying to carry five bales of material. 'I must have all of these,' she insisted.

'Mandras ... ' I muttered, trying to broach the subject carefully, 'what will he say?'

'Oh,' she flicked her head back dismissively, 'he will have to put up with it. It's for my new patchwork design: these colours are a must.'

I smiled and conjured up an image of Andrea walking in the door, laden with carrier bags and Mandras's face, or rather his mouth, opening as wide as a goldfish bowl.

After this, Andrea managed to drag me into five more shops, including some classy shoe shops. My feet were aching from all the walking around, plus I was carrying half of Andrea's bags. 'God, no more, Andrea please, my feet are killing me. Can we go and have a coffee now?'

Andrea shrugged her shoulders and smiled. 'Yes, it's OK. I think I have what I need now, but ... ' I hung onto the word "but".

'But what?' I asked when we were seated with our coffees.

Straight to the point as ever, 'When are you getting married?' she asked. I accidentally flicked some cigarette ash onto the table, coughed and then admitted to her that I had just met someone, not mentioning the internet, God forbid. She looked me straight in the eye. 'Ah, good, bring him around for a meal.' I accepted her invitation gracefully but somehow dreaded asking Paul, knowing what he could be in for.

As I left for the British Museum I had unsettling images of Andrea throwing question after question at Paul then dismissed such thoughts as I turned the corner to see the museum ahead, with its grand Doric Columns. A tall figure appeared from behind one of the columns.

'Hi,' he smiled.

'Hi,' I replied nervously.

He appeared so tall but then I conceded that I was unusually short. His height brought about a feeling of being protected, his eyes appeared soft and thoughtful. A brochure purchased, we headed for the Parthenon gallery, the home of the Elgin Marbles. We walked into a large rectangular room, two long walls containing the Parthenon sculptures portraying a procession of horsemen and other Greek figures. They were both grand and magnificent. At opposite ends of the room, there were some large, incomplete statues of the Greek gods including a grand statue of Apollo. Leaving the statues we walked over to the south frieze which displayed a motif of a soldier wearing a helmet and riding a chariot. The brochure read: "Elgin bought the frieze to England. The frieze was not so much a work of art but a prayer of stone." As I looked at it, I felt that it had a story to tell; a story of ancient Greece.

'Well, what do you think?'

'Incredible, just incredible, though they should be returned,' I said, suddenly passionate about my Greek heritage.

'What do you mean, returned?' Paul asked, staring at me.

'Easy, two-thirds of the Parthenon should be in Greece and the other third here. No, wrong, the whole lot should be in Athens.'

'Well I guess you're right, but that's how it went at the time, what with Lord Elgin … ' he said, looking perplexed.

Like lava erupting from a volcano I suddenly shouted, 'It's not good enough!'

A group of Japanese tourists stopped clicking their cameras and stared at me. Paul quickly took my arm, leading me away to the other side of the room and asked what was wrong. I felt an absolute idiot, thinking that this was a good way of destroying a new relationship. I told him that my dad was Greek and I had always wondered whether I had any other relatives in Greece.

Paul smiled and after a moment's hesitation asked, 'Would you like to come with me?'

I stood there dumbfounded for a second. 'Go with you … where?'

He looked at me. 'To America, Greece … my research; I told you about it.'

'Well … I … ' I stammered.

'Please, think about it. I know we haven't known each other for that long but perhaps you could find some of your relatives,' he suggested, leaning up against the wall.

The images from my holiday brochure popped into my head, along with thoughts of hot sun and Greece. His proposal came as a surprise. I was tempted, but like he said we'd only known each other for a short while. He told me I would need to make a decision soon as his editor was chasing him. I agreed to think about it carefully.

We walked to the end of the room and stood close to the Apollo statue. I found myself looking first at the statue and then Paul: both were tall, slender, and distinguished. Which one was my Apollo now?

'Can we go back to the west frieze, that's if you've calmed down?' he asked quietly.

'Yes, fine, sorry about that,' I replied, hoping I hadn't totally destroyed my image.

I followed behind him. There was the west frieze again, depicting a number of soldiers on horseback. I stared at one of them: a magnificent creature, full of fiery spirit and about to go into battle, gallant and heroic. I imagined wearing the helmet of Athena, standing next to the Parthenon, looking over the great sunlit city. The heat of Athena in my blood, my imagination fired. Lost in an imaginary world, I suddenly heard Paul's voice, 'Katalina, over here!'

Helmet, horse, Parthenon slowly disappeared from my thoughts. Back in the gallery again, sunlight replaced by artificial light, I followed him to another part of the room, where the east pediment of the Parthenon lay, showing the goddess Athena being born from Zeus' head. Athena had arrived on the scene fully grown and armed for battle. 'Athena, great Athena,' I announced.

Paul's perplexed expression returned as he slowly moved over to take my arm. 'This isn't going to be another one of those moments, is it?'

'No,' I reassured him, but then added, 'Athena coming from Zeus' head, it reflects her character, a character defined by logic and wisdom and a goddess passionately overseeing and protecting her city.'

Paul stopped in his tracks. 'Impressive, you know something about these Greek gods?'

I knew quite a bit, and told him my belief that the gods could reveal much about our own characters and what they represented. Incredibly he asked me to continue; I couldn't believe it. Someone was taking me seriously.

Outside the museum I told him about Andrea, saying that she wanted to meet him and reassuring him, or maybe I was reassuring myself, that she was friendly. 'Yeah fine,' he said and then offered to lend me a book on Ancient Greece. He really was keen for me to go with him, I thought, as we arranged to meet at the restaurant at the end of the week.

Back at home I sat down with a cup of coffee and logged onto the Athelia self-help website:

> **Dear Aphrodite** **I like him, he's not like other boyfriends I've had. He's decent, intelligent and he likes ancient Greece and we've met up over the weeks. And now he's asked me to travel with him What do I do?**
>
> **Dear Katalina** **Don't panic, just think about it – what do you really want?**

I wasn't really sure at that moment.

> **Dear Hermes** **I think I have my chance to travel. I look at you and see your winged sandals and how you fly up into the clouds above. I wish to fly above the clouds too, to look down on the land of the gods.**
>
> **Dear Katalina** **I'm impressed you know something about me. Yes I do fly into the sky delivering messages**

**to and from the gods and I do
wear winged sandals. All I can
say is that sadly you cannot have
winged sandals, but perhaps an
aeroplane will do?**

Having spoken to my immortal gods, I looked up "Indian dancing" and "Saris". Suzanne had palled up with the two students from the cafe, jet black hair and peroxide blonde, and had persuaded me to join them this evening at an Indian restaurant for a special night of dancing. Curious I was keen to find out more. What do you wear for such things? I looked at the screen.

"The Sari is both concealing and revealing. It is alluring, practical, demure and tantalising." The word "tantalising" captured my imagination, invoking a scene of floating, seductive Indian dancers. The quote continued.

"The Sari is surrounded by fantasy and legend and is made in various materials and worn in different ways. A full-length gown is sometimes used to cover a topless woman. It is usually draped over the body and shoulders."

Later that evening, I approached a small Indian restaurant near Soho, noticing two tall women dressed in short red skirts standing on the other side of the road. Suddenly, I spotted Suzanne. As arranged, we were meeting each other outside, along with the girls from the café. I recognised them instantly. With their jet-black and peroxide blonde hair further enhanced by their black and white dresses they reminded me of a chessboard. We walked to the back of the restaurant then down some narrow stairs into a square room, the vibration of Indian music pulsating in the background. In the corner, a small bar with an Indian barman eagerly awaited the first customer. A girl in traditional dress came up to us and pointed to a notice on the wall, written in bright red letters.

"Indian Dance Night! Have more fun – rent an Indian sari and experience the Indian culture as never before."

She ushered us into a small room where a clothes rail took up the length of one wall. Mesmerised by the display of materials, colours and dresses, I inspected them closer. The shimmering sequins, delicate silks and bright colours reminded me of Andrea's patchwork.

'Are you going to stand there all day?' Suzanne demanded.

Our two companions dived in quickly, pulling off their chessboard dresses. Suzanne introduced them to me as Monika and Angie, and I watched as Angie struggled into a small pair of sequinned sandals, whilst her friend, Monika, squeezed into a tight sequinned bustier.

Suzanne was rapidly losing patience with me, as I still couldn't decide what to wear and wasn't prepared to wear a flouncy sari. She had opted for a lavender petal skirt with a seductive slit up the side, and a sequinned belt. Not my personal choice, but after a heated discussion with Suzanne, I finally conceded to her judgement. I eventually settled on a pointy halter in deep purple with shiny sequins and thin straps cut in a v-shaped design. This had the desired effect of covering up my belly button.

'Here, try these.' The Indian girl passed me numerous bracelets in gold and silver, encrusted with tiny gemstones.

We sat at a small, round table with wooden stools and waited to be served. I looked around to see more people arriving. Some were already dressed in exquisite Indian dress; others were being led off to the changing room.

A tall, dark, slender man dressed wearing a white and gold buttoned tunic and trousers appeared at the table, holding a tray of Indian nibbles. I picked up one of the vegetable samosas and took a bite. 'God, that's strong, the spices nearly blow your head off!' I said, looking at Suzanne who by now was eating her fourth onion bhaji, only just managing to keep the crumbs off her sequinned outfit. Angie and Monica seem to be bulldozing their way through samosas, bhajis and various dips and relishes.

'They'll never be able to dance with all that food in them,' I said. Suzanne told me not to fuss and insisted that I drink a glass of wine. Suzanne had a habit of encouraging me to partake of alcohol, and in large quantities. This meant that I frequently found myself declining her invitations. Tonight, though, felt different. The music started and the first couple walked onto the dance floor.

'Come on, here's our chance,' cried Suzanne, grabbing my hand, and leading me onto the dance floor.

The pungent smell of incense filled the room. Monica and Angie were already in the swing of things, swaying their arms and circulating their bodies like exotic Egyptian belly dancers. Looking around, I could see everyone following some intricate footwork. I, on the other hand, hadn't got a clue and looked over to Suzanne trying to get her attention. Suzanne was in a world of her own, totally oblivious to my situation as she carried on dancing. Now desperate, I stood straight in front of her, waving my hands in front of her face. 'What do I do next?' I yelled.

'Just follow him, look.' Suzanne turned around still waving her hands in the air, her hips gyrating to the beat, and indicated for me to do the same.

Suddenly, a tall, dark, slim man, dressed in traditional Indian clothes grabbed me and swung me around. Looking directly at me, he said, 'Feel the goddess within you. Move your feet to the beat of your heart.' He continued to move to the rhythm of the music, saying again, 'Feel the goddess within you.'

I felt like a worm trying to wriggle away. The dancer stood directly in front of me and took my hand. I didn't have any choice. My dance leader continued, 'Follow your inner beat.'

The movements were quick and snappy with a quick turn of 360 degrees followed by a pace forward and back. I felt myself flow into the movements. He was about to take my other hand, when Suzanne appeared and snatched me back, pulling me away from the dance floor.

'What happened, why did you do that?' I asked her.

Against the backdrop of beating music, she yelled 'I rescued you. You don't want him, you want Paul, the one you've been chatting up on the internet.' Giggling, I told her that Paul had asked me to travel with him and asked her what she thought about that. She looked up, shocked, brushing away some crumbs of batter. 'I don't know, just think about it carefully. He sounds interesting. Just make sure you have your mobile with you. We don't want you being abducted, do we?'

The Indian music continued to play in the background, as I contemplated my friend's off- the-wall sense of humour. 'Thanks Suzanne your comments make me feel so much better.'

'I'm only joking,' she said, giving me a hug.

'Well we're meeting again soon and he wants an answer. Something about his editor wanting him to get on with the work,' I said

'Well, what have you got to lose? You don't want to work in a cafe all your life, do you?'

No I didn't. Perhaps she was right. I loved the Indian dancing, the sequins and even Suzanne but perhaps there was something else.

DECISIONS

Next morning, my legs were aching and thoughts of sequins and saris seemed distant now. Perhaps I should become a Hindu and run off to India instead. Taking my mobile I found more information on Buddhism, words of enlightenment, peace, causes of suffering, cessation of suffering; the four noble truths appeared. The text revealed the unfamiliar word "Dukka". I logged onto the website and spoke to Athena, goddess of wisdom:

Dear Athena   **I am tired and my legs still ache, and I'm about to go to work and what is Dukka?**

Dear Katalina   **Dukka means incapable of satisfying. Perhaps grasping is another name for it. In your case, maybe you do not know what you are grasping for.**

Dear Athena   **Please tell me!**

Dear Katalina   **How can I tell you? It is for you to find out. I suggest that you go to work.**

It was the beginning of December and Christmas was just around the corner. The streets were clad with the usual decorations – sparkling angels and stars lined up alongside an inflatable Father Christmas. A real live Father Christmas sat in the middle of the shopping centre with a bag of presents. Walking into the supermarket, I purchased my regular brand of Marlboro cigarettes and walked back past Santa who was by now surrounded by children with their scream of "That one," "No, that one."

Suzanne greeted me at the cafe door, peering at her watch. 'You're late, where have you been?' I made an excuse, saying that I'd woken up with a headache, not telling her that I'd been surfing the internet. 'Sorry, I can't help thinking about Paul, you know his proposal.' Suzanne could see that I was deep in thought and was just about to speak when Angie and Monika walked up to the counter. 'Well I think you should go, I mean it'll be an experience of a lifetime.'

'What will be an experience of a lifetime? Monika asked.

Suzanne looked at her then at me. 'Katalina's met this chap and he's asked her to go round the world with him.' I looked at her in dismay. Monika and Angie now had their eyes on me, waiting for further explanation.

'It's not around the world, it's Europe, Greece actually.' They immediately said I should go, that I'd got nothing to lose. I thanked them for their succinct advice. Suzanne disappeared for a second, so I served them. Overhearing their conversation, I asked what they were studying. Monica stopped in her tracks. 'Oh, psychology, it's really interesting but that paper was tough this morning. What was that psychologist called, you know the student of Freud?' she asked, looking at Angie.

'It was Jung, Carl Jung,' I interrupted.

Angie looked at me in astonishment. 'Yeah you're right, oh bugger! I never put that.'

I walked away in dismay. I could have done better. I vaguely remembered a psychology teacher telling us how our childhood traumas could stay with you, unless of course you went into therapy.

Suzanne was back behind the counter, serving a customer with a bag of Verona coffee. As I picked up my holiday brochure, she glared at me so I closed the book. Turning, I saw Paul in the doorway. He walked towards me and handed me the promised book on Ancient Greece. I felt my cheeks burn a crimson red, as I heard mumblings from Monika, Angie and Suzanne. 'Oh that's him, that's what he looks like.'

Paul, seeing my embarrassed face, turned to them and said 'Good morning ladies.' They giggled like a bunch of school girls. I ushered him to the other side of the cafe, telling him to ignore them. He smiled and asked me again about his proposal. I replied that I was still thinking about it and would let him know when we met later at the restaurant. He kissed me on the cheek and left. That was the easy bit, as I then faced Monika, Angie and Suzanne who just stood there gawping.

'What is your problem?'

'Um, um, nothing, just go with him,' they exclaimed.

My exasperated reply was interrupted by a customer who was keen to purchase some ground coffee. Unfortunately she was undecided as to which brand she should have. I told her that the Cafe Verona and the Columbian coffees were the most popular brands. She said she wasn't sure which one would go best with her evening meal of fish. 'Look, listen to this,' I said reading from a leaflet, "Cafe Verona has an exotic aroma, Latin America has a deep rich taste;" here smell the beans.' I placed a cupful of the dark brown beans under her nose. She moved forward and inhaled deeply. 'Umm, they do smell good. OK I'll take the Latin American, thank you.'

Mr Cotterill came in and ordered his usual English brand of coffee and ' … that especially large scone on top there, Katalina. The weathers awful Katalina, awful.'

'Yes, I know Mr Cotterill; it is, isn't.'

He proceeded to tell me that everything was so expensive lately and, as he put it, he was ' … only a pensioner.'

Suzanne came across and remarked that my apron looked a bit dirty. Hadn't I thought about taking it home to wash?

I sighed and said, 'Yes, at the end of the week.' I wasn't prepared just to hand-wash one silly apron when it could go into the washing machine with all my other clothes at the weekend. She snorted and carried on serving another customer.

Harry and his mum arrived and sat down. Immediately Harry's mum pushed a book into his tiny hands. 'Now, you look at this nice Father Christmas book, I've bought you. You don't want to dress up today do you?' she pleaded.

Harry shook his head, sweeping a glance over to the dressing up box. I walked over. 'My, that's a nice book,' I said. Harry looked at me disappointed and glanced longingly at the dressing up box.

Later that evening, I drove to Andrea's. Stopping at traffic lights, I looked up towards the clear night sky. There in the distance the stars twinkled. Lost in thought, I hadn't noticed that the lights had changed to green until I heard the car behind, furiously beeping its horn.

Andrea answered the door. 'You made it then,' she said, giving me a warm hug.

'Only just! I got stuck at the traffic lights, staring up at the stars.'

In the hallway, a Greek flag, at least 5ft tall, stood in the corner – not of Andrea's choosing. It belonged to her husband Mandras, a proud Greek. Just then Mandras appeared from the kitchen holding a bottle of wine in one hand and a corkscrew. 'How are you then?' he asked, leaning against the door jamb.

'Fine, thank you.'

Andrea interrupted. 'Except for being stuck at some traffic lights, whilst looking up at the stars!'

Mandras laughed and shook his head. 'You need children, a family; that's what it is.'

I groaned, 'Oh please, no. I don't.'

Andrea looked at me. 'He's right; you should be married by now.'

'Leave me alone, I've come round for a meal, not to face the Spanish Inquisition.' Andrea smiled, shrugging her shoulders, and led me into the dining room. The table was set beautifully with pristine white table clothes, silver place mats and expensive cutlery. Andrea explained that the children were out at a friend's house, so it would just be the three of us. Conversation darted between the latest family events, Andrea's passion for patchwork and, of course, Mandras's successful Mediterranean food business.

'Business at the cafe going well then?' he asked.

'Yeah, fairly busy,' I replied.

'How about that Greek coffee of mine, has that been selling?'

'Yes, sort of.' I didn't want to embarrass him, but the real answer was of course, no, not at all. Greek coffee was far too strong for the average British palate. Andrea quickly intervened, knowing that her husband's ears would prick up on hearing the words "sort of".

'Katalina, have you met any interesting people lately?' she asked, looking directly at me.

'Yes, if you mean Paul, the one you asked me to invite over.' I looked back at her, wondering what would come next. I looked towards Mandras sweeping back a strand of hair over his head and wondered if his hair looked slightly darker. Had he been using Andrea's hair dye again?

'Yes that's right, I mean Paul he sounds as though he'll be good for you.'

'Please Andrea no wedding bells yet,' I said, tired of her relentless match making.

The front door opened then slammed as thuds of footsteps marched up the stairs. Mandras looked up. 'Is that you, Stelios?' The footsteps stopped and I heard a faint mumbling of the words "Oh God."

'I heard that,' Mandras retorted.

A mass of dark curly hair appeared around the door, 'Yes, it's me Father.'

'Where have you been?'

'Out with friends, of course,' replied Stelios.

'Out with women, no doubt!' Stelios gave his father a glare and backed out from the room. 'I will talk to him tomorrow,' said Mandras, 'he should be training for the priesthood not running after women.'

'Oh shut up' said Andrea.

Mandras looked back at Andrea. 'Shut up? You mother him too much, that's your problem.'

Andrea stared back at her husband. 'No, that is not my problem you are … '

I coughed, hastily changing the subject, asking Andrea how her patchwork was coming along. Andrea conceded defeat and led me into the lounge to show me her latest design. A dress maker by trade, she now designed her own patchwork products, selling them to a specialised buyer situated in Bond Street. Squares of patchwork embroidered with silver threads and gold sequins were laid across the floor. 'They're lovely, Andrea.'

'Thank you, I am pleased with them,' she said, carefully brushing cotton off a square.

Mandras walked in. 'Sorry ladies to disturb you, I just remembered I have to feed Hercules.'

'Hercules, who's Hercules?'

Mandras looked at me as if I should know what he meant. 'My fish,' he exclaimed. I looked towards the fish tank strategically placed on a teak sideboard. One large orange fish – Hercules presumably – and two smaller fish swam out from behind a group of plants, surrounded by five miniature Greek temples. 'Ah, that's better, he was hungry. I'll leave you ladies alone now.' I wondered what he thought about the other two fish. Did they have names?

The evening ended; outside was pitch black. Mandras walked me to the door. 'You know, you shouldn't take Andrea or me too seriously with the match making.'

'No, I don't. I think it's quite sweet really. Anyway, I'd better go now. Thank you,' I said, giving him a quick kiss on the cheek.

During the evening I had asked Andrea if she would take me to see my dad's grave. I needed to visit the place where he had been buried – his funeral seemed like years ago. After work the next day, Andrea picked me up and we drove to the cemetery. I remembered visiting him in hospital just before he died. He had cancer and wasn't very lucid but kept insisting that I retrieve a red book from his bedside locker. It was written in Greek and I had assumed it was a bible. All I could remember was feeling terribly upset at seeing him like this. A week later he had died.

After some searching we found the grave. He had been buried alongside a plot designated for the Greek community. I asked Andrea why he hadn't been buried with the rest of the Greek community and she told me that my brother couldn't afford it. Facing the headstone, I bent and began to scrape away at the green moss that had begun to collect on the stone to reveal the inscription

SOKRITOS, STAVROS

Born 21/11/28

Died 25/4/02

My knees sunk into the grass below and sadness overwhelmed me. I didn't know what to think or feel. Tears started to fall as Andrea passed me a handkerchief. 'Here take this,' she said, placing her hand on my shoulder.

'I never really knew him. I just have odd memories.'

Andrea looked at me concerned and I asked her what she knew of my dad. She told me that he was a man with a troubled past and when he died they found piles of letters that he'd written to the Queen. Confused, I looked at her. 'Letters to the Queen?'

'Yes, he'd written them over the years demanding money back, compensation if you like, for the loss of money from his family business in Cairo. He had British citizenship, having come from Cyprus originally. For years he sent letters to the palace – he was a very determined man – but they kept sending them back. The rest of his life was a lonely existence working in a newsagent's shop.'

I was stunned. 'It's just I feel there are parts of me missing. It's horrible, it's … '

Andrea pulled me up. 'It's okay; you have us and you know you have your nephew, Father Stamitos, and your niece Sirena in America.' I agreed with her but somehow I felt that I had other relatives somewhere.

Later that evening, Andrea took me to see my nephew. I hadn't seen him since his wedding and I felt rather nervous, wondering whether he and his wife would remember me. They greeted us with their two little girls, Neola and Melinda. We chatted for a couple of hours and Father Stamitos suggested that if ever I had a chance, I should visit Sirena in America. It was good to see him again and for a fleeting moment I felt connected to my Greek family. As we drove away I didn't tell Andrea about the

33

possibility of leaving the country with Paul, I just reminded her that she would be meeting him tomorrow. Not having my mobile at hand to access the website, I imagined a conversation with Poseidon, god of emotions:

> **Dear Poseidon** **Help, I visited my dad's grave today. I now feel an overwhelming sense of loss.**
>
> **Dear Katalina** **Sorry, the pain of loss runs deep, but remember your father's spirit is inside you.**
>
> **Dear Poseidon** **Thank you, I think that helps.**

Later that week I got ready to go the restaurant. For once, I managed to arrive on time. Seated opposite each other, we looked at the menu: zucchini pesto pasta enveloped in pesto sauce flavoured with olive oil and lightly toasted pine nuts, topped with Parmesan cheese. Luigi appeared with a bottle of wine and poured some into our glasses. Paul asked what I had thought of the museum, to which I replied that it was excellent. I then had a sudden image of myself shouting and embarrassing myself in front of the Japanese tourists. He watched as I fiddled with the waistline of my skirt. I remarked that I wasn't used to wearing a skirt and that I would have to eat the pasta slowly to avoid my stomach blowing up like a balloon. He looked at me, slightly bemused.

'Well, have you thought about it?' he asked, getting straight to the point.

I fidgeted nervously. 'Yes I have … I will go with you,' I exclaimed, feeling a little apprehensive. But Suzanne was right, I didn't want to work in a cafe for the rest of my life, I wanted something different.

Paul glanced at me and smiled. 'Excellent I'm so pleased.' He leaned across and gave me a kiss on the cheek. 'I know we haven't known each other that long but I know we'll get on great together.' I smiled hoping that he would be right. 'Luigi' he called. Luigi appeared very quickly, smiling at Paul. 'Your best Italian wine, I think.'

'Celebrations eh?' asked Luigi.

'Yes,' said Paul, 'most definitely.'

I glanced at a picture of an old Sicilian village then turned and asked Paul how we would travel. He raised his eyebrows. 'Well, by aeroplane, of course!' he said.

Laughing at my foolishness, I thought about Greece and the possibility of finding my relatives. I'd only flown once before, ten years ago, and the prospect made me nervous, but the chance to get away from London was enticing. Luigi appeared and, giving Paul a wink, placed a bottle of wine on the table.

GREY CLOUDS NO MORE

Just before work that morning I practised some Greek. *Geiasas, me synchoreite, Antio*: Hello, I'm sorry; Goodbye … The language had seemed so difficult at first, but now I felt like I was beginning to grasp the basics.

As I entered the cafe, Suzanne looked up at me. 'Well, what happened? Did he ask you again?'

'Of course he asked me,' I said, deliberately delaying an answer.

'And?' she persisted, becoming noticeably more agitated.

I paused. 'Yes, I said yes!' Suzanne congratulated me telling me that I wouldn't regret it.

Christmas approached and I found myself crawling around the cafe loft; in the corner stood a rather crumpled-up tree in a torn box. I dragged it downstairs along with the few decorations we had left and stuck it in the corner of the café just by the play area. Fixing the tree in place, I arranged a few of the decorations on the branches then climbed onto a chair, attempting to position a rather worn gold star on top. Mr Cotterill, sitting nearby, had been watching. 'Haven't you got an angel?'

'Sorry, this is all I could find.'

'I guess it'll have to do,' he said, taking another slurp of his coffee. Must be religious, some people are never satisfied, I thought.

Harry was back, with his mum and her friend. 'Now, I want you to sit here and look at this new book we've just bought. It's your favourite, all about animals.' Another new book – I wondered whether he had read the last one. Harry looked over towards the play area. I could see him eyeing up the dressing-up clothes, looking at a little girl wearing the princess dress. Harry sighed and started flicking over the pages. I delivered two coffees and a chocolate milkshake to their table. His mum and her friend started chatting and were soon so deep in conversation they didn't notice Harry sneaking off to the play area. A few minutes later, Harry had persuaded the little girl to relinquish the dress in

36

favour of the cowboy outfit that his mum had suggested earlier. They stared at each other and smiled. Harry's mum looked up, aghast. 'Oh God, not again, Harry!'

Her friend stopped her. 'Just leave him, he'll be OK.'

'I'll blame you if he has a problem with his sexuality in years to come.' The friend shrugged her shoulders and they continued their conversation.

That evening I logged on to the Internet, typing in "Cyprus," and spent a few moments hoping to find any update on the Greek, Sokritos. Had the police caught him yet? Having found nothing, I typed in the word "Buddhism." A stream of text filled the screen quoting the Second Noble Truth, the origins of suffering and the attachment to desire.

The doorbell rang and I quickly logged off. It was Paul, picking me up to go to Andrea's. There he stood tall and distinguished wearing a smart suit, holding a bunch of flowers. 'Hi,' he said, handing me the flowers. He stepped into the hallway. 'Wow this is tiny.'

I looked at him, wondering what sort of place an archaeologist lived in: a castle perhaps. I realised that not only was I scruffy, but my flat also had the same uncared for appearance. I had decorated the archway to the lounge with silver tinsel which was now drooping from where it had originally been hung. Paul walked through, his head catching the tinsel on the way. I ran up and tried to retrieve it but by this time it had wrapped itself around his chin. He pulled it away and smiled. I could see that the decorations in the lounge had caught his attention, as he looked curiously around the room. The settee was covered with presents and Christmas paper. I found myself apologising once more. He looked towards the floor where the pink suitcase with yellow flowers lay open. Books lay in the middle of the case, with the odd piece of underwear stuffed in the corner.

'I can see you've started packing.' He picked up my book on the psychology of Greek gods and Myths. 'Ah, this is where you learnt so much about the gods, is it?' he enquired, opening it and scrutinising the inside cover.

'Yes, yes it is, it's a fascinating book.' I suddenly wondered where I'd left my mobile.

He put the book down and smiled at me. 'Hopefully you are going to pack some clothes for the journey.'

'Of course, just haven't really thought about that bit yet.' Changing the subject, he told me that his research would start at Vergina, the birthplace of Alexander the Great and the location of his father, Philip the Second's tomb. I nodded, telling him that I knew all about that. He looked impressed then told me that we would be meeting a Professor Yannis who would give us any necessary information we needed. I was intrigued, but began to wonder whether I would have the time to find any of my relatives.

We left for Andrea's and drove along the streets adorned with Christmas lights and decorations. Andrea's house was no exception – a large Christmas tree in the middle of the garden stood at least 8ft tall. As I stared at the glittering tree, Paul caught hold of my hand. I immediately pulled away. He turned to face me. 'I only want to hold your hand,' he said, looking rejected.

'Sorry' I said, slipping my hand back into his.

Mandras, who was not as tall as Paul, must have used a ladder to decorate this tree. I noticed their rooftop, also adorned with lights. How on earth did he get up there? I was amused by the image of Mandras struggling up a ladder, carrying a string of lights whilst swearing in Greek.

'Are we going in?' asked Paul. I could sense his apprehension, as he brushed down his jacket.

'Oh sorry, yes. Come on, let's go in.'

'Geiasas, Geiasas Katalina and this must be Paul,' said Andrea. They shook hands and Paul offered a tentative smile.

In the hallway Mandras and Stelios appeared. 'Ah, Katalina,' said Mandras, giving me a hug. He walked up to Paul, and enveloped him in a big Greek hug. 'You must be Paul'. Mandras stood at just 5ft 5in tall against Paul and the encounter amused me, Paul's face, an expression of disbelief at this gregarious

Greek greeting. 'Hi, yes, I'm Paul,' he murmured, stepping back from Mandras. Andrea led us into the lounge.

'Have you recovered yet?' I whispered, smiling.

'Yes, I think so. I'm not used to men hugging me every day!'

Andrea's lounge looked sophisticated with its colour scheme of blue and gold. Another large Christmas tree stood in the corner whilst a small wooden ship adorned the windowsill. This traditional Greek symbol acknowledged St Nicholas, patron saint of sailors. Andrea had once told me that Greek ships never leave harbour without an icon of the saint onboard. The small ship was a reminder of this tradition.

'Have you told her yet, about the trip?' Paul whispered.

'Um, no, I'll leave that until later,' I said, feeling anxious at having to face their reactions.

Mandras appeared with a bottle of ouzo and four glasses. 'Here Paul, have a glass of our national drink,' Mandras offered as he removed the lid. Andrea and I looked at Paul's rather shocked expression.

'Perhaps lemonade might be better,' I suggested looking towards Andrea, who readily agreed.

Mandras appeared a little disappointed and, shrugging his shoulders, mumbled under his breath, 'He's not Greek, what could you expect.'

Andrea turned towards Paul. 'Please just ignore him. He loves his ouzo but assumes that everyone else does as well!'

Mandras frowned then introduced Paul to Hercules, his pride and joy; the large goldfish surrounded by classical Greek temples. Paul agreed that Hercules certainly was a grand fish as we watched it swallow copious amounts of the flakes that Mandras poured into the tank. Hercules swam to the front of the tank. 'Are there any other fish?'

'Yes, somewhere in there. I know what you are thinking, there are more temples than fish!' I laughed.

Aware of some of the Greek customs surrounding Christmas, I asked Andrea whether she had managed the traditional forty days of fasting. 'Yes, I've managed pretty well, but hated not having being able to eat any meat. I've made *kourabiedhes* and *melomakarana* – traditional Greek biscuits,' she explained for Paul's benefit, before disappearing into the kitchen.

On the coffee table stood a wooden bowl suspended by a piece of wire. A sprig of basil wrapped around a wooden cross lay on top.

'What's that for?' asked Paul, looking curiously at the bowl.

'It's a traditional custom that some Greeks like to keep. The basil is supposed to keep away the *killantzaroi* from the house.' Paul looked bewildered as I continued. 'It's a mythical half-animal, half-human monster that runs wild, breaking furniture, eating the food and causing general havoc everywhere in the house.'

Paul stared at the sprig of basil. 'Sounds pagan to me.'

Andrea suddenly appeared. I gave Paul a quick nudge, hoping that she hadn't heard his last comment. She led us to the dining room where the table was laid with a small Greek flag displayed prominently at the centre. I could see Paul staring at it and then looking towards Mandras. 'He's Greek, get my meaning?' I whispered.

Andrea told us that Stelios, their older son, planned to go out later that evening, so we would have the place to ourselves. Mandras interrupted. 'Yes, out with a woman no doubt.' Andrea told him to shut up reminding her husband that their son was only nineteen. Then came the killer blow as she launched her first attack. 'Tell me Paul, what do you do for a living?'

Paul coughed nervously. 'I'm an archaeologist and I also work for *The Times*.' Andrea and Mandras nodded, looking very impressed.

Andrea spoke again. 'So, you earn good money then?'

I could see Paul looking agitated. 'Yes good money, I guess I do.' I sat there wincing, wishing Mandras would say something, anything. Eventually, he asked Paul what he was doing at the present time. Paul sat back, relieved to be away from Andrea's interrogation. Paul told him about the Aphrodite statue and his theory that it could be Greek. Mandras said that of course it was Greek and it was Paul's job to prove it.

Paul smiled. 'Yes well, that's what I hope to do and it's great that Katalina is coming with me as well.' Paul looked towards me. 'Oh and you'll meet my folks to when we get to America,' he added, placing his hand on mine. He hadn't mentioned that in the restaurant. Andrea suddenly dropped her cutlery and Mandras's mouth fell open. 'But you are not married … '

'I know but it's a good chance to find my relatives,' I answered, hoping that this might soften the blow.

Andrea went quiet, and started flicking her hair furiously over her shoulder. 'Well, perhaps it is a good idea. You should go to the archives in Athens. I'm sure your father had some relatives there.'

Mandras chipped in, 'Yes and you must see our beloved Parthenon as well.'

' I would love to,' I said, thinking about the picture my dad had showed me.

Thank God the worst was over, except for Mandras telling me that it wasn't right for me not to eat meat, that I was half Greek after all. Andrea worried that I couldn't speak Greek and insisted that I should ring her throughout our journey, reversing the charges. Paul stepped in and reassured her that most people spoke English. 'Of course, I know, but … ' she said. Mandras hit the roof and suggested that postcards would be better. I smiled at Andrea, knowing she would quietly have her way.

And that was it. A few weeks later I was off, goodbye cafe, goodbye. I was a little sad to leave the regular customers: Mr Cotterill with his gentle griping; Harry and his mum – I wondered how he would turn out; even Suzanne. On my last morning, they presented me with a small goodbye gift – a picture of a coffee bean with their signatures around the edge.

Having never been there before, Heathrow airport appeared very large. A Boeing 737, I was impressed. 'Wow,' I said.

'It's not that large,' Paul gently remarked as I handed my bright pink suitcase with the yellow flower print to the girl at the desk. The thought of not being able to smoke for eleven hours filled me with dread, so I persuaded Paul to wait whilst I had a final cigarette in the designated smoking area. I sat huddled on a stool, next to other people desperately inhaling their last shot of nicotine. A woman in front of me kept flicking ash onto the floor. I thought this strange, considering the area had numerous ashtrays lying around. Taking my mobile out, I quickly conversed with my Greek gods:

Dear Athena   **I know it's a bit late now, but I'm anxious about Paul. Will we get on and will I find my relatives? Oh and flying. I'm still nervous?**

Dear Katalina   **It's only natural to be anxious about a new relationship. You will need Aphrodite on your journey and Hermes to help you with your fear of flying.**

I stubbed out my cigarette and found Paul again. He suddenly asked, 'Why do you smoke so much?'

'Easy,' I replied, 'I'm nervous of flying at this precise moment.'

Next we took a visit to Boots. Taking hold of a basket, I threw in garlic tablets, cod liver oil, Kalm tablets and a bottle of Vitamin C.

Paul looked inside the basket. 'What do you need all those for?'

I pointed to each bottle in turn. 'This one for fighting foreign bugs, this one in case I have to run anywhere and … '

'Run, run where?'

I hesitated for a second. 'You know, run. Run to get my suitcase off the carousel before it disappears.'

He looked at me puzzled. 'Disappears? It doesn't disappear. The case comes back round again.'

'Oh, right,' I said, feeling as stupid as ever.

'Anyway, I get the picture. We'd better hurry; our flight number has come up.' Paying for my collection of medications, we walked outside and found our flight number on the arrival board. I stared at the board, mesmerised by the clicking sound as each destination flicked over. Still nervous of flying, I imagined myself sitting elegantly in my seat, sipping cocktails then accidently pressing the button that would cause my seat to suddenly recline backwards, inelegantly, smacking into the person behind me, just like that old TV advert. I burst out laughing. Paul looked at me perplexed as I relayed this story to him. He said that that was unlikely to happen.

'Oh,' I said thinking he was being a bit too serious.

Finally we boarded the plane. I sat by the window with my fingers in my ears, furiously sucking sweets as the plane took off. As it rose into the sky, my stomach gave a leap and for a second, I wished I hadn't sat by the window. I closed my eyes as I didn't dare look at Paul knowing that he might think it was funny – he was used to flying. When the plane levelled out, I opened my eyes to look out. Down below, bits of England remained. It did seem like bits: bits of land, bits of buildings, nothing fully discernible as it slowly disappeared. Then the clouds – of course there would be clouds. You had to have clouds above England. I imagined myself sitting on one of those great clouds; they looked so soft and light. I didn't know how long I had been staring out of the window, when Paul asked me if I was okay. I said I was fine, and opened my Los Angeles guidebook – Hollywood! Surely we could visit Hollywood – the stars' homes, Sunset Boulevard and the Walk of Fame.

I showed Paul the pages and smiled. 'Well we can go there, I suppose,' he said, somewhat reluctantly.

'We have the Queen – you Americans always rave on about royalty. You have Hollywood which we Brits swoon over, so here is my chance' I said.

'I guess that's one way of looking at it,' he said as he placed his cup down. 'It's just that I grew up around there, so it's not such a novelty.'

Time passed quickly as I flipped through my travel book and watched some of the in-flight entertainment. Switching off the TV screen I asked Paul how he had become an archaeologist. Placing his book down, Paul's eyes peered above his glasses, giving a look that seemed to ask, "Do you have to interrupt me now?"

'Well, when I grew up in the States, I was originally interested in film-making, like my uncle.'

I interrupted. 'Film-making?' My eyes were as large as golf balls. I thought of the picture of Jayne Mansfield's house in my travel book.

Paul sat back looking as though he would have to explain everything. 'Yes, film-making. When I went to college, I studied journalism and ancient history. It was the ancient history that got me, the fascination that artefacts can tell us stories about generations and cultures that have existed over the centuries – I was hooked. After my degree, I was offered a place in London for further study, that's how I came to England. The ancient history took off along with the journalism.'

The overhead announcement broke into our conversation, informing us that we were to land in 30 minutes. Instantly, almost a quarter of the passengers stood up, squeezing past each other to get to the toilet. I watched them lining up along the aisle and became convinced that the plane would tip over, as most of the occupants were on one side of the aircraft. I voiced my concerns to Paul and he reassured me everything would be OK.

Looking through the window I could see the tips of buildings. This was Los Angeles. I felt a moment of sadness as this was the place where my brother, Stephanus, had died of a heart attack whilst working as a diplomat for the Greek government, leaving his distraught wife and two grown-up children behind. I'd only met him a couple of times, the last being at my nephew's wedding in London. I remembered that day well – my brother was pleased to see me. He had looked after me that day, buying me cups of coffee and chain smoking his way through countless cigarettes. A month later he was dead. I wished I could have turned the clocks back.

LOS ANGELES

'Put your finger on the gel and then on the mirror, ma'am,' the guard instructed. Gel, what gel? And what mirror? I took out my passport, only to drop it a second later. Staring into the eyes of the immigration officer, I proceeded to put my index finger on the mirror and then the gel. He glared at me. 'Please ma'am, the other way round.'

'Oh, now I see.' I giggled nervously. Paul shook his head in dismay.

Then came the baggage collection; horror upon horror. Three pink suitcases with yellow flowers sailed by and I was about to grab one of them, when a lady with a broad American accent claimed that they were all hers.

'But one of them is mine,' I insisted. She ignored me as her partner snatched up all three cases. I stood back as Paul grabbed his battered old case. Mine turned up moments later.

We worked our way through the airport lounge to see a barrage of people leaning over the rails awaiting their families and friends. I stopped to admire some beautiful African clothes displayed in a glass cabinet. One blue dress had silver threads around the waist; another, a strip of gold thread running along the edge of the hemline.

Paul took my hand 'Come on honey,' he announced in an American drawl.

Honey? Oh God! 'Honey or is it marmalade? That's what you put on your toast and belongs to Paddington bear in London,' I called out, as Paul marched ahead. I wondered if he'd heard me.

We took a rental car to the hotel. Everything loomed large: the pavements were as wide as English roads; the palm trees and high rise buildings lit up with neon signs. The Hotel Figueroa, along Olympic Boulevard, was a mid-range, exotic-looking place; a mixture of artefacts and wrought iron, with everything hand-painted, including the elevators, doors and ceilings, not forgetting the Mexican tables and chairs and huge pots filled with unusual plants. That evening, we tested out the Indian clay-pit restaurant, which served both Indian and Mexican food. The Mexican food had a distinctive flavour and a piece of red chilli caught the back of my throat, making my eyes water.

'So, what's the plan for tomorrow?' I asked, trying not to choke.

'Easy, find the museum where the Aphrodite statue is housed. I need to check it out and … '

Thinking of Hollywood, I blurted out ' … then go to Beverly Hills?'

'You must be joking. I grew up around there. It's so … ' He stopped as he saw the pained expression on my face. 'I don't see what the big deal is anyway,' he finished.

'I told you – we have the Queen, you know the royal family that you Americans are always so interested in. You have Hollywood. We watch all your blockbuster films, so … '

'Yes, yes, I remember what you said before,' he retorted, looking at me impatiently.

'So please, a quick tour?' I pleaded.

'Ok. I'll take you around after we've been to the museum.'

Los Angeles County Museum was located along Wilshire Boulevard and consisted of five buildings around a central courtyard. There it was – the Aphrodite statue in all its glory. Its size suggested that it had been created for some sort of public place. A grand piece, possibly commissioned by Alexander the Great, it towered above me, as I stretched my head back and looked up. The graceful curves of white marble seemed to pirouette from top to bottom. I turned to walk away and an eerie silence predominated until the sudden clip clop of my boots resounded on the floor beneath my feet. I stopped to see if anybody had noticed me – only Paul, who turned and looked down at my feet. I shrugged then whispered in his ear, 'I am not going to take these boots off, if that's what you're thinking.'

'The thought never crossed my mind,' he replied, looking down at my boots once more.

We walked around in silence, an eerie silence except for the incessant, embarrassing clip clop of my boots on the shiny floor. The museum attendant appeared solemn. I wanted to poke him to see if he would speak. I stopped to look at the floor mosaic of Perseus. Delicate pieces of ceramic had been put together to create another Greek masterpiece.

Outside the main building, the weather had become cold and wet. Unbelievably, the British weather seemed to have followed us. Having a sudden craving for nicotine, I tugged on Paul's jacket sleeve. 'I've got to have a cigarette, that silence has freaked me out, but where do I smoke? I've heard about LA and the laws on smoking – I don't want to end up in jail,'

'You make me laugh. I'll go and ask the attendant over there,' he said, and promptly walked off, returning a moment later to point me in the appropriate direction. 'Over there, just outside the doors. Go and have your "fag," ' he said, deliberately putting on an English accent. 'I'll wait here.'

Outside the museum, I sat on the wall, lit a cigarette and looked at my watch. It was 2pm and I wondered what Suzanne would be doing. It would be 8pm in the evening back home – perhaps she was watching television or going out with peroxide blonde and jet black hair.

Hollywood was next. I held the map on my lap, scrutinising all the famous names.

'I want to see Robbie Williams, Elizabeth Taylor, Steve Martin and … '

Paul slammed on the brakes. 'Stop! You'll see them, but let me take a look at the map.' Snatching it from me, he told me that we couldn't hang around the houses too long, because the security police would think we were "staking out the joint." We ended up going round Beverley Hills quickly, although I did manage to see some rather large mansions, more wide roads and thick, tall trees. These stars really had loads of money. One house, belonging to Steven Spielberg was so huge, I asked, 'How could he have the conscience to live there? You could fit six families in there!'

Paul said, 'Well he doesn't live there he lives … oh I don't know, can we move on again?'

Paul drove on, as I carried on about the plight of starving children in Africa, which he did agree on, so at least we had shared some common ground on the affairs of humanity.

On the breakfast menu next morning were American pancakes with syrup. Paul suggested that I should try one. I complained, saying that normally I only had pancakes on Shrove Tuesday and they were terribly fattening.

The waiter peered down at me, listening to our conversation. 'You're Australian, aren't you?' My mouth dropped open and I told him, indignantly, that I was half Greek and half English. The waiter wrote down our order. 'Oh wow, English, I'm always getting you English mixed up with the Australians.'

I shuffled in my seat. 'Why do they say that? Our accents are entirely different!'

'Not to many Americans, they're not,' replied Paul, looking at me disconcertingly.

Driving out from Los Angeles and along the famous 405 freeway towards my niece's home, our conversation revolved around me remarking that everyone was driving on the wrong side of the road, to which Paul reminded me that it was only the British and Australians that drove on the left. I admitted defeat and kept my mouth closed at that point. Just before we arrived at my niece's I started wondering how we would get on. The last time I had seen her was at my nephew's wedding – would she even remember me?

The car slowed down as we entered Lancaster, a new city in the middle of Antelope Valley. Sirena came out to greet us. Inside, her husband Daniel and their children welcomed us, along with Georgette, my brother's widow. Sirena showed us to our rooms.

The sound of twittering birds woke me the next morning. I was in America and found it was strange to hear birds singing; somehow, I had the peculiar idea that twittering birds only existed in England.

In the kitchen, Georgette gave me a small velvet pouch. 'Please open it' she said. Gently, I pulled the tiny cord and placed my hand inside to pull out a ring – it was solid gold with a figurehead of Athena. Georgette looked at me. 'It was your father's originally then your brother wore it. They both loved Athena.' I loved Athena as well, so perhaps there was some deep-rooted Greek connection after all. The ring was too big so I hooked it on to my necklace.

I thanked her and went off to find Paul. Walking into his room, I placed the ring under his nose. 'Here look at this,'

He peered down at it. 'Right; a ring – what's so special … ?'

'It's a figurehead of Athena. It was my dad's then my brother's. They both liked Athena and so do I.' I glanced at the pinstripe suit he was wearing. 'That looks really smart, it reminds me of Al Pacino' I said, thinking of the Mafia.

Paul smiled. 'Thanks; I know you don't like it.'

'Yes I do, it's very smart,' I replied

Later that morning we went our separate ways. Paul went to the museum and had arranged to meet his father afterwards; something about some unfinished business. I stayed with Sirena and her family and they took me to Universal Studios. I thought of all the films I had seen, many beginning with the famous Universal Studios logo splashed across the screen. We queued up for the tram that took us round the outside locations of famous film sets. The tour guide told us about the trip, explaining how long it would take. I quickly snapped a few photos on the way and then realised that I'd probably forget what all the pictures were anyway. At least it would be proof I had gone there. The tram stopped again. 'Here are the aeroplane remains used for *War of the Worlds*, with Tom Cruise,' the guide announced, as we saw a fabricated aeroplane crash, with one half of the plane upright and the other half upturned on a bank.

Carnage everywhere – it looked so realistic. As I stared at the mess, I shuddered – I had just been on an aeroplane myself. The thought of a crash was too horrifying to consider. The tram moved on. *Jaws* was next as we passed a small pool with a plastic figure of a shark emerging from the water. Then the theme rides, including *Back to the Future*, *The Mummy* and many more. *Back to the Future* nearly gave me a panic attack, as we were shut in *that* car, with a virtual reality 3-D film around us. The car sped into space over planets, across rocks then suddenly plummeted down to the ground. The movements were fast and jerky. *Shrek* was next. Sitting in a cinema wearing 3-D glasses, Shrek the Ogre leapt out as donkey sprayed water on us with a sneeze. Yuck – but very effective.

Next stop, Hollywood Boulevard and the Walk of Fame; I had imagined the California sunshine, beating down on some exclusive, segregated area containing these much sought after paving slabs. Wrong! Unfortunately, it was raining heavily and the star pavements were ordinary paving slabs. After getting over my disappointment, I took the map that listed the names and numbers so that I could find my favourite star – Johnny Depp, no 7018. Sirena followed me. First we walked in the wrong direction then we turned around again and there, under some workmen's scaffolding, lay the stone marked "Johnny Depp." I quickly whipped out a camera and took a few shots.

In the evening, they took me to a Greek restaurant: tables of blue and white-checked tablecloths, along with some vaguely Greek-looking waiters, whom Sirena described as looking more Italian than Greek. We ordered fire feta, a Greek dip served with pita bread. The waitress opened out a folding table onto which she placed a small stove and a frying pan. She put the feta cheese in the pan and lit the stove. Brilliant red and yellow flames arose from the pan as the cheese fried. Suddenly, two swing doors were flung open as a belly dancer appeared, gyrating her hips to the music which seemed more Arabic in origin than Greek.

Georgette looked across at me suddenly. 'You know, your dad always wanted your brother to be a priest but Stephanus said it was impossible, as he liked women too much.' I thought about poor Stelios and his dad, how Mandras wanted him to be a priest!

Later that evening Paul returned. He appeared deep in thought and took me out into the garden so that we could have some time alone. I asked him what was wrong, how the meeting with his father had gone. Paul sighed. 'He just didn't listen, criticising me, not accepting that I was an archaeologist, he just kept on at me.'

'Do you still want me to come with you to meet him tomorrow?' I asked, feeling apprehensive.

'Yeah sure, don't worry he's looking forward to it,' replied Paul, smiling tentatively.

Returning to the kitchen, we sat down and Georgette passed me some photos of my brother. The photos brought a lump to my throat; he was gone. If only I could have turned the clock back, anything so I could have got to know him better. I had only met my brother twice – once at my dad's funeral, the next time at my nephew's wedding. I took hold of a photo taken at my nephew's wedding; it was striking, a side shot of him, wearing a smart wedding jacket with a crimson tie and a rose in his top pocket. Georgette passed me a photo of my father dressed in army uniform, taken when he lived in Cairo. Sirena told me more about him; that he was born in a village called Nata, in Cyprus. His parents were farmers and had been quite poor. They emigrated to Cairo in the 1930s and the family built up a successful clothing business, only for it to be taken away years later by President Nasser. My father had a British passport and Nasser wanted to throw out people who had British citizenship.

I stopped Sirena. 'Andrea said something about a British passport and writing letters to the queen, to get his money back.'

'That's right. My father, your brother, found those letters when they were clearing your dad's house out.'

It was the next piece of information that got to me. My dad had been working as a clerk when he was arrested by the Arab police, taken in for questioning and tortured. Miraculously, my dad's first wife knew the wife of a police commissioner and

convinced her that my dad was innocent. She in turn convinced
her husband. My father was helped to escape by an accomplice
dressed as a washerwoman who exchanged clothes with him.
My dad's wife got him on a ship to England, knowing that if
he had been caught, he would have been executed. James Bond
or what? This was so surreal, I was stunned. Paul looked at me
blank faced. I asked Sirena why my dad had been taken in for
questioning, but she didn't know.

Alena and Damario, Sirena's children, came running into
the kitchen. 'Look what he's wearing!' said Alena, as her father
lifted her up in his arms. Damario, with his cute looks loved
Father Christmas, in fact anything to do with Christmas. There
he stood wearing a red hat and red costume. Everybody stared
and then burst out laughing.

'Hey big guy it's not Christmas!' said Daniel

'I know,' he squeaked. Daniel made me think about my own
father.

That evening, I surfed the net in search of some consolation
from Zeus, the king of the gods:

Dear Zeus   **A father? Fatherly love??**

Dear Katalina **We have not spoken before.
Fatherly love. That is a good
question. I have been a father
and these are the things I've
managed to give my children:
to Artemis, the goddess of the
hunt, I gave bows and arrows,
if you like physical courage; to
my daughter Athena wisdom,
courage and the ability to
negotiate in times of war. Above
all else, I gave protection to all
my children.**

Dear Zeus Wow, but you were the god of all gods, where does the power bit come in?

Dear Katalina Please don't belittle me but you are right. I was a proud father, but like any human, well, god and human all rolled into one, I made mistakes. At times, I could be too controlling and too overbearing.

Dear Zeus Thanks, but what about lifting your children up, you know, holding and cuddling them?

Dear Katalina You need Poseidon.

Poseidon speaks Yes, my brother is right, I was the emotionally responsive one and would often lift my children up, laugh and play with them.

Dear Poseidon Thanks, I never really experienced that from my father. But what were your faults?

Dear Katalina Please! I'm the god oh … no, Zeus was honest and right, yes, my faults were my anger. If things didn't go right, an onslaught of rage would surge up through me; my children did run away at times.

Dear Poseidon My emotions were further disturbed today, as I was told that my dad was tortured, the pain and the injustice, it's unbelievable? All I can imagine

is seeing him sitting with his head in his hands, in a small concrete prison jail, wondering what his fate would be.

Dear Katalina **Yes, I'm sorry your emotions were stirred from hearing such a tale.**

Dear Poseidon **It wasn't a tale. It was true.**

Dear Katalina **Yes I know, give me a chance! I feel your pain; humankind can be cruel, misunderstood and vengeful. My advice is keep in touch with your emotions over the next few months; they will teach you many things.**

Just as we were leaving next morning, I walked into Paul's room to find papers and books sprawled across the floor. 'God a bomb's landed,' I exclaimed, wondering how long it would take him to pack everything up.

'Yes OK, but listen to this,' he said picking up a large book. "*Alexander the Great, born 20th July 356 BC. One main source, the biographer Plutarch, writes that Alexander's father Philip II, King of Macedonia, married Olympias. Alexander inherited a troubled past. A disunion of hearts between his parents was to lead to his estrangement from his father. The great Aristotle influenced Alexander at the time but Alexander was a doer, not a thinker.*" Paul looked deep in thought.

'What do you think of that – something to do with your father, perhaps?' I suggested making a wild guess.

'Perhaps,' he said returning to the book once more.

Later that morning we said our goodbyes. I looked at Sirena's face. I knew she was sad that I was leaving but at least I had made that fleeting connection with her. We had got on well together. If only things could be different; there was so much more I wanted to know.

Along the freeway Paul remained silent, a heavy silence. I hated long silences, they reminded me of the time when my dad had had a row with my mum. I was only five and had stood between them as we walked along a street in Southampton. It had been awful.

Still silence as I turned towards Paul. 'What's wrong?' I asked wondering what the problem was.

'Oh nothing.'

'It doesn't look like nothing to me.' Still no answer. I decided to leave it for another ten minutes, timing it exactly by my watch. 'You're not looking forward to seeing your father, are you?'

'Got it in one, OK!' he snapped.

'OK, OK.'

'Because I was the youngest, he always thought I would go into the acting business. My older brothers had gone their own way by this time.'

'Oh I see what you mean. I think … '

But I had no time to answer as we arrived at his father's house in a beautiful residential neighbourhood called Hancock Park, just south of Hollywood. Paul's father Alberto, a rather tall, thin man with dark hair and a beard came out to greet us and Paul introduced me. I shook his hand and smiled. Alberto introduced me to Francesco, Paul's uncle, a short, stocky man. An image of Laurel and Hardy came to mind. Swift greetings were exchanged as Alberto led us out into the garden, to a display of bright flower beds with fancy statues scattered across the lawn. I told Paul's uncle that it looked like a picture postcard. He smiled at me, saying I had good taste.

Paul smiled, not saying a word. His dad beckoned us to a table situated on the main veranda overlooking the gardens. An Italian style salad was followed by a regional dish of lasagne and white wine.

'So, what about this research?' Paul's father asked suddenly. 'How long will it take you?'

'I'm not sure; it depends how easily we can get hold of the information.'

'God, you could have made a film by then,' his dad snorted. Paul was just about to open his mouth when I gave him a nudge in the ribs.

Uncle Francesco butted in, leading the conversation in another direction. 'It sounds really involved and important.'

Paul calmed down and focused on his uncle, saying that it was a country's pride that was at stake and that the Greeks had already had years of disputes with the British over the Elgin Marbles.

'The Greeks,' his dad interrupted, 'what about the Italians?'

'Well that's just it, that's why my work is so important, to try to find out where this statue originated from,' said Paul, sending a further look of disapproval.

I suddenly blurted out 'Cor blimey,' trying to lighten the conversation. 'If it's not the British it's the Americans or someone else.' Paul's father looked confused, Paul's eyebrows lifted and Uncle Francesco took a sip of wine. They all glared at me. So I chose to shut up and had an imaginary conversation with Athena:

Dear Athena	I feel a fool. I have three men now looking at me as if I was from another planet.
Dear Katalina	You are not a fool and not from another planet, just keep your mouth shut for a few more seconds then the 'cor blimey' will be forgotten.
Dear Athena	Thank you so much.

After a moment, Uncle Francesco asked why I was being so quiet. I told him I was thinking about the Greek gods. Paul's father stated that the Greek gods had a lot to offer the acting profession. I looked at him perplexed, imagining my Greek gods dancing on a stage.

Paul looked away, scooping up another mouthful of lasagne. Alberto continued for the next ten minutes, ranting on about the acting profession and the scripts he hadn't written in the past.

Then he recalled *The Godfather.* Commenting on what a great film it was. 'You know, Paul, we are related to the Mafia.'

'Oh no, not that story again,' said Uncle Francesco huffing. 'He is convinced that our family is linked through previous generations to the Mafia. You'll never stop him now.'

Paul looked stunned. His father raised his hands with full blown Italian passion for this long-held belief. I glanced at Paul's pin striped suit. Paul's father continued, telling us that a distant great grandfather was part of the Mafia and lived somewhere in Sicily.

Paul interrupted. 'You cannot be serious, this is a joke.'

'No, it's not. You have relatives by the name of Campano, who live in the town of Catania, on the east coast of Sicily. You must visit them, after you go to Rome. It's my other brother Carlo and his family. They are always inviting us over. Here, I'll get the address.'

He stood up and swiftly retrieved a piece of paper with the address on from the writing bureau. 'See you must visit them, they'll be delighted to see you,' he said, handing it to Paul. I perked up, saying that it all sounded exciting.

Paul frowned. 'Exciting? What is it with you British and glamour?'

'Half Greek, please! It's the dull weather we have; we need some excitement from time to time.'

'See, your girlfriend is interested,' said Alberto.

Dinner consumed and now feeling full of pasta, we got ready to visit Paul's mum. She lived in Venice Beach, one of many beaches along the Los Angeles coast line.

'Please, give my love to your mother,' Alberto cried, as we stepped into the car.

'That's a fine thing,' Paul mumbled under his breath. I told him to shut up, thinking that he could be so tactless.

We headed towards Venice Beach. The sun was out and the weather felt warmer now that the clouds had finally disappeared.

I asked Paul whether she knew I was coming. I felt slightly anxious, wondering how he got on with his mum.

His hand left the steering wheel and he gently patted my knee in reassurance. 'Yeah, sure she does, it'll be fine.'

Car parked, we walked up a side street and over a small bridge that had a river running underneath; very picturesque site, which made me think of pictures of Venice with its gondolas. 'A little Venice,' I remarked clumsily.

'Yes,' he said, 'hence the name, "Venice Beach".' I did know about Venice – the one in Italy though.

Crossing the main street, we headed towards the beach. Further down, we turned left and met a long promenade that housed numerous apartments, all with their own unique style. Some were very minimalist, with glass balconies, others in a Tudor style with dark wood. 'That's her apartment, there.' Paul pointed towards a two-storey apartment that had a white painted front and a balcony. We walked round the back and climbed up a few steps. He remained silent and I sensed a feeling of apprehension as he rang the bell.

A tall woman appeared with long auburn hair and bright blue eyes. 'Hi, come in. I'm Angelina, and you must be Katalina.'

Perhaps that's why he's tall, and has those blue eyes, I thought, as we stepped into the hallway. I smiled as she led us into the lounge. The walls were painted white, with splashes of turquoise, blues and greens decorating the skirting boards. I looked up, noticing a number of paintings, mostly abstract in design. I walked closer to one of them: a painting of a deep crimson rose, it stood out. There in the corner, Angelina had signed her name – a talented woman.

'Wow, have you done these?' I asked.

Angelina smiled. 'Yes, I like to paint. In fact, I sold one of my paintings last week.'

She opened a door that led out onto the balcony. The sun streamed down as I walked outside and sat down. The sea breeze caught the side of my face, as I looked out at the view. In the background I could hear Paul's voice, but decided to stay put, allowing them to talk.

A few minutes later Angelina called out to me. 'Please come in and have a drink.'

I looked at Paul's sullen face and wondered if they had got off to a bad start. Angelina passed me a cup of coffee. An embarrassing silence ensued – I shuffled in my seat and was about to make another comment about one of Angelina's paintings when Paul launched in.

'Why did you leave when you did? I was only eight years old!' he choked. 'I'll never forget that afternoon. Suddenly you weren't there, just gone!'

A stunned silence filled the room. I looked at them – it was like an episode from a soap opera. I placed my cup down and waited. Angelina stood up and quickly crossed herself.

Paul pointed to a small statue of the Madonna and child. 'Oh God, and that thing as well,' he cried.

'Please Paul, Katalina's here, and don't say "God" like that. That *thing* is religion; religion has kept me sane throughout these years.' She sighed, 'No, I'm sorry, I *had* to leave. It was your father, he never understood. I was depressed, he couldn't cope. I'm so sorry.'

Paul's head dropped in shame. He had asked the question and had received a truthful, open answer. Perhaps he hadn't expected such a direct reply. Angelina could see his embarrassment and walked over to him, touching him on his shoulder. Paul flinched and stared back at her.

She continued. 'I'm sorry. Depression is a cruel thing, something that unless you've suffered from it, you wouldn't understand. That's why I paint as well, it helps.'

Sitting quietly I had been taking all this in. Shocked was an understatement. This laid-back, confident university professor had baggage; baggage that had been unexpectedly exposed. Mother and son stood up together, giving each other a tentative embrace. Paul sat down again; more relaxed now but still, a look of unease hung across his face. I wished I was back in the café serving Mr Cotterill, or anybody for that matter.

Angelina poured out more coffee. 'Why don't we go out and take Katalina somewhere? She hasn't been here before. How about the Queen Mary down on Long Beach?'

Paul looked towards me. 'Yeah, great, I'd love to,' I said; anything to get away from this stifling atmosphere.

The Queen Mary stood in front of us, elegant and refined; a magnificent ship, built in 1936, that had played host to the rich and famous, as well as being used in the Second World War, it stood there in all its glory. Angelina had visited it before, but seemed entranced by the grandeur it displayed. Tickets bought, we opted for a self-guided tour that took three hours, due to some rather small, unclear arrows that directed us around the ship in opposite directions. We walked along corridors of 1930s-style cabins that were still used today as a hotel.

'Come on Katalina,' Paul called out to me, stepping into another corridor on B deck.

I told him that I needed a cigarette then decided from the look he threw me that it would be better to wait.

As I caught up with Paul, he turned to his mother, who had stopped to admire one of the archives from this magical period in time. Angelina seemed lost in thought, staring through the glass at a reconstructed display of a first class cabin. On the bed lay an elegant 1930s evening gown, a glistening green with a V-neck. I watched her, Angelina, the goddess Aphrodite, perhaps? Tall, elegant and graceful, I imagined her wearing this gown, Paul's father taking her arm, leading her into a grand dinner hall; a day when they weren't arguing.

'You would look good in that,' I said.

'Why, thank you,' she replied.

We continued on our tour, eventually arriving outside. The cafeteria was open and we ordered cool drinks. I took mine outside and imagined myself in an elegant 1930s dress. Deciding that this wouldn't suit me, I chose to admire the buildings that stretched along the bay. After three hours of walking and with aching feet we returned to Angelina's apartment for a quick coffee.

'Well, what did you think of that?' asked Angelina, placing a pot of coffee on the table.

Paul sat next to her, still looking pensive. 'Yeah, great, and so huge,' I replied, looking at his tense expression, wondering what else was on his mind.

'Why did my father always want me to go into acting?' asked Paul suddenly.

Angelina stood stunned and took a breath. 'What do you mean?'

'Well, I have a good job in the university and a respected job at that, so why, even after all these years, does he criticise the work I do?' He glared at her, waiting for an answer.

Angelina sat down and took a breath. 'Your father had a younger brother, one he never speaks about. He looked after him and got him into the theatre, you know, acting. His brother was twenty-one when, one winter night after an evening performance, he left the theatre and stepped off the pavement … ' She hesitated. 'A car going at least 60 mph raced around the corner. He was killed instantly. Your father never got over it.'

Paul looked at her, 'Yes, but I … '

Angelina interrupted. 'He was the spitting image of you. When your father couldn't make it as an actor he became a writer instead. He was dead set on you joining the profession, especially as your brothers had gone their own way by the time you were seventeen.'

Paul sat back and took a deep breath. Angelina walked to the other side of the room, searched through some papers, and retrieved a photo. 'Here he is. His name was Paul too. Your father threw all the photos out, but I kept this one.' We peered down at the photo. I could see the resemblance: the angular jaw line, the bright blue eyes and that straight Roman nose. Paul turned away.

The journey back to Paul's father's house seemed long, full of heavy atmosphere. I could feel his anger brewing. The burning silence put my nerves on edge. I wanted desperately to break the silence, but what with – a full blown discussion of what had just been said or something completely different? Lighting a cigarette, I inhaled slowly. The wisps of exhaled smoke twirled and then evaporated in front of my nose.

'I'm sorry you never knew you had another uncle,' I said, waiting to see if the silence would break. Paul coughed a couple of times, still intent on looking straight ahead, ignoring my comment.

After a moment, he spoke. 'No, I didn't know; let alone him having the same name as me. I can't believe how stupid, how selfish, how … ' He stopped. I thought he was going to cry.

His lips firmly pressed together, he put his foot down on the accelerator pedal. As the car approached a red traffic light, he slammed the brakes on.

I had nearly finished my cigarette when he continued, saying that he felt angry at his father. I tried to soften this, saying it must have been a shock.

'I guess,' he said then went back to criticising religion, recalling how his mum used to force him to go to church. What was the point of going to confession, saying sorry asking for forgiveness, when people go out and commit the same sin again? I agreed with him, but suggested that perhaps religion had helped his mum with her depression, as it had mine.

Paul turned to look at me. 'Oh great, brilliant; so the pair of us have had depressed mothers,' he snapped.

The immaculate driveway appeared in front of us – we had arrived back at his father's. I wondered what was in store; Paul's father now had an angry son on his hands. The front door opened, and Uncle Francesco appeared, beckoning us into the hallway. We exchanged pleasantries and Paul asked where his father was. Alberto was in the kitchen and Paul marched off to confront him.

'Oh God,' I said to Francesco, 'perhaps I should … '

'Stay in here,' he said, 'and tell me about the Queen Mary.'

So I did, telling him that it was a wonderful ship, originally built in Scotland in 1936 and not the USA. Francesco smiled, as I told him that it took three hours for us to get round as it was so badly sign-posted.

After half an hour, Paul returned, appearing more relaxed and suggesting that we go to the dining room. I could smell the strong Italian herbs. His father, a more than competent chef, served up Cannelloni made with rich mozzarella cheese, served with fresh Italian bread. At the dinner table, the conversation interchanged between the weather, Italian cookery and the relatives I hoped to find on my journey. Paul seemed more relieved and I assumed that he had made up with his father.

Alberto held out the bottle. 'Here, Katalina, more wine?'

'Thank you, not too much or I'll be under the table,' I said, having a fleeting image of me lying flat on my back.

Alberto smiled at me, 'Well, that would be interesting!'

Paul turned towards his father and suddenly said, 'Thank you.'

His father looked back, stunned. 'Whatever for?'

'Because you listened to me.'

ROME

When we arrived at the airport, Paul dropped me off and went to return the rental car. I waited at the main entrance of the Tom Bradley airport terminus, and stared curiously at a bronze statue of Thomas Bradley. Fifteen minutes later Paul returned and started calling me "honey" again. I reminded him about Paddington bear and explained that honey is something you eat and not a term of endearment.

He looked at me. 'I thought you said he ate marmalade not honey.'

'Yes, yes you're right I did,' I replied, having to admit defeat.

'Anyway what's wrong with you?'

'Nothing, I'll just be glad to get away from here; all these families and their problems and "honey" just pushes me over the edge,' I said, hoping that Rome had something better to offer.

It was 10 am and not too busy. The flight was to take thirteen hours, so I made sure that I had plenty of nicotine gum and sweets at hand, and a travel book detailing all the places to see in Italy. In Rome, the Coliseum was a must, the Pantheon and maybe the Sistine Chapel. Finally, we boarded the plane. Seats found and baggage stowed, we waited for the plane to taxi down the runway. I felt sad at the thought of leaving Los Angeles and Sirena behind. The plane started to gather speed and quickly surged into the sky. For a second the experience seemed exhilarating then nerves returned as I looked out of the window. The tall buildings and spaghetti-like freeways soon disappeared from sight as overhead announcements in Italian and English were made, welcoming passengers to the flight. Paul sat in his seat, his elbows digging into me. This had happened on the way over here from Heathrow but I hadn't said anything at the time. I placed my right elbow on the arm rest, slowly pushing against his.

'Do you mind? I hope to get some reading done,' he said, pushing his elbow back again.

'Sorry, it just feels so squashed here,' I said, feeling quite stressed at the thought of being twenty thousand feet in the air again.

'Buongiorno,' said the air hostess, passing over two coffees.

'Buongiorno' I replied, asking her if she had any chocolate. She pointed towards a small range of chocolate bars. 'Yes, that's ok, I'll have that one.' The air hostess passed across a Snickers bar. I took it for a second and stopped. 'Sorry, I've changed my mind; I'll have some crisps instead.' Paul gave me a stern look. The air hostess smiled tentatively. 'I'm nervous of flying. This is only my second flight,' I said.

'Oh, I see, Madame.'

'It's not Madame actually, we're not married.' Paul looked at me again. 'Oh, and by the way, how long will the flight take?'

The air hostess pursed her lips, trying her best to remain civil. 'Around thirteen hours.'

'Oh God! Thirteen hours of not smoking.'

'Keep your voice down,' insisted Paul.

'There is no smoking in the toilets either,' the air hostess added before moving on.

'Are you going to be like this all the way to Rome?'

'No. I can't find the Italian word for no,' I said, flicking through the pages of the little phrase book. 'Oh look, it's "no," just like in English. Here try this: *arrivederci, si, grazie*.' My hand knocked into his face.

'Careful!' he said, crossly.

'Oh, mi scusi,' I said, thinking he was being a spoil sport.

Looking annoyed, he firmly pushed my hand down into my lap. 'No, I won't.'

'You know some Italian then.'

'Not a lot; I had no reason to learn it, growing up in America,' he said, pushing papers into a file, 'and thankfully, where we're going most people speak English.'

'I suppose, but my uncle in France always said that we were lazy, precisely because of that. We rely on others always to speak English.'

66

'Well, have you learnt any Greek?'

'Only smatterings, like *parakalo* for please,' I said, feeling proud that I had at least bothered to look at my native language.

'Well I guess that could be pretty handy in Greece, asking for drinks when looking for the odd statue,' he said, bending down and finding his legs rather squashed by the seat in front of him. A few papers went flying onto the floor. His long body looked awkward, scrabbling on the floor. 'Uno, due, tre … '

I looked at him. 'I thought you didn't … '

'No I don't, just a smattering like you,' he smiled.

Fiumicino airport, Rome, also known as Leonardo da Vinci; I thought of paintings and the fact, which I remembered reading somewhere, that Leonardo never did get on with Michelangelo.

After a long flight, we eventually found ourselves at the hotel, the Hotel Del Sol Pantheon; a grand building in the middle of Rome, which overlooked the Pantheon building. A posh hotel – Paul had requested the best. It dated back to 1467 and was the oldest hotel in Rome. I glanced through a leaflet in reception which said that the poet Aristo and the philosopher Jean Paul Sartre had stayed here.

A twin bedroom with a hairdryer, satellite TV, radio and mini bar welcomed us. The decor was stunning, elegant and colour co-ordinated. Andrea would approve of this, I thought, as I felt the texture of the thick velvet curtains; perhaps I could take back a small sample for her. I walked over to the patio window and looked out to see a cobbled street below and the famous Pantheon. Returning to the main lounge, I wondered where Paul had gone. From the bathroom I could hear the sound of running water. I walked in to see a large room housing an elegant marble shower and a large oval bath adorned with gold taps. There was Paul, naked amidst a pool of white bubbles.

He looked up at me and smiled. 'Hi, come on in, there's room for both of us.'

Standing in the doorway, I suddenly felt embarrassed. This was stupid, I knew that staying together would move our relationship on further, perhaps a bit too quickly for my liking.

'Um, yes well, perhaps later, I haven't finished exploring everything yet.'

'Exploring everything – what do you mean? Haven't you stayed in a hotel before?'

'Yes … well, no, not quite like this one,' I said clumsily. My eyes took in another glimpse of his body. He caught my gaze. 'I like the gold taps,' I stammered.

He looked at the taps and stared back at me, confused. 'Oh well, please yourself,' he replied, looking a bit dejected.

Feeling awkward, I returned to the lounge, exploring every electrical device going and spotted the mini-bar. Too early for a small glass of whisky, I wondered?

The next day we visited the Pantheon, an immense structure with Greek-style columns. Beyond the grand entrance lay a conically shaped building. The main entrance led out to a large circular structure with a massive domed ceiling. Sunlight streamed through a hole at the top, bouncing onto the floor and surrounding walls. Standing against a pillar, the light from the ceiling reflected down onto my legs. It made me think of Apollo, the sun god, radiating his warmth onto the people of Rome. A number of gold-plated icons hung from the walls and the floor was decorated with delicately patterned mosaic tiles which splayed outwards from the centre.

Outside the Pantheon, we found a small café. I sat at a table, thinking about the beautiful mosaic floor and how the sunlight made it sparkle. The waiter appeared to take our order and soon returned with cups of steaming espresso and tall glasses of ice cream. I lifted my cup, pushed the saucer to one side, and took a sip of the strong Italian espresso then plonked the cup down on the table. Paul glared at me and stretched forward, picked up my saucer and abruptly placed it back under my cup. I lifted the cup up and pushed the saucer out of the way. An annoyed look reappeared on his face.

'I hate saucers, they always get in the way,' I said, thinking how picky he was being. Looking irritated, he took my cup back again, placing the saucer underneath. I snatched it back then placed the saucer defiantly on the floor.

Paul said, 'There's no need for that. This is a decent Italian café; you should have a saucer, it doesn't look good.'

I looked at him. There he was in his black jacket and white shirt, telling me what to do with a saucer. I picked the saucer up and put it back on the table, to one side. 'There, happy now? Not on the floor, but not under my cup either.' It was incredible and I was stunned by his petty behaviour. I lit a cigarette, taking a deep inhalation of smoke and then exhaled, watching the circling smoke evaporate in front of my eyes. God, this was only Italy, what about the rest of the journey?

A group of young Italians sat down behind us, giggling and shouting. I turned around and wished I were with them or even back at the cafe. The aromatic smell of ground coffee seemed very appealing. Turning back to the table, I asked him what his plans were.

'We have a good two hours to look round Ostia then Professor Bettulini will meet us on the corner of Via Adria,' he replied.

'Sounds a bit cloak and dagger; I thought we were going to meet him in the museum.'

'I was, but when I spoke to him on the phone he changed his mind, telling me that the Italians would not be too keen to hear about the statue being discussed again, so he suggested a different place to meet.'

He continued, telling me that the professor believed the statue should live in its rightful country. However, he had to be cautious, as certain people in his department would not be too happy about his benevolent assistance in the matter.

One hour later, the ruins of ancient Ostia lay ahead of us. The name Ostia derived from the Latin word "ostium", literally meaning "mouth". It was one of the great a seaports of Rome. Paul stood with his hands on his hips, looking into the distance. 'There is so much to see here. I've read so much about this place. The Baths of Neptune are supposed to have a beautiful preserved mosaic.'

The Baths of Neptune were indeed very beautiful. A mosaic floor depicted a sea god riding a chariot drawn by four prancing horses. It was huge, measuring 55ft by 36ft, and I did not want to miss an inch of it. Collecting a guidebook, we sat down to get our bearings. The amphitheatre was wonderfully preserved, containing a series of steep semi-circular stone seats that would have held 3,500 spectators. The tiny stage was intact and I imagined a group of Ancient Roman actors performing a theatrical drama. Sitting in the auditorium, I could almost hear the shouts and laughter of the spectators. Beyond the public baths, we walked around a cluster of apartment buildings that, according to the guidebook, had been inhabited by middle-class families.

'These living dwellings remind me of a site I excavated back in England, near York; the number of vases and artefacts we found was astounding.'

'So where exactly did they find the Aphrodite statue?'

'Right here in Ostia.'

As we sat down, Paul took out a book from his bag. He looked anxious as he diligently studied every page. He retrieved a notebook from his bag and a gold tipped pen, the same one he had in the restaurant at our first meeting, and scrutinised a page of scribbled notes.

'What are you looking for?'

'I need to confirm a date with the professor,' he said, returning to the notes in front of him.

'Do I come with you, or what?'

A firm "no" was the reply. I felt put out, but understood that now wasn't the right time to question his motives. He left me at the excavation site, so I continued to walk around, finding a small marble fountain to sit by. The sun was pleasantly warm and I could feel its gentle heat on my face. The surrounding scenery was stunning, a mixture of old ruins combined with the rawness of nature; the trees and flowers prolific.

An hour later, Paul returned looking deep in thought. We sat and had coffee as he explained about his meeting with the professor. Apparently when the statue was housed in the LA museum, the original carbon dating analysis had suggested

440BC, which conflicted with the idea that the statue had belonged to Alexander the Great. The professor was surprised to hear that Alexander the Great may have commissioned the statue and told Paul that he would need more information.

I was feeling decidedly hungry by now and the café's menu was too much of a temptation to resist. We both ordered Fettuccine Alfredo, another Italian dish to savour, and by no means free of calories. It was similar to macaroni cheese, but prepared with vast amounts of cream and cheese. We finished our meal with the classic Italian dessert, tiramisu, which literally translates as "pick me up", presumably because of the combination of espresso and cocoa powder. I recalled attempting to make this dish a few years ago as part of an Italian cookery course that I had attended with Suzanne – hers was a striking success, whilst mine turned out like jelly.

Seated outside, different Italian voices echoed around us. I picked up a menu and ordered corretto, an espresso coffee with a smattering of alcohol. The waiter quickly returned, placing the cup in front of me. Eager to taste it, I took a large gulp then pulled a face. The waiter looked at me, smiling.

'Signorina, I think you need to take small sips, it is strong, yes?' he exclaimed.

I sat back in my chair, still gasping. 'Yes, I think you're right.'

Paul gave me a whimsical look, remarking that I couldn't wait to taste the alcohol. I smiled.

Back at the hotel, I turned on the television and slumped into a chair, still feeling giddy from the alcohol and coffee. Watching an Italian newsreader in full flow I was entertained by his hands and voice until I heard the sound of running water. I tiptoed to the bathroom and peered around the door. In the bath, Paul sat with his hands above the water, reading a book.

He looked up at me. 'Are you coming in?'

'No I'm okay, just watching this Italian newsreader; can't understand a word he's saying.' Paul stared for a second then returned to his book.

Next day, sitting at the breakfast table, the smell of the coffee woke me up. 'Vorrei il caffe, grazie,' said Paul, looking at the waiter.

'Si, caffe,' I replied.

Paul looked impressed. 'Wow, you've actually used that phrase book.'

'Hardly, only looked at it occasionally,' I said, pretending to be more confident than I felt. 'You should have a go,' I urged, pushing the book to him.

Paul pushed it back. 'No thanks, I'll get by.'

That morning we headed for the Coliseum. Approaching its massive archways, I stood in awe for a few minutes thinking about the film *Gladiator*. I had heard a lot about the film but never got round to watching it, mostly because of the gore and violence.

'Grand, but bloody,' I announced.

'Pardon,' said Paul. I told him about the film and said that the Italians were a bloodthirsty people. He ignored me and walked on. We explored the interior of the Coliseum, with its circular rows of seats. I imagined the shouts and screams from the audience, as a poor animal or slave was about to be dragged into the arena, ready for the fight to begin. Paul was yards ahead of me on his hands and knees examining the structure of the walls. He appeared deep in thought.

'I'm forty-four, ancient, a bit like these walls.'

Stunned, I stepped back. 'Oh, so you're forty-four. Why tell me now?'

'It's these walls, if you like; they're ancient, made me think of my age. I dreaded telling you. I thought if you knew my age, you would never have come with me. I didn't like deceiving you.'

'Please, it doesn't mean a thing, it's not a problem.' I said, gently patting his shoulder.

Standing up, he looked relieved. Presumably his conscience felt lighter now. I didn't mind that he was older. If anything, it made me feel protected.

Taking my hand he led the way, 'Come on, I want to show you the underground vaults.'

The vaults were small and poky and smelt damp. 'Go on; tell me what they were used for.'

'They were used to house the animals and slaves.'

The Coliseum was magnificent, and to think that it had stood here for centuries. I was pleased to leave knowing that years ago nearly a million people had died in the bloody games. Minerva, the Roman goddess of war and peace, was linked with the city of Rome. The Minervan warlike qualities seemed very fitting as I walked away from this gruesome place.

OPERA

Next morning, I was awoken by a strange burbling sound. Throwing the bed covers on the floor, I ran over to the chair and grabbed my bag. There at the bottom, a tinge of blue light was flashing: my mobile phone. It was Andrea, asking how I was getting on. I told her that we were in Rome. She said that she couldn't talk for long as Mandras was due back anytime and would hit the roof at the prospect of a large phone bill. Andrea asked after Paul, wondering how we were getting on. I said that we were getting on and she reminded me to keep in contact. When she had rung off, I suddenly felt lonely. I missed Andrea, even though she could be pushy at times. Placing the phone back into my bag I felt a flat square object inside – it was my gift from the people at the café. I looked at the picture of the coffee bean with the initials round the edges. F.C. – that was Mr Cotterill – I wondered what he would be doing; probably still moaning about students.

I was about to take a book out when suddenly a loud explosion vibrated through the room. Stopping in my tracks I looked around; everything seemed to be in place. I walked over to the window.

Paul raced out of the bathroom and stood next to me. 'What was that?' he demanded, looking shocked.

We could hear screams and shouts from outside. Looking down, we saw people running everywhere, smoke and flames swirling up into the morning sky. Towards the far end of the square a car, torn to pieces, lay across the pavement. Twisted lumps of metal, rubber tyres and other indistinguishable parts spread across the ground. A few moments later, the sound of a police siren pierced through the air. Instantly, I thought of the Greek, Sokritos, the one who had shot a Turk across the Green Line.

A shudder ran down my spine. 'You see, it's the Mafia, just like your dad said.'

He stood back from the window with a look of disbelief. 'Oh please, you don't know that it's the Mafia, it could be some European political group; anyone for that matter,' he said, trying

74

to convince me. I shrugged my shoulders as he pushed a packet of cigarettes into my shaking hand. 'Here, have this.' Paul passed me a small glass of whisky then poured a glass for himself.

Managing to take hold of a cigarette, my hands shaking, I lit it and inhaled. 'Are you sure you're OK?'

'Yes, I'll be all right in a minute, when this whisky has done its job.'

Downstairs in the restaurant, guests talked amongst themselves, asking all possible questions. The hotel manager informed us that nobody had been hurt and that the car had belonged to a middle-aged man. The man had left his vehicle and gone into a local café. I was relieved to hear that nobody had been hurt but still couldn't shake off the impact of what had happened.

Returning to our room, Paul took out his papers, intent on staying in. I, on the other hand, had recovered with the help of another glass of whisky and had my mind set on a pair of Italian shoes. Undeterred, I put my jacket on and grabbed my bag.

Paul looked up, peering above his glasses. 'You're going out?'

When I told him of my plan to buy myself some genuine Italian leather shoes, he said I was nuts and urged me not to go. I told him that the shops were in the opposite direction from the blast and that although I appreciated his paternal concern, he wasn't my father. Not waiting for any more comments, I walked out, slamming the door behind me. I was on a mission for red leather shoes and it would take more than an explosion to put me off.

As I walked down the street, away from where the bomb had exploded, a trembling feeling quickly emerged. I could see police officers examining the spot where the car had been. As they looked up at me, I hurried away, hoping they didn't think that I'd had anything to do with it. Perhaps it was the Mafia. More than likely, I thought, even if Paul wasn't convinced. Then I remembered Paul's uncle telling us that his uncle in Sicily had some relatives linked to the Mafia. My thoughts lurched between thoughts of the Mafia and Italian shoes, which only served to increase my determination. Marching past a café, I could smell the aroma of continental coffee wafting into the air. Should I stop and have a strong coffee with a cigarette, or should I carry on? No, I decided, shoe shop first. I glanced at all the Italian signs then peered in at the shop windows. Third shop along, shoes and more shoes caught my eager eyes. Finding myself in a select boutique, there they were! Not shoes in the sense of a heel with leather around the ankle, but slip-ons, a sling-back shoe with a moccasin design at the front, in bright red. I tried them on: they fitted perfectly. The assistant placed them inside a designer carrier bag. I walked back past the coffee shop, hesitated then decided to go straight back to the hotel. Perhaps another bomb would go off. I would never see Greece, never see the Parthenon and never see Paul again. I didn't stop running until I had reached our hotel room. I pushed opened the door, slightly out of breath.

'That was quick,' Paul said, taking his glasses off and looking amused.

'I ran, well walked fast to the shop and back again. I knew where to go,' I said, smiling nervously.

He looked to see me fiddling with my necklace. 'So our brave Athena isn't so bold after all!'

'No, our bold Athena was just being cautious,' I said, sitting down on the bed.

Paul suddenly groaned, saying that he'd lost some papers. 'What about this one?' I asked, holding up one with a picture of a statue on.

'Yes, that one, thank you,' he said, snatching it from me and muttering under his breath.

Ignoring him, I opened my carrier bag and gazed adoringly at my bright red leather shoes. Paul would not appreciate them, so I kept them in the bag. The muscles in my legs ached; it was all the fast marching. Running a hot bath, I poured the contents of one of the small perfumed bottles into the bath. The strong aroma of patchouli and rose swamped the room. Bubbles flew everywhere as I moved my hands furiously backwards and forwards in the water. Leaning back in the bath, I heard the shuffling of papers accompanied by the odd moan coming from the other room. Moody and obviously frustrated; I hadn't seen him like this before. Then, like a bullet from a gun, operatic music burst through the room. My thoughts now distracted, I sat up, to hear an operatic voice accompanying the music. He was singing! He put his head around the door and held out a pair of two tickets.

'Here, tonight, tickets for the opera.' What an unpredictable man he was. The opera! Although I would have preferred an Italian nightclub, the opera did sound sophisticated.

'Great, I can wear my new Italian shoes.'

'And a dress as well,' he said, smiling.

It was 7 pm, time to get ready. A black suit, white shirt and bow tie were laid out on the bed. Very smart, but how could I match that? Easy, my new Italian shoes, but with what? I suddenly remembered the sixties-style v-necked, sleeveless red dress, at the bottom of my suitcase. I took it out and hung it by the window. The sunlight caught the iridescent red, and the silky material gleamed. I had never worn the dress before and had bought it as a joke, spurred on by Suzanne who said that I ought to show off my body more. It looked too feminine and clingy for me and the hemline fell just above the knee.

Paul had washed and dressed and looked immaculate in his suit. My turn now! I went into the bathroom to get ready. The dress fitted perfectly and yes, more of my body was showing, just as Suzanne had predicted, and my new shoes matched it beautifully. The dress clung to my skin, a feeling that I wasn't used to. I caught hold of the hem, trying to pull the dress down. It made little difference, as it bounced straight up again, clinging to my skin just as before. I made a final adjustment before walking into the lounge. Paul was standing by a mirror, adjusting his tie, and could see my reflection. He turned round and stared. Nothing, I thought, he hasn't said anything. Oh God I must look awful.

'It's stunning, really stunning, and the shoes go well.'

'They're not shoes, they're moccasins.'

'Well, moccasins then; anyway you look great.'

'Thanks, you don't look so bad yourself.'

I was awestruck by Teatro dell' Opera, a magnificent building with numerous square archways at the front. For once, I felt quite smart, and Paul certainly looked the part. I only wished we could have had our photo taken so that I could send it to Suzanne as proof. Inside the opera house, the decor caught my attention, with its glistening chandeliers and gold painted architecture. As the orchestra struck up, a shiver of excitement ran down my spine. The opera's theme was very Italian, about the life of a daughter born to a hunchback father. The daughter falls in love with a duke, who then betrays her. The father attempts to murder the duke, but instead the daughter sacrifices her own life. I wondered whether the story had any significance in my life. Would Paul betray me, and, well, were we in love with each other anyway?

During the interval, we sat at the bar. 'What do you think, I know it may not be your thing?' he asked.

I kept my real opinions to myself; that the music was too loud and one woman reminded me of a farmer throttling a hen. Paul looked at me, waiting for an answer. I told him I was enjoying it, saying that it was "emotionally intense". Paul agreed, saying that it was the intensity of the music that he enjoyed. When we returned to our seats, I gave my dress another tug, but it bounced up again. I quickly I sat down.

Act Three was traumatic as it involved the heroine's sudden death. I squeezed Paul's hand tightly.

'Ouch!'

'Sorry,' I whispered.

Later that evening we found a nearby restaurant. A waiter served up our meal: Melanzane, pomodori, parmigiano al forno. Aubergine with tomato and parmesan cheese lay in front of me: Greek, Italian and vegetarian; what a relief. We continued to talk about the opera and the fact that I was dying to get to Greece. I was not so keen on meeting his Sicilian relatives, wondering whether it would be a repeat performance of our visit to his dad, but I didn't tell him that.

I took another sip of the sweet white wine and then a spoonful of caramelised pear with Marsala and mascarpone cream. I noticed Paul once again looking deep in thought. He told me that he wasn't sure about his meeting with the professor tomorrow.

'It just feels strange, the fact that he wants to keep quiet about it, not wanting his colleagues to know.'

'So you don't want to continue?'

'I didn't say that. Like him, I believe that these antiquities should be returned to their rightful country.'

'Good, that's OK then,' I replied. 'Let's go and get an ice cream,' I suggested hoping that this might help.

'What, now?'

'Yes, now.'

Walking along a narrow street, we came across a row of shops. One of them sold Italian ice cream. 'I'll wait outside,' Paul said.

I walked in to survey the counter with its 103 different flavours. My eyes darted backwards and forwards as I tried to make a decision. In the end I chose a combination of four flavours and the vendor passed me a rather tall cone.

'What on earth is that?' exclaimed Paul.

'This is a genuine Italian large ice cream,' I announced, 'although I think you'll have to help me eat it.'

Paul was up early the next day, sorting through more papers and going over the questions he needed to ask the professor. We agreed that I would stay behind. He left at 10.30 and I took a bath, listening to Italian pop music, drinking wine and smoking strong Italian cigarettes, wondering what lay ahead. Intoxicated with cigarette smoke and ears burning from listening to two hours of Italian pop, I stepped out of the bath. My fingers and toes were shrivelled like prunes. I tried to push out the wrinkles by pressing my fingers against the side of the bath. As soon as I stopped the wrinkles sprang back.

The door opened as I ran through to the main lounge, my towel just covering me and my hair dripping onto the carpet. 'You look wet,' said Paul, looking me up and down.

'I've been in the bath, listening to pop music, drinking wine, smoking and wondering about you. It's been more than two hours.' Waiting for an answer, I looked at him indignantly. He was obviously in a daze, sitting down on the bed, clutching the papers that the professor had given him. 'It's the engravings on the bottom of the statue. Nobody questioned them at the time. Or rather, it was covered up.'

'Covered up?'

'Yes, covered up. The Americans had the money to house the statue and the Italians were determined to push the issue that it was theirs, a sort of quiet agreement between both countries.'

'Hence why people don't want things dug up again. Get it dug up again!'

Paul gave a grimace and continued, telling me that the professor had said the engravings might give a more accurate picture of the statue's origins.

'Didn't they do that carbon analysis thing on it? It doesn't make sense!' I exclaimed. Paul looked away.

After our visit to the opera, and feeling in the need of more cultural experiences, I suggested we visit the Vatican where the Sistine chapel was. Paul seemed surprised at my request. I knew that he wasn't overly religious, nor was I for that matter. I reassured him that I was only interested in Michelangelo's famous painting.

The Sistine Chapel is a magnificent structure and a popular tourist attraction. I stared up at the ceiling. Michelangelo had painted nine panels of pictures depicting the Creation, which were now illuminated. The mixture of golds and reds was a sight to behold. I watched Paul for a moment; his head craned back staring up at the painting. I giggled to myself, thinking that because he was so tall he could see the details far better than I could. Later, we found a statue of Michelangelo and a book showing some of his famous sketches and drawings.

'It's the solar plexus in his drawings; it draws you to the soul and heart of a person,' I commented, reading from the guide book. 'His drawings are those of a sculptor, every stroke of the pencil accentuates the curves and muscles of each portrait. It does, doesn't it?' I asked, attempting to attract Paul's attention.

'Yes, you're right.'

'It's the beauty and grace of it all.' I added, feeling more cultured by the minute.

Paul was impressed, agreeing with me. We were getting on together, it was great. After walking round in a contented silence, we came across a large crucifix decorated in gold. Paul glared at it at first then his expression softened.

Bags packed, we left the hotel. I turned round and looked across the road to the place where the bomb had exploded.

SICILIAN NIGHTS

The plane landed in Fontanarossa, Catania. What were Sicilian people like? I kept thinking of Al Pacino, the Godfather, and Mafia country. Were they so different from Italians – surely not? My guidebook informed me that, as with Italians, one might expect a lot of animation, hands flying everywhere. However, positive qualities included hard work, resilience, optimism and a good sense of humour. Where was Paul's I wondered?

A customs official with dark, bushy eyebrows inspected my passport and looked up at me. My hands were now rather clammy, and I wondered why he was scrutinising me. Did he have a sub machine gun hidden behind the desk? I stared back at him and asked if there was a problem, hoping not to antagonise the situation any further.

He took a pair of glasses out from his front pocket and placed them on the bridge of his nose, fiddling with them until they were in their rightful place. 'No, Signorina, everything is OK. Please, you can move on,' he said, gesturing at me to walk forward.

'What was that about?'

'I don't know, but keep going. I want to get to the hotel tonight, not tomorrow morning.' As we left the airport, Paul took my hand. I stopped to retrieve my guidebook. 'What are you doing now?'

'Listen to this,' I said. 'Sicilians often have a strong distrust of authority, especially when confronted with a silly rule. Consequently, they don't attempt to change the law, just find a way round it. A bit like the Greeks then.'

'And?' Paul looked at me impatiently, trying to lead me to the entrance.

'Perhaps that explains that customs man back there.'

'Perhaps.'

We arrived at the Hotel Albergo Modern, a three star hotel, situated near the city's nightlife. Standing at the reception desk, we waited for the keys to our room. Bursting to go to the toilet, I asked the receptionist who pointed towards a door to the right of the elevator. I opened the door, nearly crashing into a person with long, thick curly hair. At the commotion, the person turned round to reveal a man's face. He glared at me, his mouth wide open and, careful not to raise his hands in the air, suddenly yelled in Italian, presumably something to the effect of "Get out!" Stunned and apologetic I fled, dashing into the ladies' toilet next door.

'Where have you been?' asked Paul, looking bewildered.

'I got lost and walked into the men's and this man yelled at me!'

'Oh God, didn't you look at the signs on the door?'

'No I didn't, I was bursting.'

The twin bedroom was not as big as the last, but at least it had air conditioning. It was furnished in the style of the 1960s, with a minimalist look and a number of fancy accessories, such as the chrome armchair in the corner of the room. The cool terrazzo floor, smooth, shiny and cold to the feet, spread throughout the bedroom and into the bathroom. The tiny flecks of marble stone reminded me of a beach in Crete. That was the one time I had been to a Greek island, with a girlfriend. The beach had small, gritty stones that would catch between our toes.

On my way to the bathroom, I nearly stepped on Paul's papers that were sprawled across the floor. 'Hey, careful!' he exclaimed, as he quickly slid a piece of paper away from my feet.

I apologised, remembering the last time I had sat on his work, and plonked myself down into an armchair, wondering what Sicily had in store for us. Feeling bored, I suggested visiting Catania and asked Paul whether he knew that it was founded by the Greeks.

'Oh yes, more Greeks,' he muttered, trying to concentrate on his paperwork.

'What about your relatives? You're going to meet them soon.'

He looked up. 'What about them?'

'Aren't you wondering what they're like?' I persisted.

'Yes; why do you think I'm looking through this?' he snapped back, slamming a pen down on the table. 'I need to keep my mind occupied.'

'Occupied?'

'You know, keep my mind busy.'

'Oh sorry, I know what that's like.'

'Do you?' he sighed. 'She's religious, my aunt; well she used to be,' he said, shrugging his shoulders.

'Oh, that's what the problem is. Well, I guess you'll just have to bite your tongue,' I said, taking a book from my bag.

I tried to read extracts of the book to him. He quickly stopped me. 'Please don't. Just let me get on.' so I left him to it.

Sudden gloomy thoughts of meeting his religious aunt popped into my head, so I distracted myself by writing a postcard to Andrea, telling her all about the bomb and the grizzly Coliseum.

Next day we headed for the Roman amphitheatre, which dated back to the second century BC. Rather like the Coliseum, it didn't take long for me to lose sight of Paul. I found him a little while later on his hands and knees examining the limestone construction.

'Couldn't find you, I might have known,' I said, looking down at him.

The tourist leaflet explained that the theatre had a diameter of 87 metres and could seat 7,000 people. It also said that it was probably Greek in origin; I smiled. Yes, the Romans stole all of their great ideas from the Greeks.

Paul was still busily examining the stonework, so I sat down on one of the steps, and imagined a group of artists performing a Greek tragedy. Their costumes, colour and decoration were accurate in detail and I looked on with absorption. Paul appeared, and touched me gently on my shoulder. I jumped 6ft in the air, the vision instantly evaporating.

Back at the hotel, he talked about his relatives, revealing his apprehension at the thought of seeing them for the first time, in particular his religious aunt. I tried to reassure him that it wouldn't be that bad.

Next day, we drove out of the town centre into the countryside, where Paul's relatives lived on the outskirts of Catania. The landscape changed. In the distance was an expanse of thick, green North African bushes, interspersed with olive and citrus groves.

The bright Italian sun shone against a rolling electric-blue sky. I felt as though I could just carry on driving around the countryside with its stunning scenery. The thought of meeting Paul's relatives filled me with trepidation. We turned a corner into a narrow country lane. In the distance, the tips of palm trees and the convoluted rooftop of a renovated country house came into view. We had arrived. Walking up to the house, we passed through the flickering shadows of the palm trees that lay either side of the main pathway. It was impressive. The door opened and Paul's uncle and aunt and eldest daughter greeted us. Immediately, a sense of overwhelming shyness had me fiddling with my bag, nearly getting my finger caught in the strap. Nervously, I looked up at Paul's aunt. She smiled at me. Paul moved first, greeting them one by one. Each family member was gregarious in approach, with hugs and kisses all around. Pushing me forward, Paul introduced me to them. I sent him a condescending glare and the next moment found myself being squashed like a tomato, as Paul's uncle gave me a strong embracing hug.

Stepping back, I whispered in Paul's ear, 'I think I'm the one that's being overwhelmed.'

He leant forward and whispered, 'You're not the only one.'

Paul finally stood back and we walked into a large, impressive house. Marcella, the daughter, took my hand, insisting on giving me the quick tour: two large lounges, a billiard room not forgetting an outside pool. White and cream walls in nearly every room, the floors were designed in a terrazzo style, each with its own distinctive marble. A veranda looked out onto a magnificent view overlooking the luscious Sicilian countryside. The expanse of green vegetation, along with the blue sky and bright sunshine, provided a perfect setting. Marcella, still bursting with energy, led me upstairs. She showed me the four bedrooms with their balconies and the two large bathrooms. Marcella had done some of the tiling herself and she proudly pointed this out to me. The ceramic tiles in the bathroom were of typical design, comprising mainly of light blues, yellows and greens. She told me that she was at college working in art and design using ceramics and this had been one of her projects. A Greek-style design ran across the floor.

Antonia, Paul's aunt, interrupted our tour and called Paul from downstairs, where he had been dragged to the billiard room by his uncle.

'I've given you the bedroom at the end, Katalina and yours, Paul, is along here,' she said, pointing in the other direction.

Paul walked along the corridor, dumped his bags and joined me in my room. I had opened the window and stepped out onto a small veranda. 'It's quite something,' he said, placing his arm around me.

'Yes it is,' I replied, turning towards him, noticing a red mark on his cheek. 'You've got lipstick on your cheek,' I laughed. 'It must have been all that Italian embracing!'

He lifted his hand, trying to locate the offending mark. Taking a tissue out of my pocket, I quickly wiped it away.

Later that afternoon, Paul and I were entertained by Uncle Carlo. He led us into his billiard room and passed Paul a cue. I declined his offer to avoid making a complete fool of myself. I watched and listened as their conversation developed.

'So how're your dad and uncle, I keep trying to get them to come over here?' remarked Uncle Carlo.

Paul stood up, using the question as an excuse to stop playing for a moment. 'Yeah, they're both well and Dad's still busy writing.'

'Ah yes, writing; he loved stories when he was a boy. Not a very productive financial earner, but hey … ' Uncle Carlo pursed his lips and shrugged.

'Maybe, but he has sold a few of his novels and he's working on a screenplay for a film.' Paul looked over at me but I kept quiet.

'My, he's doing well then?'

'Yes. He's talking about making a film, a bit like The Godfather.'

'A bit like the Godfather – how do you mean?'

Starting to reach full flow, Paul's mouth appeared to be working ahead of his brain. 'I mean The Godfather, you know, Mafia.'

His uncle took a shot, pocketing the ball. 'The Mafia … and … ?'

'I have to ask you something,' began Paul. I looked at him, wondering what he would say next.

'Sure, what?' asked Carlo, straightening up, obviously satisfied that he had managed to get another ball in.

'It's my father. He suggested our family was linked to the Mafia.' Paul waited for a response as Carlo's cue slipped and shot across the table sending balls flying in the air.

'Oh, your father, he's obsessed … mad … We've had this conversation before. His ideas and imagination are beyond scope. He should keep such stories for his writing!'

'Maybe,' said Paul looking pointedly at his Uncle, 'but there was an explosion in Rome.' I backed Paul up, explaining about the bomb and describing how we'd both needed a stiff drink. Carlo shook his head, tutting, and insisted that his family had had nothing to do with it.

Carlo picked up his cue and went to retrieve the balls that had flown into Antonia's plant pot. 'Oh my God, her plants,' he exclaimed, taking care not to tear any of the leaves. He went on to explain the whole story. In the early 1900s, when the Mafia was just beginning to establish itself, a distant cousin had had some dealings with them. Up until the Second World War, they had operated mainly in the countryside, controlling rents and obtaining a percentage of each crop yield in return for protection. He assured Paul that no living relative had any connection with the Mafia. Hearing the click of the front door Carlo quickly checked Antonia's plant, making sure that every leaf was still in place. Relieved that they were, he stretched.

'Ah, they're back, I wonder what Antonia has bought, I'm starving!'

The rest of the family arrived. Enrico, the 24-year-old son, lived and worked as a clothes designer in Palermo. Marco, the 19-year-old, was a waiter in Catania. Still living at home, the life and soul of the party – a time-waster, as far as his father and brother were concerned. Then Marcella, the only daughter, aged twenty, still living at home.

I watched Marcella and her mother. They appeared close, dependent upon each other. It was like the relationship between Demeter and Persephone: Demeter, the ever-protecting, nurturing mother figure; Persephone, the good little girl, always doing what she was told.

The strong smell of tomatoes and herbs led everyone into the dining room, where a large table, covered by a crisp white tablecloth edged with lace and adorned with candles and floral decorations stood – no doubt Marcella's work. Pasta alla Norma, a Sicilian spaghetti dish comprising a spicy sauce of tomatoes with fried oily aubergines and grated salted ricotta cheese was served. The image of this large Italian family sitting round the table was like a scene from an exotic Italian film. I savoured every morsel of my meal and glanced at Carlo, very much the man of the house. A successful businessman, he had worked himself up through the ranks of the main banks in Catania.

'Katalina, I understand you are Greek,' he suddenly said as I took a large spoonful of spaghetti. His expression was kind but I still felt overwhelmed by "King Carlo". 'You know the Greeks were in Sicily centuries ago, in fact the first colony of Greeks arrived in 729 BC. They gave us many things,' he mused, looking down at his next spoonful of spaghetti, 'but the Italians, perhaps, have more style, unique in their own way.' Taken aback by this statement, I agreed, but felt rather cheated. To be Greek, be it only half, was to be proud of a heritage steeped in classical history and myth. I swallowed another spoonful of tomato sauce.

Carlo turned to Enrico, and asked how his clothing business was going. Enrico replied that his new design would soon be put in to production. Carlo congratulated him saying how proud he was and Enrico smiled smugly looking towards Marco.

Zeus, the infamous Greek god of all the gods, came into my thoughts, Zeus, like a thunderbolt executing his plans and desires. Carlo had established a wealthy kingdom for himself and had numerous children, for each of whom he wanted great things. Marco looked away from his father. The conversation continued as Carlo asked Marco about the food business.

'You take the mickey, father, it's just waiting tables, that's all,' Marco replied indignantly.

I felt sorry for him and looked at Paul, who sat motionless, staring at Marco. Paul's father had the same patronising view towards Paul's work that Carlo did to Marco. Bloody families!

Unable to leave it there, Carlo continued. 'He'll never get on, he just wants to party all the time; no plans for the future.' Marco's face dropped and he seemed about to give his father a piece of his mind when Carlo stepped in again asking me what I thought.

I felt an instant sense of panic. Why ask me, what did I know about the future?

I was still trying to get my thoughts together, when Antonia chipped in. 'Don't put her on the spot. Marco's OK; give him a chance, he's still young.'

'Perhaps she's right,' I said.

'Women, always sticking together!' Carlo huffed.

Perking up at the female support, Marco spoke up. 'I like reading.'

'Where's that going to get you?' his father interrupted.

I ignored Carlo. 'Reading?' I asked, turning to face Marco now.

'Yes, novels, and I enjoy going to the theatre.'

'You, the theatre? Never! Where's that going to get you?' Carlo exploded.

'Shut up, will you,' shouted Antonia, exasperated.

'Yes, I've been going to the theatre. I'd like to act.'

'Oh, not another one,' interrupted Carlo. Antonia threw him a disconcerted look.

'Oh wow, that's great, I love the theatre,' I said.

Marco's deep brown eyes looked directly at me, acknowledging a shared interest. Paul noticed his gaze. 'I must show you my books sometime,' Marco said.

I smiled. 'That would be great.'

The following day Carlo took Paul into Catania to show him where he worked. Marcella had gone to college that day and Enrico was back in Palermo.

'Here, I'll show you my books,' said Marco, leading me into his room. Along one side of the room were rows upon rows of books – all of the great novelists: Dickens, The Brontës and contemporary novels, P.D. James and more.

'You've read all of these?'

'Most of them. I'm now interested in reading plays and I'd really like to go into acting,' he added.

'Paul's dad wanted to be an actor. He's a writer.'

'Yes, I think I've read one of his books. It's a shame he doesn't live closer.'

I listened, absorbed by this interesting, fast-speaking Italian – ideas galore and plans for the future. Unfortunately, his father approved of none of them. I imagined Marco as Hermes, the eloquent god of communication, the youthful messenger of the gods, playing a role in a Greek play, wings protruding from his shoulders.

Later, when Paul returned, he told me about his uncle's bank and the fact that he really was the boss, never having to lift a finger; delegating most of his work to junior staff.

'Interesting,' I said, not as readily impressed as Paul so obviously was.

'How about you?' he asked. I told him that Marco had shown me his collection of books. 'Oh good, what else did he show you?'

'Nothing, that was it,' I said, detecting a note of jealousy.

Next morning, Antonia served breakfast. She had prepared a cappuccino especially for me in a tall mug decorated with pictures of cups and cocoa beans. It reminded me of the café in London.

'Here, you might want a spoon,' she offered.

Looking at the exploding froth I took the spoon and dived in. The bubbles evaporated as I scooped up another mouthful. Suddenly, a hand came across, stopping me.

'Please, just drink it!' exclaimed Paul.

Antonia turned and smiled. 'No, if she wants to scoop it with her spoon, it's fine.'

After one more spoonful, I then chose to drink it in the normal way, which was frustrating, as there was still a lot of froth left, which left me with a white Father Christmas moustache.

'You have some cappuccino above your lip,' Marco broke in, passing me a serviette. Paul looked first at me and then Marco, giving him an indignant glare, seemingly jealous of his own cousin.

'Oh, thanks. How's the reading going?' I asked, wiping the froth off.

'I've nearly finished the play.'

'You need to get together with Paul's dad,' I said, looking to Paul for support.

Paul looked at me, still not quite sure of his cousin's intentions. 'Oh yes, my dad is a writer.'

'And he's just starting to write a screenplay, isn't he?' I prompted, throwing Paul a scornful look.

Carlo appeared, sat down and was about to open a newspaper, when Antonia broke in, surprising Paul with a question. 'Do you go to church?'

He hesitated for a while and then abruptly answered, 'No, I don't.'

She stared back at him and smiled. 'That's a pity; I will be going to Mass tomorrow morning and I thought you could come with me. You should keep up your Roman Catholic faith; you were christened and baptised. I believe your mother is religious, isn't she?'

Carlo laid his newspaper down on the table and peered over his glasses. 'Your mother; how is she?'

'Fine,' exclaimed Paul, the expression on his face a picture. I knew that this wasn't a subject he wanted to talk about.

Carlo opened his rather large Zeus-like mouth and continued. 'Yes, your mum had her mad moments. I remember Alberto would ring saying how difficult it was for him to cope with her madness and bringing … '

'Zeus … Poseidon … anybody … ' I thought, 'help me now.'

THE GREEN LINE TO APHRODITE

Paul banged his fist down on the table, my coffee cup bounced in its saucer. 'How dare you? We came here to get to know you and instead you end up criticising my mother. You say "mad". How could you? She was depressed. Do you have any idea what that's like?' His eyes were aflame with anger. The silence was deathly as everybody waited, wondering who would speak next.

Carlo coughed nervously. 'Sorry, I shouldn't have said that, please forgive me.'

I didn't dare look at Paul's face. He would have to get himself out of this. Paul was quiet again, and a sense of calm reasserted itself, as he turned to face his aunt. 'Yes, my mother is religious and I know this has helped her over the years,' he finally admitted.

I breathed a quiet sigh of relief and said, without thinking, "If you like, I'll go with you tomorrow morning.' Paul looked at me, astonished.

Antonia smiled appreciatively. 'That would be lovely, thank you.'

The family took us out into the countryside. At dinnertime, we found a small restaurant that served homemade pizzas. I watched with fascination as the cook threw a lump of dough the size of a bowling ball onto a floured surface. Rolling up his sleeves he kneaded the dough, backwards and forwards until it formed a flat pizza base, which he flung effortlessly into the air before laying it onto a large spatula and placing it inside a hot oven. Stepping forward to the counter, I could feel the intense heat coming from the oven. Paul stood beside me, equally absorbed by the skill of this exuberant chef. Catching hold of my arm, he beckoned me to our table. Antonia and Carlo had their heads down, examining some potted plants. Paul thanked me for volunteering to go to the church with his aunt then repeated the fact that his mother had forced him to go to church and "do the confession bit," as he put it.

Carlo came over and sat next to Paul. 'Oh, your aunt, she's obsessed with plants, can't get her away from them,' he said.

We both looked over to see Antonia looking closely at one pot, after another, examining the leaves meticulously. She summoned a waiter to ask him what type of plants they were. The waiter confessed that he had no idea and suggested that she needed a gardener rather than a waiter.

Another waiter appeared and set down the homemade pizza. 'Here you are,' he announced proudly, 'served with San Marzano tomatoes. Enjoy!'

I mused at the waiter's enthusiasm for the tomatoes, unsure what that meant. Then I found myself gazing at Paul once more. Wearing a blue shirt with white collar he looked smart, as always, and I asked him why.

He shook his head. 'No reason, I just like to be. Is that OK?'

My elbow propped on the table, I smiled at him. 'Yes, of course.'

I placed my knife and fork down and was reaching a cigarette out, when my telephone rang.

'Hello!' I said, wiping away a drop of tomato that had somehow smudged across my left cheek.

It was Andrea. I told her that we were eating homemade pizza and that Paul's aunt was taking me to Mass the next day. At the word "Mass," Andrea went silent. A moment later, she reminded me that I had been christened Greek Orthodox. I agreed, trying to regain the peace. When she had calmed down, she told me she had to go as Mandras was glaring at her. I switched off my phone and put it back into my bag, wondering what else could go wrong. The rest of the afternoon was spent walking around the countryside, with Paul's aunt examining any plant that came into view.

Back at the house, I disappeared upstairs and used my mobile to log on to the Athelia website:

Dear Poseidon **I've had some great homemade pizzas but, oh God, I wish I could have got here sooner. Uncle Carlo criticised Paul's mum saying she was mad, Paul got very cross and there was this awful silence, it was too ... too ...**

Dear Katalina I think 'too much' is what
you were going to say. I send
people tidal waves, earthquakes
and much more at times. Life
experiences can so often be
made up of introverted feelings,
unexpressed emotions. I
arrive with an earthquake and
everything appears torn apart
and exposed but then comes the
time for people to move out of that
sub-conscious place, to then take a
step forward.

Dear Poseidon Thanks; a bit deep, but I think I
get your drift.

'Katalina are you coming downstairs?' a voice shouted. I
logged off and left the room.

Later that evening there was to be a special traditional Sicilian
folk dance nearby. Carlo and Antonia went every year and this
year they could share their tradition with Paul. There were three
main dances and Antonia explained them to us, as we sat outside:
the Tarantella, meaning tarantula, an Italian folk dance where
everyone dances clockwise in a circle, quite different from the
Indian dancing that Suzanne had dragged me to. The music of
the Tarantella becomes faster until suddenly everyone changes
direction. Carlo interrupted as he placed sparkling wine on the
table, informing us that the dance appeared in *The Godfather.*

Paul flinched at the word "Godfather" and watched as Carlo
poured wine into my glass.

'Here, Katalina, Sicilian wine; the best, Cin, cin!'

I smiled, taking a sip of wine, followed by another sip, and
then drank a further two glasses. Paul stared knowingly at me.

All the family joined us, sitting down to take in the cool
evening air.

'Well Katalina, what do you think of Italy then?' asked Carlo.

'Great, except for the bomb in Rome,' I replied.

Carlo apologised for his country's behaviour and informed us that the Godfather of the Mafia had been on the run for forty-three years.

'Some say he has hidden out in the country, up in the hills somewhere. Personally, I think he has fled the country.' Paul shook his head in disbelief. 'Anyway, it is time for celebrating, I think, uh?' exclaimed Carlo, slapping Paul on the back.

In front of the chairs and tables lay a circular forecourt where the Tarantella was to take place. Four bandsmen walked towards the forecourt, each holding a musical instrument. As the music started, people stood up and joined hands – the tarantula dance had begun. I took another sip of wine and noticed Marco giving me occasional glances.

'Come on, everyone to their feet,' commanded Carlo, pulling Paul up from his seat. I noticed the contrast between them: Carlo, standing only five feet tall, dwarfed by Paul's six feet. Sensing that Paul wasn't keen on dancing, I looked away. Soon all the family were up, joining the circle. The music was slow at first, gradually increasing in pace until suddenly everything changed, as people began to skip in the opposite direction.

Marco rose from his seat, and bent to take my hand. 'Come on, it is a fun dance.'

I accepted his hand and we smiled at each other until our gaze was interrupted as the pace of the music increased. A number of people started to drop out, including Paul, Marcello and Enrico. Marco and I, along with a few others, remained. My movements became so quick I barely noticed Paul, who was sitting, watching my every move. Marco grabbed my left hand, swinging me around. The circle of people rapidly decreased until finally just the two of us remained. We had now gained quite an audience. As the music changed pace into a tango, Marco continued to swing me around. Then, using one hand, he spun me on the spot. A combination of fiery footwork and passion dynamic moves had set in. My feet now on autopilot knew every step to take. Carlo watched Paul, who sat staring at Marco. He caught Paul's attention, with a nudge. Paul looked back at his uncle, whose expression indicated that he knew what Paul was thinking. Carlo quietly whispered into Paul's ear and Paul immediately walked on to the dance floor. I suddenly found myself being swung round, first by Marco, and then, my hand pulled in the other direction, by Paul. Marco let go, smiling.

'I think it's my turn now,' Paul uttered. Taken in by this impromptu move, my eyes met his. He was in charge now as he towered above me, my head on his chest. He laid his right hand behind my head, protectively. The music began to drop in pace and everything seemed to slow down. My body finally slowed down. My feelings towards him were starting to change. The evening had passed very quickly. The musicians departed and the barmen began to fold up the chairs and tables.

'Bloody womaniser,' Enrico whispered into Marco's ear as Carlo drove us home. Marco turned away from his brother, ignoring the remark. I didn't dare look at Marco. Instead I held Paul's hand.

As we walked up the stairs together, I could feel my legs beginning to ache. When we reached the top, we turned to go to our separate rooms. Paul caught my hand and looked at me. When he suggested that I spent the night with him, I looked shocked.

'What about your uncle and aunt?'

Paul insisted it would be okay and that I could sneak back to my room early in the morning. Romance was definitely in the air – the Sicilian dancing and music had been intoxicating. At 2am, I awoke to find myself squeezed up against Paul. I knew I had to sneak back to my own room soon, but first I needed to speak with Aphrodite:

Dear Aphrodite I've just experienced some Italian passion and dancing. I don't know what to say.

Dear Katalina   **Say nothing; you are moving on.**

Dear Aphrodite   **So was that Eros?**

Dear Katalina   **No, it was me, just a sprinkle of passion to start you on your way.**

I heard footsteps in the hall and the sound of somebody switching on a light. I closed my eyes and went back to sleep.

Next morning, I sipped my coffee with a dreamy expression across my face. My thoughts were far away.

Antonia pushed another cup of black coffee towards me. 'Please, Katalina, when you are ready to go.'

Oh God, I'd forgotten my promise that I would go to Mass with her. It was a tight schedule, as we were leaving for Greece later the same day.

Arriving at the church, I sat in one of the pews at the back and stared at the altar, whilst Antonia went into the confessional. I thought of what Paul had said the previous day. The church smelt of incense and candles and during the Mass, I found myself closing my eyes, putting together my own prayers. As I opened my eyes, Antonia motioned for us to leave. 'Come, we'd better go, I don't want you to miss your flight.'

Outside, Paul's family waved us goodbye.

'Give my regards to your father and uncle and get them to come and see us,' shouted Carlo, as we walked to the car. That was unlikely I thought as I saw Paul nodding politely.

Our brief visit to this romantic, passionate island was at an end. As we caught the flight to Thessaloniki, ahead of us lay the classical land of Greece. It was here that I would embark on my journey in search of my relatives, living or dead.

THESSALONIKI – VERGINA

The wheels of the plane thudded on the tarmac as we landed and the lights of the airport building shone brightly against the dark night sky. At last, I had finally landed on Greek soil. In my head, I quickly spoke to the god of travel:

Dear Hermes   **I'm here, finally here in Greece. Your wings have brought me to the land of the gods, thank you.**

Dear Katalina **Yes, you have landed, and you don't need to thank me. This, I'm sure, is just the start of your journey.**

Outside the terminus, we hailed a taxi to take us to our hotel. The driver spoke to us in broken English. Greek voices blared out from the radio sounding alien to me.

The taxi driver continued his conversation. 'You English then?' In a daze, I looked out of the window, not answering.

'Answer him,' said Paul, giving me a nudge. I told the driver that I was half Greek. He asked us if we were here on holiday.

'Sort of,' Paul replied.

'Sort of?' I whispered.

'I don't want to give anything away,' he whispered back.

At the hotel, the taxi driver got out and collected our bags. 'Efcharisto,' I said.

The taxi driver looked at me with surprise. 'Bravo, you speak Greek then?' he said.

'Only a little,' I admitted.

Next morning we sat in the restaurant, waiting to be served. A friendly waiter appeared, introducing himself as Dimitri. I had a long conversation with him all about the Greek gods and the spectacular places to visit in Greece. I got on really well with him, much to the annoyance of Paul.

'O kafes me gala, parakalo,' I said.

Paul looked at me, 'Which means?'

'Coffee with milk please,' I said, pleased that the Greek language was becoming more natural now.

'Oh, right,' replied Paul, glancing towards Dimitri.

We stayed in that morning, giving Paul a chance to review his paperwork. He told me that a Professor Marolis had originally found the site of Vergina and the tomb of Philip II in the 1970s. When he retired, Professor Yannis of Athens University took over most of the work and, since then, has found further artefacts.

I flicked through a tourist book that I had picked up in the hotel foyer. "Thessaloniki, the central location of Macedonia; Macedonia is part of the northern region in Greece. Greek history first recorded its existence in 7 BC."

Reading on, I found out that in 512 BC, the land was conquered by the Persian, Darius.

Within a hundred years it was Philip II and his son, Alexander the Great, who conquered all of Greece. I placed the book down on the marble coffee table and opened the patio door to walk out onto the balcony. A cool breeze stirred the air as the bright sun shone through into the room. The hotel overlooked Thessaloniki Bay with its blue sea stretching out to the horizon. Poseidon's glorious Greek Mediterranean Sea spread all around.

Later, as we walked through the reception area, the receptionist recognised us from the previous evening. 'Geiasas, Katalina and Paul,' she said, telling me her name was Sophia.

'Geiasas,' I said, spotting a photo on the reception desk. I craned my neck, trying to take a closer look. The receptionist smiled, turning the picture round for me to see. An old black and white print showed an elderly woman wearing a long dress.

Curious, I asked, 'Who is she?'

Paul nudged me. 'Don't be so nosy.' I swept an indignant look back at him.

'No, please,' the receptionist replied, 'it's a photo of my great-grandmother; she lives on the island of Santorini.'

'Oh, how sweet,' I exclaimed.

The receptionist bent down and retrieved more photos. 'Here, I have these as well.'

Not wanting to appear rude, I patiently looked at each photo in turn; pictures of children, families over the generations swept before my eyes. Sophia asked if I had any photos. I told her hardly any, only a few in my suitcase.

As we walked along the sand taking in the early morning sun, the sea appeared calm. Paul talked about his research and the meeting with Professor Yannis. He explained that he had e-mailed him when he was in the US. The professor had replied, confirming what the Italian professor had said about the statue, and had also offered to show him around the Vergina site. Paul told me how great the professor was. I asked why, then wished I hadn't as he launched in to tell me more about the projects and research the professor had carried out and the different artefacts he had found over the years. I nodded in the right places. It wasn't that I wasn't interested; he just seemed to carry on about it for too long.

That evening I ate my first Greek moussaka, albeit a vegetarian version based on aubergine and peppers, rather than the traditional minced lamb, followed by a milky honey dish. We had a different waiter that evening; efficient but not as friendly as Dimitri. Our meal over, we were about to get into the lift, when:

'Ah Katalina, Katalina, please have a look at this one; do you have yours on you?' Anticipating Sophia's request, I had slipped two photos of my father in my pocket to show her. Suddenly, Dimitri appeared from behind the bar and smiled at me. Paul sent him a quick glare and left me with Sophia.

The next day, we planned to visit the famous White Tower, an historical monument with a grizzly past. Built in 1430 by the Turks, it had previously been known as the Bloody Tower. Looking through my tourist guide again, I read that that the Turks had used it to massacre their enemies; slitting their throats. They would hang their bodies from the top of the tower with blood, guts and gore dripping down over the sides. Lovely, and just before breakfast!

Paul was still getting ready, so I headed down to the restaurant having arranged to meet him in the hallway. At the bottom of the stairs, I leant against a pillar. Feeling a bit conspicuous and wishing that Paul would hurry up, I stared at the pictures on the wall, pictures of Thessaloniki, Greek flags and scenes of magnificent Greek landscape. From behind the reception desk I heard Dimitri calling me.

'Kalimera, Katalina you stand there like the great Athena herself.' Shocked, I turned towards the desk, to see Dimitri smiling.

Paul then appeared from behind and tapped me on the shoulder. Looking first at Dimitri then at me he demanded, 'What did he say?'

Dimitri overheard Paul's question and repeated his words in a very pronounced Greek accent. I wished the ground would open and suck me in. Why did he have to repeat it?

Paul pursed his lip then took hold of my hand possessively and led me into the dining room. 'Athena?' he asked quizzically

'Yes,' I replied, looking wistful. 'You're not jealous?'

'Well, yes, as a matter of fact I am. I guess it's a compliment really.'

'It is. In fact, it makes me feel quite good. All I need now is a helmet and sword,' I giggled.

The sun was bright, set against a brilliant blue sky. My warm Greek sun had finally arrived. There was the White Tower, standing prominently on the sea front, its Greek flag flying. Walking towards the tower, we saw a rough-looking Alsatian dog drinking out of a water fountain. I wondered if it was lost and I was just about to stride up to it when Paul stopped me. 'Don't do that. You don't know what it's got!'

'It hasn't got an owner, that's what it hasn't got!' I said.

'Maybe, but many of these animals are strays.'

'Oh, that's awful,' I wailed, looking closely at the animal. 'Mind you, he does look well fed. Perhaps he is OK.'

'Yes, I'm sure he is. Let's get on now.'

Our next task was to climb to the top of the tower. The spiral staircase seemed to go on forever. The place felt damp and claustrophobic and I began to feel out of breath. Paul, with his long legs, had already reached the top. A few more steps and I would be there. Almost collapsing on the ground, I turned my head up to look at Paul.

He gazed down at me in disbelief. 'You made it then?'

'It's ok for you, you have long legs.'

'No, you're just not fit enough,' he replied.

'Yeah, probably true. Wow look at that,' I said, looking out from the top of the tower. The city of Thessaloniki lay stretched out behind us, a mixture of high-rise buildings, red roofs and green trees.

Walking back, I thought about the Bloody Tower, Sophia and Dimitri. As we entered the hotel, its grand white marbled-floored entrance greeted us, gleaming in the sunlight.

'Katalina, geiasas, parakalo – I have more photos,' called out Sophia. Paul immediately turned and rushed towards the lift, announcing that he would see me later. I faced Sophia, as she showed me her photos telling me about her mother who lived in Athens and who rang her every night. Sophia went through each photo, one by one, determined to secure my undivided attention. It made me think of an aunt I had in England. My mum and I would visit her every Saturday afternoon. When we arrived she would have a plate of rich tea biscuits ready. My mum would fill the kettle up and come back into the lounge to find a box of photos on the table. We would spend the whole afternoon going through every single one.

Half an hour later, I arrived upstairs. 'Thanks for running away!'

Paul peered up from his book. 'My pleasure; it's not my thing.'

I snorted and thought about ringing Andrea. Would she be in? Looking at my watch, I tried to work out the time difference – were they two or three hours behind; would Mandras answer? I dug down into my bag for my phone and dialled the number –

Mandras answered. Our conversation was short as we exchanged a few pleasantries and he went on to moan about tax returns and Andrea's overspending before hastily saying goodbye.

At 7 pm, we went down to the restaurant. Dimitri came over to our table. Paul looked at him cautiously. I looked at Dimitri, with his head held back and black hair that swept over his forehead into small wavy curls. He handed us each a menu, smiling at me as he did so. I gave a tentative smile back before quickly looking down.

'What do you think of our country then?' he asked.

Paul gave an indignant look. Before he could make a comment, I replied that it was beautiful but that, of course, we had only seen Thessaloniki so far. Dimitri insisted that we must visit "the magnificent Parthenon."

Paul interrupted him dismissively. 'We are, we are going to see it, thank you,' then continued to inspect the menu.

'Oh, that is good. I shall leave you to choose your meal. The squid is good tonight.' Dimitri reluctantly left us alone, summoned to another table.

'He doesn't give in, does he,' exclaimed Paul.

'He's Greek, just being friendly,' I said as I watched Dimitri walk away. He was unusually tall with a long stride.

'Greek, and eyes on you,' Paul added.

'Oh get away with you, just choose your meal. The squid is good!'

I realised that my vegetarian tastes were going to be a problem here – practically everything on the menu contained meat. Fortunately I managed to find a dish called gemista – vegetables stuffed with rice, pine nuts and herbs. The bitter taste of green pepper and the soft textured white rice blended together beautifully. My dessert, vyssino, a sweet dish made from morello cherries in thick syrup served with a slice of aged kasseri cheese, tasted like a dream.

Scooping up the last cherry from the bowl, I looked up to see Dimitri again. Paul looked up as well, disgruntled by his presence.

Dimitri held a small glass filled with a clear liquid. He placed it down on the table in front of me. 'For you,' he said. 'Every Greek must taste our famous ouzo.' I caught a twinkle in his eye as he turned away, doing his best not to catch Paul's eye.

I looked down at my first ouzo and, without hesitation, swallowed it in one gulp. Spluttering and choking, my throat burned and my eyes watered.

Paul gave me a disconcerted look. 'Are you supposed to drink it in that way?'

I replied in a squeaky voice, 'That I'm not sure of, but I think this is the way any good Greek citizen should drink it.' I felt light headed. 'I think I'm going to need some help to get upstairs.'

Paul took hold of my arm and led me back to the room. Seduced by the intoxicating power of my homeland's national drink, I could see that he was wondering whether this was going to be one of many scenes to come.

I awoke at 6 am with my head pounding. I remembered the ouzo and being helped upstairs by Paul. In the bathroom, I found a bottle of aspirin. I tipped out two tablets and quickly knocked them back. I thought about the day ahead – today was to be our first trip to Vergina. It was an important archaeological site that could hold vital information and clues to the statue's origins. Aspirins taken, I went back to bed. An hour later, Paul woke me up.

'Come on, get up, we'll be late.'

'Sorry, it must have been the aspirin I took earlier.'

'I'm not surprised after drinking the ouzo like that,' Paul said, pointedly.

As we approached Vergina, white washed houses with red rooftops came into view. Although it was only mid-March, I could feel the heat on my skin. In the middle of the village stood a holy shrine. These religious monuments were common throughout Greece, appearing on many of the roadsides. This one was larger than most, boasting large red roof adorned by a gold cross. In the front, an open archway contained a large icon depicting a famous Greek saint. It made me think of my father – he was a religious man and had loved the Greek icons. It reminded me of the times when he would take me to the Greek Orthodox Church. As I stood there, I recalled one of the photos Georgette showed me of my father, a young man wearing a uniform.

We stopped at a café for a drink, finding the place almost deserted. Refreshed, we continued towards the museum, approaching a flat gravelled open space leading to the main entrance. The museum contained one of the tombs found by Professor Marolis. I stood mesmerised as I looked through a glass casing, where light shone onto a gold wreath, constructed of a variety of oak leaves, which glittered and shimmered in the light. Other artefacts, including pots, vases and jewellery, were displayed within the museum. Round the corner was a large square burial casket made of gold engraved with an image of the sun. Paul had always raved about this famous casket which had originally contained the bones of King Philip II. The light shining down from the outer casing made the gold sparkle. A few steps led to a picturesque mural, depicting the abduction of Persephone by the underworld god Hades. I remembered that it was Paul's cousin Marcella who mimicked the qualities of this vulnerable goddess. Finally, we found the grand entrance to the original tomb of Philip II. Tall Doric columns framed a large door that led through to the main tomb itself.

'Wow, to think that this has stood here for all this time,' I announced.

'Yes, it's magnificent,' Paul replied.

Leaving the museum, we looked at our map and headed towards the main excavation site.

'Aha, you made it,' exclaimed Professor Yannis, standing up to give Paul an embracing hug.

Paul stepped back towering above the Professor then leant forward to shake his hand. 'Hi, I heard so much about you,' he said, nervously. The professor smiled back at him, flicking his hand in the air, as if to refute the compliment.

I interrupted their greetings. 'Geiasas!'

The professor looked towards me and smiled. 'Ah, you speak Greek?'

'Only a little; the odd word or two,' I replied.

There was something familiar about his face. He reminded me of my brother, Stephanos, with his dark, thick greying eyebrows and fixed determined expression which held me firmly in its gaze.

The professor found a space and, beckoning for us to sit down, described the excavation's progress. A document, originating from Alexandria, had been found that described how a large statue, a vase inscribed with the words "Megas Alexandros" and small figurines had been made during Alexander's lifetime. Recently, they had excavated a number of Aphrodite figurines. Paul's eyes gleamed, anticipating a link to what the professor would hopefully reveal. The professor led us to a tent where the figurines were stored in a box protected from the sunlight. He put on some gloves and passed another pair to Paul, who immediately bent down to pick up one of the figurines, admiring its delicacy.

'What about the date of these figurines?' asked Paul.

The professor took out a packet of cigarettes and offered it to us. Paul shook his head while I gladly took up his offer. Paul sent me a critical glare.

'The date … We are not sure yet.'

Paul interrupted him. 'Yes, but surely you must have some idea.'

The professor sighed. 'Your enthusiasm is good, but have patience! We've only just found these two figurines.' Paul apologised for his eagerness.

Exhaling, the professor continued, remarking that Paul reminded him of a young Odysseus, impatient to get on with the journey.

'Are there any more of these figurines?'

'Yes, we believe that there are two more, as well as a vase, which is also linked to the Aphrodite statue and the Great Alexander himself.'

'I've heard about this, but how?'

'Alexander had a teenage sweetheart called Cassandra. His father disapproved of her, but later on, Alexander commissioned a statue of Aphrodite in commemoration of her. His father forbade the relationship, wanting the young Alexander to go to war, to fight the invading Persian army. I suggest you go to the museum back in Thessaloniki to see more artefacts from that period in time.'

The movement of the professor's hands as he spoke, the way he held his cigarette, conjured up an image of my dead brother. 'How did the Aphrodite statue get to Ostia anyway?' I asked.

'Ah yes; that is a very good question. Well, Philip hated the large statue so, afraid that his father would have it destroyed, Alexander had it shipped to Rome, out of his father's reach.'

'Now that makes sense,' I said.

Paul looked at us both. 'It could still be Roman though, couldn't it?'

'It could, but that's why we need to continue with this,' replied the professor.

'He's half Italian,' I suddenly interrupted.

'Ah, well I see; but still keen to find the truth?'

'Of course,' asserted Paul.

Professor Yannis shook Paul's hand. 'Don't forget; ring me any time, well, within reason.' He shrugged. 'You must go to the university in Athens, tell them I sent you.' The professor turned to me and gave me a strong Greek hug. 'And you, take care.' He looked towards Paul and added. 'You look after her.'

Paul nodded. 'Yes I will.'

I felt embarrassed as Paul took hold of my hand. 'I need looking after, do I?'

'After last night, I think you do,' he said. Remembering the ouzo, I had to agree.

We drove back to Thessaloniki and found the museum. Inside a glass cabinet stood a number of amphora vases dating back to between 378 and 321 BC which fascinated Paul. Walking across the other side of the room I fell in love with a piece of gold and turquoise jewellery.

Returning to the hotel, hot and tired, we changed into our swimming costumes and made our way to the indoor pool. Much to my amazement, Paul swam a few lengths, whilst I chose to lie on my back and found myself staring up at the blue ceiling with its sculpted figurines. My mind started to drift and was soon dominated by thoughts of the Greek gods and the journey ahead. Paul swam into the side of me and woke me from my dream.

That evening we decided to sample Thessaloniki's nightlife. I pulled out the skimpy red dress that I had worn to the opera. Jewellery was the next item to consider. Assorted clothes flew out of my case, as I searched for a small white box. I found it tucked under a T-shirt. Inside lay the silver necklace with its Greek key design. As I tried to unclasp the catch, I dropped it. Paul came up behind me and picked it up. Carefully he placed it around my neck. 'That's it, I've got it now.' I turned round, looking in the mirror. He smiled at me. 'That looks stunning.'

Dimitri stood at the bar serving our drinks. 'Ah, Katalina and Paul, you are going out tonight?'

'Geiasas, yes; we thought we'd sample some of the nightlife before we leave,' I replied.

Paul turned away, pretending to examine a painting on the wall.

Dimitri then announced in a pronounced Greek accent, 'Oh my, Aphrodite herself, her silky hair and beautiful necklace and … ' Paul turned round sharply and was about to raise his right arm towards Dimitri when I stretched out my arm and stopped him, just in time. Dimitri added, 'She's strong as well.'

Keeping hold of Paul's arm, I asked, 'Well, which one am I, Athena or Aphrodite?'

'Easy, both,' Dimitri replied.

Paul glared at us; a glare that reminded me of Zeus, the god of power, of thunder, now directing his thunderbolt towards Dimitri.

Paul turned to us and asked whether all Greeks were so self obsessed. I felt a tinge of embarrassment, as the joke was now wearing thin. I couldn't believe what I had just said.

'No, it's a joke,' insisted Dimitri.

'Oh, so she's not beautiful now?' demanded Paul.

'Of course, she is like a special treasure; a treasure that needs to be taken care of.' Paul backed down and I continued to feel embarrassed as Dimitri poured our drinks.

'Here, these are on the house.'

We made our way onto the streets of Thessaloniki. Relieved that things had calmed down, I could now see the humour of that the situation. I suddenly realised that Paul was exceedingly jealous. I didn't know what to think at this point. I was in Greece and did not want to be detracted from my mission.

Along the sea front, we found a fish restaurant. Next to our table sat a small, lively family. The mother was having great difficulty keeping control of her younger son.

'Come back now! You've only eaten one mouthful.' The boy ran back down to the water. Moments later, back again, he took another mouthful and ran back to the sea. The mother looked exasperated, the father keeping his head in his newspaper. It made me think of Harry, the small boy from the café.

'Must have some attention deficit disorder,' I said

'Attention what?'

'You know, they can't sit still for long, they get easily distracted.'

'That wouldn't happen if it was my child,' remarked Paul.

The waiter appeared and placed a menu on the table. The Greek word "kalamari" appeared with the English translation "squid." I chose a cheese dish, "saganaki," deep-fried squares of kefalograviera cheese doused with lemon juice.

'Try some kalamari, it's really good,' Paul insisted, offering me a piece.

'No thanks, I'm happy with the cheese.'

With an unexpectedly strong Italian accent, he continued, 'Eh, you are missing out! It's good.'

'Missing out? No, I prefer the idea of an octopus swimming in the sea, not sitting on a plate in front of me.'

He smiled and we continued to eat. Greek salad with feta cheese and olives followed. The squid had beaten him so we skipped the main dish and ended our meal with saffron and honey pears. The pears reminded me of the caramelised pears I had eaten in Sicily.

Next morning, with our bags packed, we went into the restaurant. Sophia called out to me. I walked over to the desk with Paul following behind. 'Ah, kalimera to you both. You are leaving us today?'

'Yes, that's right,' answered Paul, happy to speak to her now that we were leaving.

Sophia showed me some more photographs and wished us both well for the future. I felt privileged that she had shown me her photos: it made me think of the relatives I hoped to find. In the restaurant, Dimitri served us breakfast and also wished us well, saying he hoped there were no grudges or hard feelings. Paul shook his hand and replied that there weren't, but I suspected otherwise.

London – A display of the Elgin Marbles inside the British Museum

Los Angeles – Universal Studios

Los Angeles – Long Beach. The Queen Mary

Rome – Magnificent paintings on the ceilings of the Vatican

The Parthenon where ancient Greek mariners oversaw the great city of Athens

Athens – Some wild cats in the shade from the hot mid-day sun

Running for Greece – the olympic stadium in Athens

Greece – The magical site of Delphi and where the navel stone stands

Cyprus – A lizard makes a sudden appearance and scurries across the rocks!

Cyprus – One of the many beautiful house of mosaics found in Paphos

Cyprus – A small wayside shrine in the village of Nata. A time for reflection

A Greek icon painting

ATHENS 1

The car stopped as Mount Olympus and the other grand mountain peaks lay before us, emerging like giant whales from snow-white crusted waves in the thick swirling mist of a brewing storm. I took a deep breath of the clean, sharp air. These mountains represented the mystical home of the gods. This was the home of Zeus, most powerful of all the gods. I took out my camera and snapped a few shots of this immortal view. As we continued on our journey I fell asleep and dreamt of Zeus seated on a gold throne, keeping a watchful eye over his country of Greece.

'Wake up!'

I felt my arm being nudged. Slowly my eyes opened and Zeus disappeared from sight. In the distance I could see the sprawling city of Athens and, on the horizon, like a volcano about to erupt, the Parthenon standing proud, just like the picture my dad had shown me all those years before. As we journeyed into the city, the buildings loomed closer. The Parthenon disappeared from sight, as we drove into a subway.

When Paul asked for the map, I passed him a crumpled sheet of paper. 'How can I see that, it's all screwed up?'

'No, no, it's ok, I'll just flatten it out a bit,' I said as, with the sheet sprawled across my lap, I attempted to push the creases out.

Paul stopped the car. 'Here it is, just below that small crease there.'

'I can't see that, you have your finger on it.' Abruptly I pushed the map into his lap.

Feeling the need to lighten the atmosphere, I told Paul the story of Athena and Poseidon, how they fought for ownership of Athens. Poseidon had put forth a seawater spring and Athena had planted an olive tree.

'Who won?'

'Why, Athena, of course.'

'Who else, I might have guessed?'

I added that the olive branch was a symbol of peace. 'Great!' he replied.

We pulled up to the Andromeda Hotel, close to the Acropolis, a small, yet luxurious hotel with spectacular glass doors and a patio decorated with an assortment of plant pots. The reception area was equally lavish, adorned with soft furnishings and modern Greek artworks.

The receptionist handed us our keys and we went to our room. The furnishings in the main lounge were a sumptuous cream and white like a slab of marble cake. The large bedroom, in shades of blue, was cool and calming, the spacious bathroom tiled in a Greek key design.

I opened the balcony doors and stepped out to see the Parthenon. 'Look at this!'

Paul stood beside me, observing the smile of satisfaction on my face.

The hotel had two restaurants, one on the ground, the other on the top floor. This spectacular roof-top restaurant overlooked the northern side of the city, providing yet another magnificent view of the Parthenon. As it was only open in the evenings, we decided to sample the open-air cuisine. Our table, situated at the edge of the restaurant floor, directly overlooked the streets below. People were still around and the city was bustling even at that time, unlike some places in England where everything seemed to come to a halt after 5.30.

'Vraidi, or should I say good evening,' said the waiter. He was fastidious, straightening the cutlery then examining the glasses to check that they were clean.

'Ah, that is good, this is a top restaurant; everything must be perfect,' he remarked as he straightened one last fork. As he passed us the menus, he inadvertently knocked over one of the glasses he had just meticulously inspected. I looked at him, noticing his name badge – "Nico."

'Except for that one, that's not perfect now,' said Paul,

pointing to the glass that now lay on its side. I gave him a look. Had his petty, critical behaviour surfaced once more?

'My deepest apologies; I will have it replaced immediately.'

'Perfect but clumsy,' Paul added after he had gone.

'Give him a break!'

'Ah, siding with your Greek countrymen; a true Greek patriot.'

'If you say so,' I countered, annoyed by his childish display.

Nico returned with a new glass, apologised profusely, and insisted that the soup for the evening was excellent. I watched him as he walked away. He was short in height with unusually short blond hair. Then I returned my gaze to the Parthenon which stood like a tall castle, just waiting to be explored.

A middle-aged couple were seated at a table by the window. The woman, of average height with grey hair and glasses, stood up, holding a walking stick. She walked over to a painting on the wall, examined it, and then walked back to her table.

'Why do people do that?' I asked.

'Do what?'

'Use a stick when they don't need to.' Paul looked at the woman just as she was sitting down, and asked me how I knew that she didn't need a stick.

'Simple,' I told him, 'she wasn't hobbling.' Gesturing with my hands to illustrate my point, my arm suddenly connected with something. I hadn't noticed Nico returning with our soup and I knocked the bowl to the floor. With a loud crash, beans and more beans spread in a pool around our table. 'Oh, me synchoreite!'

'No, it's ok, I will get another bowl,' said Nico.

'I can't make it out who's the more clumsy; you or the waiter,' said Paul with a smirk.

Trying to recover from my ordeal and conscious that the other customers were looking at us, Paul's sarcastic remarks made me keen to get my revenge.

Next morning, we were late to awake and ended up sharing the bathroom, me cleaning my teeth, whilst Paul shaved. The opportunity was too good to miss and I was in the mood for confrontation. When Paul turned his back, I snatched his toothbrush and squeezed shaving foam onto it. I watched him take the brush and place it into his mouth. Trying to stifle my giggles, I walked back into the bedroom and peered round the bathroom door.

'Oh God, yuck, this is shaving foam. Katalina!' He stood, his mouth bulging with shaving foam.

'Yes,' I gulped, trying to contain my laughter. Was he going to be angry; would he laugh or cry?

'Why?' he asked, walking towards me.

'Why what?' He glared at me for a minute as he walked towards me. As our eyes met, he swiped some of the foam from his face and slapped it onto my nose. I swiped the foam from my nose and slapped it back onto his.

'Sorry I had to do it; had to get my own back, what with Nico and the soup last night.'

'Oh right, so it was payback time?'

After breakfast we walked to the metro station, which was modern in design, bright and metallic, containing many artefacts. Inside the station were magnificent statues behind glass casing. Some were headless, others armless, but all were massive. I wanted to reach out and touch them. They represented the centre of the universe, the centre of a place steeped in powerful classical history.

We soon reached our destination, the family archive. I felt anxious; would I get anywhere? Would I find what I was looking for? At the reception desk stood a man reading a newspaper, a cigarette between his nicotine-stained fingers. I approached him and spoke to him in English. He immediately began waving his arms around, mumbling in Greek, interspersed with the odd word of English. He pointed to the lift, and wrote the number five on a piece of paper. In the lift, we stood in silence. The door opened and we walked out into another reception area. This time, there was a Greek woman who spoke more English. I explained what I was trying to do. She listened intently then said that I needed the next floor. Back into the corridor and into the lift which took us up to the sixth floor. Out of the lift, we were faced with yet another receptionist.

'My name is Katalina Sokritos; I've come all the way from England, I'm half Greek and I've come here to trace my family,' I announced.

The woman stared at me and nodded. 'Do you have your passport?'

I leant down into my bag and searched; no passport. 'I'm sure I put it in here this morning. Oh this is so unfair; I'll have to go back to the hotel.'

'I'm sorry Madame, but we need to see your passport.'

'Well it only took us half an hour to get here. Come on, we'll go back and get it,' replied Paul.

Exasperated, we walked back into the lift, back to the metro then back to the hotel. Having retrieved my passport, we retraced our journey to the archive, and ventured straight to the sixth floor. Seated at a computer, I took my brother Stephanos's birth certificate out of my bag and typed in his date and place of birth. We waited to see what the database would turn up. The name and date had been registered and we were directed to the archive bookshelves to look for further details.

'Here it is,' said Paul.

He held up an old, leather-bound book with Greek lettering on the front. It contained many Greek surnames beginning with "S." Placing it down on the table, I began to turn the pages. Although it was in Greek, a translation sheet had been placed just inside the front cover. I came to the name "Sokritos," written in Greek followed by the forename "Stephanos." We'd found it, but the rest of the entry was in Greek.

I looked at Paul in dismay. 'Well, I guess it's to be expected.'

'I suppose so,' I said, feeling the impact of my disappointment.

'How about the girl at the desk; perhaps she could translate it?'

Carefully picking up the book, we walked over to the main desk. The girl spoke English and translated the entry, revealing a miraculous and surprising picture of my dead brother – he had another brother called Leandro. Although Leandro was dead, he had three children. At this point, the girl's boss appeared, insisting there were other were other people needing assistance.

That evening, the restaurant felt cold as I kept going over events of the day. My brother had a brother! Although he was not alive, there were three children. I felt a sense of relief that my search had begun but impatient that it wasn't going to be as straightforward as I would have liked. I noticed the couple from the previous evening seated by the window and decided to name them "George and Mildred." As on the previous evening, Mildred still had her walking stick. I listened across to their conversation.

'Oh I don't think much of this Greek food, it's too oily, and as for having to pay for a glass of water, well that's disgusting!'

'Bloody cheek!'

'What?'

'Mildred.'

'Who's Mildred?' Paul asked, looking round.

'You know that couple sitting behind you, the one with the stick. She said she didn't like Greek food, that it's too oily.'

'Shhh, they'll hear you.'

That evening a different waiter appeared. He wore a crisp white shirt, bow tie and cream coloured waistcoat, and a badge with the words "Head waiter – Christos."

'Ah, you must be Katalina and Paul?'

'Yes, how do you know?' I asked.

'Ah, my friend Nico told me about the accident with the soup.'

'Oh, that,' murmured Paul.

I gave a half smile and then began chewing my lip.

'Well, my name is Christos and I will be serving you tonight. I recommend the moussaka and a very special Greek wine,' he said, giving me a wink.

Paul glared at him. 'She's a vegetarian.'

'Me synchoreite?' queried Christos.

'I said she's a vegetarian. She doesn't eat meat, and she's half Greek,' said Paul, determined to antagonise the new waiter.

Christos turned to face me. 'Is this true, you don't eat meat?'

'Most of the time. Please ignore him,' I said, pointing to Paul, 'the meat in the moussaka will be fine.' Christos shook his head in disbelief and walked away.

'What is it with these Greek waiters? If they're not looking at you, they're recommending their local dish.'

'Yes I know, it's rather sweet,' I answered. 'What was that about the meat thing?'

'Well it's true; I thought you were a vegetarian.'

'Yes, but not a strict one.'

The moussaka tasted good and the meat didn't matter – I pushed most of it to the side of my plate, much to Paul's disgust. The aubergines were fried just enough to give a succulent oily consistency. The thick cheese sauce with the occasional slice of tomato added a distinctive flavour.

Christos appeared and placed a bottle of wine on the table. 'Here, try this; you won't regret it,' he smiled, quickly unscrewing the lid.

Paul was just about to stop him but he had already walked away. 'Pushy, isn't he?'

'Yes, but let's try it anyway'

After an hour, I had managed to drink two thirds of the bottle and it showed. First, I started singing a rendition of Robbie Williams' "Angels." I followed this by telling everyone that I had two nephews and a niece but wasn't sure where yet.

Christos appeared. 'See, that's how good the wine is; drink and be happy!'

'Epicurus,' I cried.

'You know about Epicurus?' Christos asked.

Not giving me time to answer, Paul hauled me up out of my chair and directed me towards the door.

'Kalinychta,' cried Christos, waving his hands in the air.

'No, this is what wine can do,' replied Paul, trying to pull me away from the restaurant.

Next morning, all I remembered from the previous evening was somebody mumbling the words "God, how embarrassing".

Over breakfast, I tried to explain what "epicurus" meant.

Most people assume it refers to pleasures of the body, be it wine or sex; however, the Greek philosopher, Epicurus, taught people that they should rely upon their senses as a way of relaxing their anxieties; in other words, listen to what your body tells you. In my case, my body seemed to be telling me to get drunk. I wondered idly whether Epicurus ever got drunk.

Paul remained quiet for a moment then asked, 'Do you think I don't know about Epicurus?' He could be so smug at times.

Back in our hotel room, Paul reviewed his papers, reading aloud that Alexander the Great conquered country after country. Asia Minor, Egypt, Babylon, all were conquered by this legend. He continued to tell me that Alexander had entered Cyprus in 333 BC with engineers and divers, men of every rank, the Cypriot people welcoming him into the Persian occupied island.

'Fascinating,' I said, but the mention of Cyprus got me thinking about the Greek, Sokritos, who had shot a Turk. Not wanting to dwell on this, I retrieved the picture of the coffee bean from my suitcase and reminisced about the café. I wondered how Mr Cotterill was, whether Harry was still driving his mum mad. Then I thought of the computers and how I had met Paul on the internet. Now, here I was in Athens with him. What did I think of him and what did he think of me? Were we getting on, and how would this journey end? I recalled having once read "*In order to understand ourselves in the present we need to understand our past.*" This made perfect sense to me; it was the very reason I was here. The history books tell us that the Greeks brought about the birth of western civilisation, their philosophy, ideas and general way of living still shape the world today.

'Finished!' Paul suddenly called out, interrupting my thoughts.

'Finished what?'

'Looking at these papers, ready for the university tomorrow.'

'If you're ready, maybe we can get something to eat outside,' I suggested.

'Yeah, fine.'

'So what did I do last night in the restaurant?' I asked. Paul reminded me of the waiter, the bottle of wine, the singing and the fact that I was telling everyone about my nephews and niece.

'Oh,' I said, feeling my toes curl.

After our meal, we went for a stroll. Near the base of the Acropolis we found a small café. I ordered a glass of lemonade and sat outside to smoke a cigarette. Refreshed, we continued our walk, climbing the steep, uneven pathway up to the Parthenon. I stopped, breathing heavily.

'God, you are so unfit,' Paul remarked.

'It's the smoking,' I replied.

Eventually, we reached the steps to the main gate. At the top of the steps, we walked across a wooden platform and under a stone archway. There it was, right in front of us – the Parthenon built by Pericles, the great Greek architect. To the left of the Parthenon stood the Erechteum; a small temple with statues of women. I walked over and stared up at them.

'Wow; Athena and more Athenas!' I exclaimed. They appeared so large and grand that I imagined one of them winking at me.

Paul tapped me on the shoulder. 'They're not Athenas; they're Caryatid maidens, put there to replace the columns that once stood there.'

'Well, they're Athenas to me.'

A cat sat on a stone. I walked over to stroke it.

'I wouldn't do that, they're wild cats.'

I ignored him and was just about to reach out when the cat suddenly darted behind a rock. 'See what I mean?'

The stony ground felt uneven beneath my feet. This was my moment. I knelt down, the stones digging into my knees. I grabbed some of the stony soil then let it trickle through my fingers. 'I'm home,' I thought. Paul glared at me, astounded and embarrassed. Picking myself up, I rubbed my legs. 'There, that's better!'

A group of tourists were staring at me as Paul took my hand and led me along the west side of the building. 'What on earth are you doing?' he asked.

'I'm home. I'm touching the very soil I came from, that's what I'm doing.'

Next, we visited the Parthenon museum which was laden with statues. The Greeks believed themselves to be at the centre of the universe, their statues represented human gods. The Greeks became the gods themselves as they secured and protected their city from foreign invaders. The relief mural of the "Mourning Athena" caught my eye, Athena's left hand on a lance with her right hand resting on her hips. Why was she mourning, I wondered? We moved to another room which contained a replica of the west pediment of the Parthenon – a scene of the quarrel between Athena and Poseidon. Athena had won and to this day there still stood an olive tree to prove it. We found the grand replica of the eastern pediment showing the birth of Athena from Zeus's head. Miraculous, I thought, placing a completely different perspective on childbirth. Both pediments showed the other gods: Persephone, Aphrodite and Hermes. Handing Paul the camera, I asked him to take a picture of me in front of the east pediment. I stood, posing with my hands on my hips. Almost immediately, a fierce Greek attendant appeared, screaming the words "No posing!" Paul had already pressed the button and, feeling humiliated, I apologised profusely. Paul led me outside.

Out in the open air, I took a deep breath, relieved to be away from the scornful gaze of the museum attendant. Walking along the south side, I looked again towards the Parthenon. Despite the scaffolding obscuring the view, I could picture the great ivory and gold statue of Athena standing proud in the middle of this magnificent temple. I turned back to see the sun god Helios and his horse looking down upon me. To think that this great building had stood up to wars, just like my dad had said.

'I'm coming back here!' I suddenly announced.

'Are you?' Paul looked surprised.

'Yes, I am.'

Paul didn't question me on this, putting it down to my wild imagination. We continued through the archway and back down the steps, making our way to the base of the Acropolis where a gift stall stood at the bottom of the hill. My eyes greedily took in the jewellery, statues and ornaments. Beside the stall stood a number of Greek flags; I had to have one. The question was, large or small.

'You are not going to buy a flag are you?' Paul asked in a derogatory tone.

'Yes, I don't know which size though?'

'Small, small, please,' he said.

With automatic defiance my decision was made. Large it would be.

'I think I'll have this one,' I said, pulling out an immense flag, handing it to the assistant. Paul sighed. Stuffing my purchase into my bag, I wondered what to do with it. Surely, there were more things to do with a flag than hang it up.

Sitting at the bar that evening, I watched Nico serving other diners. Paul sat opposite me, fidgeting with his tie. 'I wonder what he'll manage to break tonight.'

'What do you mean?' I retorted.

'Well, will he spill a drink, knock a bottle over?'

'Ssh, he's coming over.'

Nico walked over to our table and laid out fresh napkins, setting them down meticulously by our placemats. He took our order for drinks and left. We sat in silence until the sound of breaking glass distracted us. Turning round we saw the remains of two broken glasses at Nico's feet. Christos handed him a dustpan and brush.

'God, not again,' exclaimed Paul. Giving him a disconcerted look, I kicked him under the table.

'He's just unlucky,' I said, looking on sympathetically as Christos brought our drinks over.

'No, just born clumsy, how he ever got to be a waiter beats me!'

Having drunk the last drop of wine, we left the unfortunate, accident-prone waiter and headed for a Greek taverna, aptly named "Zorba's," which specialised in traditional Greek dancing. A large national flag was prominently displayed, pictures of Greek landscapes dotted around the room.

At the back of the taverna was a dance floor with a stage. I settled for tender chicken with feta and mozzarella cheeses oozing out of it, giving a very distinctive taste. Once again Paul chose squid.

'I thought you were vegetarian,' he said.

'I am, but I fancy something different.'

A group of musicians began to play as waiters came round the tables bearing trays of ouzo. One of them came to our table and slammed down two glasses.

'Drink up, it's time to dance.'

'Oh no,' groaned Paul, watching as I swallowed my second glass of the fiery national drink.

One of the musicians announced the next dance, "Hassa pose rukos."

I watched as people stood up, linking shoulders with each other. I wished that I could join in but felt too inhibited. An array of bodies wearing T-shirts and vests formed a semi-circle. In the middle, a woman wearing a skimpy blue top was obviously enjoying herself, unaware that her boobs were bouncing up and down, almost on the verge of escaping. Suddenly, as she kicked her leg forward, her silver sequinned sandal flew off, landing at a waiter's feet. I burst out laughing. This caught Paul's attention and he couldn't stop staring at her breasts. I gave him a sharp kick. My Greek blood, fired up by the sound of the music, was overruled by my English reserve. I so wanted to dance. If only Suzanne was here. She was the kind of friend who got you really sozzled so that inhibitions disappeared. The woman with the bouncy boobs sat down.

'I want to dance!' I announced.

Looking disinterested, Paul replied, 'Go on then, I'll stay here.'

'No, I want to dance with you!'

He pointed towards the dance floor. 'No you go ahead; enjoy yourself.'

I reminded him about our experience in Sicily. Suddenly he stood up and reached across the table.

'Take my hand, I insist.' He led me to the dance floor. 'What's the Greek word for love?' he asked, sliding up closer to me.

'Agape, I guess,'

'Ok then,' he replied, as his eyes met mine.

Midnight, and back in our hotel room, we stood opposite each other. He breathed in and remarked on my seductive perfume.

Minutes later, we found ourselves in the shower together, screaming and spraying bubbles everywhere. God only knows what the other guests must have thought.

In my head I spoke to Aphrodite:

Dear Aphrodite **Last time I asked you if this was Eros. You said it was just you. I believe Dionysus had something to do with it this time. This time it felt different.**

Dear Katalina **You are right about Dionysus and yes, this time was different. A sense of wholeness is coming into shape, a sense of belonging with a sprinkle of passion.**

Dear Aphrodite **Thank you, you are right. Also, I think being on Greek soil helps!**

ATHENS 2

'You have a good night last night, eh?' asked Christos, pouring coffee into my cup.

My cheeks started to turn crimson, as I didn't know whether he was referring to the Greek dancing or our noisy escapade in the shower. I wondered whether anybody had heard us.

'Ah, yes, a really good night,' I replied.

Paul smiled. 'Yes thanks, but what makes you ask?' Presumably he was also wondering about our shower antics.

'Ah, my friends at Zorba's, they said you were dancing and drinking ouzo.' Christos looked towards me.

'Yes, that's true. It was Katalina drinking the ouzo though.'

Arriving at the university, Paul introduced himself and asked if, with the permission of Professor Yannis, he would be allowed to see the archive materials. The girl at the desk peered above a pair of red, angular glasses and said that she would have to check with her boss. Permission granted, she showed us to a back room. Large books lay alongside a wall and a computer sat on a desk, scattered with, paper and pencils. As Paul sat at the computer, I thumbed through the books, pretending to know what I was looking for. It was quite interesting to start with: the findings of some professor or other, artefacts found on such and such a date.

I was just about to go outside for a cigarette, when Paul looked up, announcing, 'There, got it, there's something here!'

I looked at him. 'Got what?'

'This information that backs up what Professor Yannis said.'

The information revealed that in the 1970s, a Professor Marolis had suspected that there was an Aphrodite statue buried in Rome. In addition, it revealed that there was probably another statue.

'Another one?' I asked, expectantly.

'Yes; apparently when Alexander entered Cyprus he discovered that his childhood sweetheart had been murdered, so he had a small statue made in memory of her, but that's all it says.'

The text then went on to give details of the carbon dating analysis used at the time. Paul attempted to explain the procedure to me.

'Oh, I see,' I said, feeling none the wiser. I suggested that coffee and nicotine were needed. Paul nodded but declined my offer of nicotine.

Outside, I lit a cigarette, inhaled deeply and slowly blew out a stream of smoke. Two statues – how bizarre was that? And if there were two, how long would this mission take? I stamped out my cigarette. Walking back into the building, I asked the girl if it was okay to take drinks into the room. She frowned, then eventually conceded, telling me to be careful, as there were some very old books. I strategically placed Paul's cup on the edge of the desk as he told me that he'd rung Professor Yannis, informing him of the possible existence of a second statue. The professor had confirmed this, much to Paul's surprise then went on to tell him about the engravings on the base of the statue.

Back inside the metro station, I noticed a stately mosaic behind glass, its terracotta colours seeming to merge with the beige background. A statue of Poseidon, the magnificent sea god, formed an imposing presence in the grand foyer. Walking through the ticket machine and down a few steps, we caught the train.

Back at the hotel, Paul slumped down into an armchair to peruse his notes. I decided that it was a good moment to catch up with Andrea. She insisted on calling me back. I told her what we had been doing, Vergina, the Parthenon and the frantic Greek dancing. I decided to pass on the details of our evening in the shower. I began to tell her about the furnishings in our room, the blue, beige and cream decor. Incredibly, she asked me to describe the blue. Was it turquoise or sky blue? Mandras would go nuts if he could hear our conversation. I told her about our encounters with the Greek waiters, that Nico was clumsy and Christos gregarious and rather in your face, but in the nicest possible way. She laughed and told me that Stelios had a new girlfriend, which inevitably turned the conversation to marriage.

Had Paul proposed? A wedding in Athens would be fantastic. 'No,' I said, rather more forcefully than I intended.

Paul looked up curiously from his book. I looked at him and mouthed "Andrea."

'Oh right, you've been on the phone for ages, Mandras will have a heart attack,' he muttered, looking back down to his book. I ignored him and said my goodbyes.

Later that evening as we were sitting in the restaurant, Nico came up to our table.

'Oh no,' said Paul.

Nico leant over and straightened the glasses and cutlery, ensuring that everything was just so. Paul sat back in his chair, holding his breath. Nico handed us the menus and disappeared. Paul began to speculate on the possibility of two statues; his editor would be delighted at this turn of events. Nico returned to take our orders.

'That Greek chicken thing and some white wine will do, thank you,' said Paul.

'Efcharisto, sir'

Paul looked at me. 'Sir?' I said.

'Yes, you see he can be polite; clumsy, but polite,' I said. 'George and Mildred are always sitting by the window, and they've ordered fish and chips; that's so uncultured.'

'Well, you sometimes sit by the window,' Paul remarked, looking as though he was thinking about other things. Mildred looked up glancing straight at me – oh God! Had she heard what I'd said? Nico returned with our coffees.

'Well, no accidents I suppose, but not like Luigi back in London' Paul remarked, once he had gone.

'Luigi?'

'Yes, at the Italian restaurant I took you to, remember?'

'Oh yes.' Luigi: the one who had given me an insinuating look.

'Well, Luigi was perfection, not clumsy and always efficient.' I sneered and returned to my coffee.

Next morning, I was back at the archives at 10.30, determined to find the next piece of the jigsaw puzzle. Sitting at the computer, I typed in my family name and located the three children belonging to Leandro, my estranged brother. Three names appeared: Sophia, Philip and Sebastien, together with their birth dates and addresses. Reading through the information on the screen, I came across another entry for Sophia – date of death 8 November 1997. I felt a sickening feeling in the pit of my stomach. Only two children were left. Philip lived on the island of Santorini and Sebastien lived in Athens. I pulled out my diary and noted their addresses then sat for a while wondering what Philip and Sebastien were like. Were they tall, short, dark? More to the point, would they want to meet me?

I now began the task of tracing my father and his parents. I returned to the shelves of old leather books. Once again, under "Sokritos", I could only find an entry for my brother, Stephanos, no mention of Stavros. Frustration, anger and disappointment welled up inside. Ask, I thought; ask the girl on the desk. She showed me an alternative way of searching the database and eventually I found an entry for my father, but no mention of his parents. I paused and stretched, my back aching from the prolonged search. Turning, I noticed a smartly dressed man seated two rows away from me. He seemed to be staring straight at me. I continued with my task for another twenty minutes. With a gasp of exhaustion, I sat back and looked around again. The man was still there, glancing in my direction. An uneasy feeling came over me which I tried to ignore. After a few more minutes, my anxiety got the better of me. I hurriedly gathered my belongings and left. Along the street, I passed a row of gift shops and decided that a little retail therapy would help calm my jangled nerves. Later, I giggled as I anticipated Paul's reactions to my purchases: a delicate blue and purple vase, an ashtray, a small Athena owl and a pen.

Back at the hotel, Paul was looking despondent. 'Absolutely nothing,' he said

'Nothing?' I asked, unwrapping my gifts and admiring the paper imprinted with the word "Athens".

'No, just the same as before; the statue was found in Ostia

in 1747 and is now stored in the LA museum. I knew all of that already. No information on the whereabouts of the second statue at all. I came across more personal information about the Great Alexander; you'll love this!'

'How so?'

'Well, Alexander's father remarried. Alexander confronted his father in rage at a cousin's banquet, and his father banished him.'

'Sounds a bit like your father,' I said without thinking.

Paul glared at me. 'Can I continue?'

'Yes, sorry!'

'I came across a biography that described Alexander at the beginning of his career. The writer talks about him as if he was Achilles, the heroic hero who turns into Hercules as he conquers more land, and then becomes Dionysus; a transformation and a spiritual release. And so it went on,' he said, smacking his papers down on the table.

Unsure how to react to this outburst I focused on the statue. 'What do you care, you'd rather it remained with the Italians.'

Paul looked really frustrated now. 'Oh excuse me, give me a chance.'

I decided to change the subject and told him about my day: my lack of success at the archives and the strange man who had seemed to be staring at me. Paul insisted that it was my imagination. I didn't bother to argue with him but I still felt uneasy. Paul said that he was going to e-mail his editor, so I decided to leave him to it and went to take a shower.

That evening, Christos appeared in the lounge. 'Kalispera! Enjoying Greece?'

'Efcharisto,'

Ignoring Christos, Paul picked up a leaflet.

'Have you visited the Olympic stadium?' asked Christos. 'It dates back to … ' he looked towards Paul for the answer.

'How far back?' asked Paul, trying not to show too much enthusiasm.

'I'm not sure,' Christos replied. 'It's very good though, you can imagine the great athletes running round the track.'

Paul nodded. 'No doubt we will visit it sometime, thank you for the recommendation.'

Returning to our room we came across Nico leaning against the reception desk twiddling a string of beads.

'What's that you have there?' I asked, my usual curiosity getting the better of me.

'Kolomboi.' At my puzzled expression, he explained. 'Worry beads; a Turkish word, God forbid. It's a way of passing the time. I take hold of each bead and pray to our mother Mary.'

'What, pray for another job?' Paul muttered under his breath. I quickly stood on his foot.

Nico looked up. 'Pardon me?'

I jumped in. 'He said that you pray for good health.'

'Yes, as well, you could say that.' I hurried Paul along, directing him towards the stairs.

Back in our room, everything was spotless. In the bathroom, all the bottles had been lined up in a row, just like soldiers. The one time I stayed with my father I remembered seeing rows of bottles on the kitchen table. Was this a Greek thing or some ordinary human peculiarity?

The Olympic stadium in the middle of Athens was a large racetrack surrounded by marble seating. Above the stadium flew the Greek flag. Paul told me that the stadium was completed in 1906 and laid claim to the rebirth of the Olympic Games. I agreed with Christos's earlier comments – I could see the muscular Greek athletes running round the track. Paul stood reading the marble plaque that listed the dates and places of previous games. I walked onto the racetrack and imagined the spectators sitting on their exquisite marble seats.

Sitting in the bar that evening, we made plans to return to Zorba's. I noticed that for once, Paul's shirt wasn't tucked in. A small detail really, but it seemed to me that this distinguished shirt-and-tie man appeared to be more relaxed. Nico served our

THE GREEN LINE TO APHRODITE

usual glasses of wine. We talked about the Olympic stadium and how magnificent it must have been when the games re-started. Paul looked up and noticed Nico in front of him, cloth in one hand and spray in the other. He just managed to avoid knocking Paul's glass over.

'Oh not again!' said Paul, rescuing his glass as Nico wiped the surface. I giggled until my glass was toppled spilling all its contents onto my lap.

'Me synchoreite,' cried Nico.

'God, he needs help,' said Paul. I rushed upstairs to change.

After we had finished our drinks we set off for Zorba's. Ah, you are back, good to see you. How's Christos?' asked the waiter.

Looking surprised at such over-familiarity, I replied, 'Oh yes, fine.'

'God, they know everyone, don't they?' said Paul.

Yet again, Paul ordered the squid. 'Did you know that the octopus is very intelligent? I saw this programme once, where they had to swim through a maze. Also they like to play.'

Paul slammed his knife and fork down on the table, telling me that I wasn't going to put him off. I told him that was the last thing on my mind.

A bouzouki suddenly struck up. The familiar melody of the Hasapiko, made popular by the film "Zorba the Greek" pounded through the air. People linked arms and began the exuberant movements of the dance. The passion of the music seemed to run through me. I wanted to join in, but not just yet, as I had another idea.

'Come on, this way!'

'Where are we going?' asked Paul, sensing that he wasn't going to have any choice in the matter.

'Just follow me.' We arrived back at the Olympic stadium. It looked quite different in the dead of the night – lamps glowing, lighting up the racetrack. 'Ready?'

'Ready for what?' I could see the apprehension on his face

as I announced that I was going to become a Greek athlete. 'Oh, no, you can't do that; are you nuts?' he exclaimed attempting to catch hold of my hand. Too late; I didn't care. Paul couldn't stop me now. Fired up like a bullet, my feet sped round the track. I felt fantastic. I was an athlete, running for Greece, running for Zeus, and I was going to win. To win meant being awarded the famous crown of olives. Zeus himself would award this triumphant trophy. The exhilaration and the liberating feeling of running and running was intoxicating. Suddenly, I heard the wail of an approaching siren. I reached the finishing line, gasping for breath. Looking up, I could see Paul talking to a police officer and a police car.

'Bugger!' I thought, but worth it.

Paul strode up to me. 'Satisfied now? I told him that you are half Greek, half mad, half English and wholly drunk; you are lucky not to be arrested.'

In my head I spoke to Hermes:

Dear Hermes **Thanks, oh thanks, my dear God of travel. That was great; I ran for Greece.**

Dear Katalina **Any time, all part of the journey. But that wasn't quite what I had in mind.**

As I was trying to catch my breath, I noticed a familiar looking man by the police car. I was puzzled but couldn't recall where I had seen him before. I smiled at Paul. 'You'll have to carry me back, my legs are killing me.'

ATHENS 3

A stream of sunlight shone across the carpet. My legs heavy, I recalled the excitement of the previous evening: Greek dancing, plates smashing, my exhilarating sprint around the Olympic stadium. Suddenly, in a moment of clarity, I remembered where I had seen the police officer before.

'That's where I saw him!' I exclaimed.

Paul, engrossed in his paperwork looked up, startled. 'Who … where?'

'The archives; he was the one staring at me. Remember? I told you about him.'

Later that morning, Christos appeared in the restaurant. 'Kalimera; so, we have an athlete among us!' he cried.

Paul turned away, embarrassed. 'Oh, you heard.'

Christos went on to ask whether I had timed myself. Perhaps I should enter the next Olympic Games.

Mouth wide open in disbelief, Paul interrupted. 'Timed herself? Hell, the police were there.' He shook his head. 'Amazing, you Greeks, you're completely mad!'

Christos and I shrugged. 'English, American, they just don't understand,' I said.

'Ochi,' sighed Christos in agreement.

After breakfast, I returned to the archives whilst Paul continued to the university. Logging on to the computer, I found Sebastien's address, on the outskirts of Athens. I wondered what he looked like. What work did he do? Did he have children? My next task was to try to trace my grandparents again. Last time, I had managed to locate my dad, Stavros Sokritos, but when I had searched for my grandparents, only the name "Sotorio" had come up. I decided to try a new approach. A search on the origins of Greek surnames revealed that Sotorio was an earlier version of Sokritos. Relocating the entry for Sotorio, I finally found my grandparents. They had lived in Cyprus in a small village called Nata, just as Andrea had said. Back out in the fresh air, I passed a newspaper stand. Glancing at one of the newspapers, a headline jumped out at me: "Sokritos". I snatched up a copy and hurried back to the hotel.

Nico was at the bar, cleaning up. 'Kalimera, Katalina.'

'Kalimera, Nico.' I replied, placing the newspaper down on the bar. 'Can you translate this for me? Here … '

'It says a Greek Cypriot named Andreas Sokritos shot a Turkish soldier.' I thought of my internet search in London. 'It was because the Turk had taken down a Greek flag near the Green Line, you know, the border between north Cyprus and south Cyprus. The police believe that he left Cyprus and could be hiding out here in Athens.'

Taken aback, I thought about the police officer turning up at the archive and the stadium. Was there a connection between me tracing the name Sokritos and his sudden appearances? 'Efcharisto,' I said and ran upstairs.

Paul returned to a roomful of smoke. 'God, get the fire extinguisher; better still, make that a gas mask,' he spluttered, trying to slice his way through the fumes to open the window.

'What's wrong with you?'

'It's that policeman, my name, Sokritos, archives, Greek guy shot a Turk a few weeks ago and, and … ' I babbled. I took some deep breaths to calm myself and began again, telling him about the article in the paper, explaining my suspicions.

'I can see what you're thinking but you can't prove that he's been following you. Anyway, have you shot a Turk recently?' Seeing that I still looked worried, he sat down and took hold of my hand. Gently he asked whether I had managed to find anything about my family. I explained about the different surnames, how I had confirmed that my dad came from Cyprus and that I had found a nephew, Sebastien. In return, Paul told me about his discoveries: further carbon analysis had dated the statue back to 440BC, not around the time of Alexander the Great. He had also found a form of Ancient Greek/Egyptian alphabet that had been used for only about 50 years. The alphabet had been devised by Alexander as a form of code, a way of keeping vital information from his enemies. Professor Yannis had mentioned a vase that had been made at Alexander's request when he took back Macedonia from the Persians. On each side of the vase was an image of Athena and a thunderbolt and on the base, the words "Megas Alexandros" meaning "Alexander the Great." There should also be two small symbols: the owl of Athena and a thunderbolt representing Zeus.

Paul looked harassed. I sensed he needed time alone to ponder these revelations, not deal with an uptight female worried about a man following her. Choosing to take a philosophical approach, I launched in with the story of Hercules and the twelve labours. 'Hercules had to perform these labours at the request of his cousin Eurysteus. One was the lion of Nemea; another Leranean Hydra, and … '

Paul sat back and asked me to stop. 'Please, I will try to explain some technical jargon to you. One procedure is … .' I tried to listen, but it was becoming complicated, so I stared out the window. 'Have you been listening? I listened to your story about Hercules, so hey, how about something back?'

'Sorry, what did you say just then?' I felt awkward, knowing that I had ignored him, my mind focused on the shooting of the Turk.

'I said that I'm sure that this statue does date back to Alexander. I came across a newer method of analysis, luminescence dating, which gives more precise results.'

'So more digging required then?' Paul shot me an indignant glare. 'Sorry, I didn't mean to be funny; maybe I'll go outside for a cigarette.' He nodded, affirming that this was a good idea.

In the shower that evening, I thought about the various men in my life: my nephew, Sebastien; the mysterious police officer; and finally Paul. I was beginning to feel insecure about him, his increasingly indignant looks, his frustration with his work. As I was drying my hair in front of the mirror, he came into the bathroom and told me that he'd just rung Professor Yannis. The professor had suggested that he e-mail the museum in LA, instructing them to carry out the luminescence analysis. Relieved to be doing something positive at last, he leant against the bathroom wall and watched me.

'This evening, let's go for a drink and then walk around the Parthenon,' I suggested.

'If you like, but you can't go into the Parthenon at night, it's closed,' said Paul.

'I know, I meant just walk around the area, I want to see the lights. It's supposed to be beautiful at night.'

Walking along the streets of Athens, we came across a small taverna near the base of the Acropolis. Retsina was another new powerful drink for me to try, this time served with Greek salad and creamy feta cheese. Paul quickly took my hand, just as I was about to take yet another sip.

'Stop, for God's sake, I thought you wanted to walk round the Parthenon later. At this rate you'll be crawling.'

'No, I'm fine. I think this retsina is better than the ouzo!' Sipping, I looked up towards the Parthenon. The great temple was illuminated and the added glow from the moonlight gave it a magical feel. Jumping up from my chair, I grabbed Paul's hand.

'Come on, this way,' I urged as I raced out of the restaurant. I didn't stop until we reached the main gate of the Acropolis. Paul pulled me back.

'What are you doing?' he asked, looking anxious.

'Come on, nobody will see us. You've got to see the Parthenon at night.'

'Yes, but … ' not leaving him any choice in the matter, I pulled him through the hole in the hedge. 'Oh no, first the Olympic stadium now this. How much retsina did you drink, for goodness sake?'

Holding my forefinger out, I moved it slowly towards my nose. 'See, complete focus. Only two glasses, I think.'

Walking up the steep pathway at night time was precarious without the benefit of daylight to guide the way. Finally we reached the top. Spotlights lighting up the Parthenon, a totally different but magical picture appeared in front of us.

'Now this would have been the time to pick up the soil, there's nobody here,' Paul remarked.

'Oh don't be a prude. At least people were entertained that day.'

'Well now, the question is, why are we here and what are you going to do?' We really shouldn't be here.'

Undaunted by his comments, I insisted, 'I told you that I would be back here. It's just so different here at night.'

'Yes I guess, but that hasn't answered my question.'

He walked over to the west side and looked out towards the city. I sat on a rough stone, wondering what or who had brought me here. An image started to unfold. I faced the Parthenon and raised my arms up high towards the night sky with its shimmering stars. In my imagination I spoke the words "Almighty Athena." The scaffolding started to melt away and the floor of the Parthenon tore open. A small, bright light began to glow from the centre of this magnificent building then burst through like a frenzied tornado. Glowing and intense, the light spread outwards, revealing a grand Athenian temple. Flames of light spread around the sides as I saw white marble statues, large as Hercules, appear at each corner. I could see the Elgin Marbles, the great frieze surrounding the temple, a centaur and a Greek soldier situated above the main temple. The sculptures were brightly coloured, almost fluorescent. Pericles, the great Athenian, had constructed this glorious temple. Zeus, the father of all the gods, stood next to Athena. Athena, the people's goddess, the goddess of warfare, the protector of the city, stood proudly, her face and body made of ivory wearing a Greek Attic helmet, carrying her shield and spear; her breastplate, encrusted with gold and copper, her bracelets and necklace shimmering in the light. This was the glorious temple built for the Athenian people. They entered, bearing gifts and treasures for the goddess. A young woman, wearing a red chiffon dress, her dark braided hair adorned with a silver band stepped forward; an old man draped in a long tunic followed behind. Each of these ancient Greeks bore the faces of my ancestors. People with faces resembling my father, brother and aunt sat at a table. A passer-by handed me a crown of gold leaf and pointed me towards the goddess. I walked over and placed it at her feet. Athena smiled. The land of the gods had come alive. I saw Greek sailors boasting among themselves as to who had brought the greatest gift to Athena.

'You can see the gold tip of her helmet from the sea,' I heard one of them say. 'Yes, it is true, and her gold shining spear,' replied another.

My father appeared in front of me, smiling as he passed me a small golden box. He told me it was from Athena herself. I thanked him and opening the lid … At once, an eerie silence fell. Darkness returned, as my image faded.

'Where have you been?' cried Paul.

'I don't know, I was … just around the corner,' I stammered.

For a moment, I stood motionless, thinking about what I had just seen.

Paul looked at me curiously then took my hand. 'Anyway, let's go now, before somebody comes.'

Back at the hotel, I had the intense feeling that it was time to let go – but let go of what? The Buddha and the second noble truth talked about letting go: "Desire should be let go" – no! I suddenly realised that I was going straight for desire; the arrows of Eros had finally struck. I ran into the bathroom, took a hasty shower then sprayed myself with perfume. I was exhilarated by my experiences at the Parthenon, my dreams alight from past to present. Feeling dynamic and passionate and without hesitation, I snatched the Greek flag, wrapped it around my body and leapt onto the bed.

When Paul walked into the room, I stood, ripped off the flag and announced, with a grin, 'The great Athena … no … Aphrodite lives!'

Paul stood, dumbfounded. The first time he had seen me fully naked, not shy and almost sober.

'Are you sure about this?' he asked, staring at me.

'I wouldn't be standing here like this, would I?'

'I agree, you wouldn't, but you have been drinking.'

'I have, but blame Dionysus for that. Anyway that was ages ago, my head is clear, I'm Katalina, I'm standing here on this bed and I want your body now. Is that ok?'

Paul looked stunned. 'Yes, that's more than OK!'

Jumping down off the bed, I started tugging at his jacket. 'Careful, that cost … On second thoughts, carry on.'

Jacket removed, I unbuttoned his shirt and took the large Greek flag and spread it across the bed. 'Here just touch me,' I murmured, pointing to my chest.

'I am, I am, give me a chance. By the way, please don't fall asleep,' he said.

I knew then that he must have thought I was a half drunk and completely mad. At that moment, I didn't care. 'In the name of Athena, no, Aphrodite, I will not fall asleep!'

In the restaurant next morning, Christos greeted us. 'Kalimera to you both. You only have a few days left, eh? You will have some good memories to take away with you, yes?'

I blushed as I remembered the previous evening: the flag, the drink and … I had let myself go – oh God!

Christos continued to look at me. 'Strange, it was my night off yesterday and I had a few drinks with my friends, here in the city. It was around midnight and for some reason I looked up towards our great Parthenon, and … ' he hesitated before continuing ' … well, I saw this magnificent shining light coming. I've never seen anything like it!'

I stared at him. 'Oh did you … ' I stammered nervously, 'perhaps it was the moon.'

'The moon; are you crazy? No, it was coming from the Parthenon. My friends thought I was drunk.'

I looked down at my fingernails trying to think of something to say. At that moment, Nico called Christos over to another table.

Paul and I looked at each other, not saying a word. Paul finally broke the silence. 'You're unusually quiet.'

'Oh, it's nothing.'

'No it's not. Something's troubling you; what is it?'

'Nothing, just last night,' I said, looking away.

'Last night was great, the flag – where do you get your ideas from? No, perhaps I shouldn't ask,' he said chuckling to himself.

'It's not funny, I feel embarrassed. I'm not normally like that.'

'No I agree, you are not normally like that, but don't be embarrassed. Tell me though, why do you have to drink so much?'

That stopped me in my tracks. He was right of course, but I was in Greece, I needed to experience everything I could, with the aid of alcohol if necessary.

'I don't drink that much!' I exclaimed, in total denial. At his look of disbelief, I relented. 'Well, I'm in Greece now; I have to do what all Greeks do, don't I?'

After a busy day sightseeing, we decided to spend the evening at the Herodicus theatre. The performance was due to start at 8 pm and I was just about to go for a shower when my mobile rang – it was Andrea. Feeling the need to unburden myself, I told her about my vision at the Parthenon the previous night and how one of the waiters had also seen something strange. Andrea was silent and I realised that she didn't understand. I changed the subject, telling her about my relative living on the island of Santorini, our plans to visit, and about my research that had led me to discover my nephew, Sebastien. When I told her about my antics at the Olympic stadium, she gasped. I heard her calling out to Mandras.

'She ran round the Olympic stadium!'

Mandras roared with laughter and asked her if I was drunk.

'Probably … ' she replied. Once again, our conversation was cut short by Mandras muttering about the phone bill.

'Have you finished yet?' Paul called out. 'We're going to be late. Poor Mandras will be footing a heavy telephone bill.'

Eventually, dressed and ready, we walked out onto the busy Athens streets. The theatre was situated beside the Acropolis. Illuminated against the night sky, it looked spectacular. We took our seats in the open air auditorium. The show was *West Side Story*, performed in Greek. Looking at the programme, I noted the name Sokritos, alongside the word "choreography". 'Look at that,' I said, pointing to my name and pushing the programme towards Paul.

He screwed his eyes up. 'Oh – another one of your relatives?' he asked, laughing sarcastically.

'Perhaps, you never know,' I said, snatching the programme back.

The night air was cool and stars sparkled like jewels. Turning my head away, I looked towards the Parthenon and re-lived the previous evening's events.

After the performance we went to a coffee bar – an exotic place serving all types of coffee as well as cocktails. Returning to the hotel, I looked across the road and saw a man looking at us, the same man from the archives and the Olympic stadium.

Next morning in the restaurant we heard a clatter as Nico frantically piled a dozen plates on top of each other. Christos appeared, giving Nico the watchful eye. Nico looked back at him, now taking each plate in turn with caution.

'He's back then,' said Paul, raising his eyebrows.

'Yes, I'm going to miss him, when we go,' I said. Paul grunted dismissively.

Nico walked over. 'Ah, Kalimera, what can I get you this fine morning?' he asked, straightening the cutlery.

We sat with our arms by our sides, keeping everything out of his way.

Paul whispered, 'Watch out!' I gave him a sharp kick under the table.

'Oh, café megala and cereal … no … bread, efcharisto,' I ordered. Nico marched off. We chatted about the day ahead. I told Paul that I was feeling anxious about meeting Sebastien. He reassured me that it would be fine.

We arrived at the metro station for the last time. One station later, we parted.

Paul kissed me on the cheek. 'Good luck!'

'Thanks, I'll need it.'

I took another train to the outskirts of Athens. I had arranged to meet Sebastien at the station. I got off the train and remembered what Sebastien had said on the telephone. He would be wearing jeans and a white T-shirt, holding a newspaper under his arm. It felt like a scene from a James Bond film. I felt quite anxious, wondering whether Sebastien would like me, whether I would recognise him. What if he didn't turn up, what if … ?

I turned to see the back of a man dressed in jeans and a T-shirt. I hesitated then took the plunge. Walking up to him; I tapped him on the shoulder. Swiftly, he turned round. It was not Sebastien.

'Me synchoreite,' I said, as he glanced at me curiously then walked away. I looked at my watch – Sebastien should have been here by now. Feeling an overwhelming sense of panic, I wondered if he had changed his mind. I looked in my bag for a telephone number – nothing. Disappointed and downcast, I headed back to the hotel.

Nearly collapsing at the reception desk, I saw Christos. 'Are you ok?' he asked, obvious concern in his voice.

'No, not really; he wasn't there. I don't have a phone number … '

'What, your fiancé Paul was not there?' He looked at me, confused.

'No, Sebastien, my cousin; he wasn't there at the station. I must have I missed him. I came back here to see if I can find his phone number.'

Christos put down a glass on the counter and filled it with ouzo. 'Here, have this, it'll calm you down.'

I snatched the glass and started to drink the strong aniseed-flavoured liquid then stopped. 'Oh my God, no, I'll never get there if I drink that!' Christos shrugged.

I ran upstairs and looked in my suitcase. Nothing, no telephone number, I couldn't find it amongst the information I had noted down from the archives. I sat on the bed close to tears then realised there was only one thing to do. I had to return to the archives and find the phone number. Back downstairs my half glass of ouzo was still waiting on the counter.

Christos looked up at me once more. 'Ah you're back, did you find it?'

'No, I'm going back to the archives,' I replied, taking one last mouthful of ouzo.

Christos smiled, 'Drank like a true Greek. Good luck!'

Back in the archive building, I quickly found the telephone number. Scribbling it down, I took out my mobile then stopped. What if Sebastien had changed his mind? I knew that it could be risky tracing relatives. Putting my doubts aside, I hastily dialled in the number.

'Yassus.' It was Anna, Sebastien's wife.

'It's Katalina, where's Sebastien? I … I couldn't find … ' I stammered, finding it difficult to hold back my tears.

'He's at the station … no, wait!' said Anna. I could hear another voice in the background – Sebastien. 'Katalina, he's here, he's just come back from the station.' She passed the phone to Sebastien.

'Are you OK? We must have missed each other.'

'Yes, yes, I'm OK.'

'I'll meet you at the north end of the terminal, there's a large statue of Hercules there; you can't miss it.'

I returned to the metro station, found the Hercules statue and waited for what seemed like an age. Eventually, Sebastien arrived. I looked at him, noting his appearance: average height, stocky but not fat; dark brown hair cut short to the nape of the neck, brown eyes and a prominent Greek nose. He led me to his car then and drove us to his apartment. Anna was there to greet us. As is customary in Greek hospitality, she had prepared a few snacks.

We sat in the lounge. I didn't know where to start. It didn't take long for Sebastien to begin firing questions at me: where had I been in Greece; what was my home like in London? And so on.

Sebastien told me about his sister, Sophia, who had died in a car crash. He passed me a photograph: long, dark curly hair and a winsome smile; such a young age for a life to end. Then he spoke of his other brother, Philip, the aloof one. 'He lives by himself. He was a fisherman before he went to university and now he writes.' I sensed an element of disapproval but chose not to question him further. 'He's the one who knows all the family details, births and deaths, that kind of thing. I think that your dad had a sister.'

'Really?' I asked, wondering whether she was still alive.

'Yes, Philip is the one to tell you more.'

Anna offered more snacks and drinks and I accepted gratefully. Sebastien explained that he worked as a builder and as a barman, ' … to help pay the bills,' as he put it. Anna stayed home and looked after the children. She showed me a photo of them, Eleni, aged 6 and Leandro, aged 10. She asked whether I had children and when I replied that I did not she looked at me, perplexed. Sebastien showed me a photo of Sophia. Anna suddenly spoke, asking whether I'd like to visit her grave. I was stunned. It seemed almost like an intrusion, but somehow it felt like something I needed to do.

We took a taxi towards Athens. 'Now go up this narrow lane and I'm sure it's there,' said Anna. 'Oh no, this isn't it,' she sighed. Sebastien glared at her, the taxi driver groaned. 'Just carry on up here,' she ordered.

Finally we arrived. 'Can you wait for us?' asked Anna. With an expression of disbelief, the taxi driver agreed.

A large cemetery with gravestones lay ahead of us. I wondered if Anna knew where the grave was. 'This way,' she said, striding ahead, like the commanding officer of a regiment in a battlefield. She came to a halt again. 'No, it's this way,' she said, pointing in another direction.

'Do you know where you are going, woman – we have a taxi driver waiting for us!' snapped Sebastien.

Anna ignored him. 'Just follow me.' A few moments later, she stopped, crouching beside a headstone.

'Thank god, I thought we'd never get here,' said Sebastien.

I knelt down beside her. It was like a replay of the time I had visited my dad's grave in London. I read the simple inscription.

SOPHIA SOKRITOS
DIED 8–11–97
AGED 21

Anna placed a bunch of deep blue irises on the grave. I looked around to see other graves decorated with the same flowers.

'They are lovely, but so unusual,' I commented.

'They're named after the goddess Iris, a symbol of authority and religious belief. She is supposed to guide the spirits of girls and women into the afterlife,' Anna explained. 'Come on, the taxi driver will be waiting.'

'And charging us a small fortune,' commented Sebastien, frowning.

As I left the apartment, Anna wished me well. Sebastien took me back to the station. On the train, I tried to take make sense of everything. It had been wonderful to meet Sebastien and Anna, Sophia's grave had left me feeling sad, reminding me of my dad and making me question my search. Could I cope with any more anticipation, any more loss?

When I returned to the hotel, I logged on to the Athena website:

Dear Poseidon **I see you riding in your chariot, drawn by magnificent white-maned horses. Last time you spoke of earthquakes and great tidal waves. I was frightened when Sebastien wasn't there; I thought he didn't want to see me. And I felt so alone.**

Dear Katalina **Fear is a destructive emotion. It opens up great holes in the soul. Once the fear comes to the surface, it has the chance to turn into great courage. Remember the outcome. You found Sebastien and Anna and they welcomed you into their home.**

Dear Poseidon **I am beginning to see what you mean, but then they took me to the grave, Sophia's grave. Oh god.**

Dear Katalina **That's true, but you obviously went of your own accord.**

Dear Poseidon **You are right, I did agree to go, I needed to see it. I don't have any regrets.**

Dear Katalina **Continue onward with courage. Athena herself will help you.**

Later that afternoon, I met up with Paul and told him about my meeting with Sebastien and Anna, how it had started so badly but turned out so well with the revelation that my Dad may have another sister. I hoped that Philip would be able to supply more information.

As it was our last night in Athens, we decided to have a drink in the bar before exploring the nightlife for the last time.

'Ah, your last night,' said Christos, undoing the cap of a wine bottle. 'So where will you go tonight?'

'The place with the smashing plates,' I said, raising my eyebrows.

'You mean Zorba's?'

'Oh no, not there again!' groaned Paul. 'Oh well, I guess it's our last night.'

'Have a good night,' said Christos, and went off to serve another couple.

'What will this Philip be like then?' asked Paul.

'Aloof, according to Sebastien; a writer, he said.'

'Interesting. What does he write?'

'He never said.' I stared at an abstract painting on the wall, full of intense sprays of red, yellow and gold. It reminded me of a bonfire on Guy Fawkes Night. The surrounding black provided a deep contrast.

I turned to see Paul looking at the same picture. 'It's the lines in between the colours, they make me think of the engravings on the statue,' he said.

'That's abstract,' I replied.

The front doors of the hotel suddenly swung open. A group of Englishmen carrying beer cans tumbled into the foyer. One of them belched as he came face to face with Christos. Nico had just come on duty. He looked up as the men collapsed on the floor, laughing and shouting.

His face went a deathly white, as he just managed to catch hold of a bottle of wine. Christos stepped out from behind the bar and walked towards the men. One of them stood up and held his palm out as if to make a high five. Christos frowned.

'Oh God,' I said.

'What's wrong?' asked Paul.

'Well, to you Americans, holding out your palms means "high five", but to a Greek it's an insult, meaning excrement on your face,' I replied.

'Oh shit!' exclaimed Paul.

'Exactly!' I said, shocked at his sudden use of an expletive.

Nico, still white and shaking, looked at Christos, waiting to see how he would react. Christos politely asked them to leave. Three of them got up and moved toward him, menacingly. With the courage of Zeus, Christos stood his ground and repeated his instruction, this time more forcefully. His dignified presence had the effect of defusing the situation.

Sobering now, one of the men said, 'Oh shit, we don't want to stay here anyway lads. Where's Zorba's?'

'Turn right and then left. It's at the end of the Andromedas Street.'

'Come on lads!' They tumbled out of the doors, leaving their beer cans behind.

Christos walked over and, picking them up, mumbled, 'Bloody repressed English.'

'Repressed English?' I enquired.

Christos looked at me, 'Nei, me synchoreite, Katalina. Yes, repressed! We Greeks can tolerate so much, but … '

'You sent them to Zorba's,' exclaimed Paul.

'No, in another direction; just far enough to get them away from here and any other Greek bar, God forbid.'

'I think we will stay in, what you think?' asked Paul, turning to me.

'Coward!'

' 'No, I just don't want any trouble on our last night.' Spoilsport!

'What's on the menu tonight then?' asked Paul.

'Moussaka, and oh, squid,' replied Christos.

'Excellent, we'll stay here.'

The roof-top restaurant was quiet that evening. I could see the Parthenon: my last night taking in that spectacular sight.

'Brave, wasn't he?' said Paul.

'Who?' I replied, staring up at the brightly lit Parthenon.

'Christos, standing up to those men.'

'Yes, like a true Greek hero,' I said proudly.

'Greek hero? Which one … Zeus, Hercules?' he asked. 'Now you've got me at it.'

'Oh, I think Zeus, it was the voice.'

'If you say so,' he said, giving me a tentative smile. 'Touchy though, that high five … '

'Well yes. I guess each culture has its own ways.'

As we were tucking into our food, George and Mildred came up to our table. 'I couldn't help but hear your English voices; I don't know what you think of the food but … '

'Well, I'm half English and half Greek, and I think the food … ' I glared at her. Paul glared at me, Mildred froze. ' … is good, I like it.'

Paul looked away with embarrassment and Mildred walked off in a huff.

'Well you handled that discreetly, didn't you?'

'Yes I did,' I said, feeling my cheeks turn crimson.

A flicker of sunlight peeked through the curtains. It was mid April and I awoke thinking about the island of Santorini. Briskly I jumped out of bed and ran over to the balcony to take one last look at the view. Taking our bags downstairs, we headed for the restaurant. As Nico served us, I noticed how steadily he poured the coffee.

'Kalimera to you both,' he said.

'Kalimera Nico' I answered, as Paul gave him a tentative glance.

'That's a first, no accidents,' said Paul.

'Yes, perhaps you made him nervous.'

'Me? Don't be silly, he was like it with everyone, glasses and plates smashing to the floor.'

'I suppose.'

Finishing our breakfast, we went up to reception. Christos and Nico said goodbye and wished us well.

As I picked up my suitcase, Christos cried, 'Katalina, look after yourself, us Greeks must stick together!'

I smiled to myself, as Paul looked away.

We walked out into the sunshine and waited for the taxi to take us to the airport. 'Are these Greek waiters all the same?' he grinned.

SANTORINI

A final drive through the city of Athens. I looked back to catch a last glimpse of the Parthenon. This wonderful building shone like a bright light in my soul, now masked by confusing feelings.

My fear of flying was secondary; Paul's intermittent moody and jealous behaviour had finally got to me. Arriving at the airport, we collected our cases. As I strode off with my bags, Paul called to me to slow down; I ignored him. Finding a British Airways check-in desk I asked the attendant for the next flight back to London. She tapped away at the computer and was just about to speak when Paul came up behind me.

'What are you doing?' he demanded.

'I'm going back to London,' I said firmly.

'Why? For God's sake, tell me why?'

'Because … '

Queues started to build behind us, the attendant becoming impatient. 'Please, Madam, if you would like to step aside until you've decided what you are doing I would be grateful,' she said, looking pointedly at the other customers behind us.

'Oh I suppose so, I'm sorry,' I apologised.

Paul pulled me away from the desk. 'What's wrong, what have I done?' he asked, looking confused.

'It's just this relative thing, it seems too much, and you, and … ' I fell silent.

'Yes, go on, please tell me.'

'You are so jealous all the time. Those waiters are only having fun, and … ' I hesitated, ' … you're moody … sarcastic … '

Paul thought for a moment then admitted that he was jealous; perhaps it was his Italian blood. Suddenly, he announced that he loved me, that he had too much to lose if I left now.

'Lose what, your precious statue?' I snapped.

Stunned, he glared at me. 'Well if that's what you think, fine. However that precious statue is Greek, and you are Greek, think about the connection.' He paused for a moment and sighed. 'I'm sorry, I have been moody; it's this statue. I feel like I have so much invested in it.'

'I suppose so.' I muttered, still unconvinced.

'Don't give up on your relatives. I'm sure you'll find out more from your nephew. What was his name – Philip? I'm sorry if I appear jealous. It's because I love you.'

The desk attendant beckoned for my attention. 'Do you want these tickets, Madam?' she asked.

'No, I don't think so, thank you,' I said, taking Paul's hand.

During the flight, I looked out of the window to see the whitewashed buildings of Santorini. Once outside the airport, we took a taxi to our apartment in Fira, situated on the edge of a cliff, overlooking an expanse of translucent blue sea. From the window we were greeted by a spectacular sight: the sky, the sea, the sparkling whitewashed buildings. The bright colours of the rooftops caught my attention, the subtle mix of reds and oranges reminding me of the abstract painting in the hotel.

'The home of Atlantis,' said Paul, unpacking his bags.

'Pardon, what?' I stood still, mesmerised by the panoramic view. I half listened as he told me about Atlantis, a mythical island, and of the people who had supposedly lived there centuries before. Of all the places that had laid claim to the myth of Atlantis, Santorini had been considered the most likely, based on the ideas of Plato. The geographical structure of the island and its history of volcanic eruption gave plausibility to the story.

He walked over to the balcony, placing his arm around me. 'You heard every word of that didn't you?'

'Um, yes every word,' I murmured as I leaned forward to kiss him.

Paul disappeared to the bathroom as I stared out at the deep blue sea. Moments later he reappeared, wearing scruffy blue jeans and what looked like a Hawaiian shirt. I stared in amazement; the profusion of colour made him look different. The open-necked shirt in differing shades of yellows, reds and browns, with Celtic lettering splashed everywhere, was perhaps not so Hawaiian after all.

Leaving the apartment in search of a local supermarket, we found that the main door led out onto a back street. The apartment was at the top end of a street which descended down into the main village. Black cobbled stones, taken from the island's volcanic eruption, paved the street. Walking down was easy, but I dreaded the thought of walking back up again. Admiring the brightly blue and yellow coloured fronts of the tiny houses, I found it so refreshingly different to the grey landscape of London. Halfway down the street sat an old woman dressed in black, just like the photographs in tourist books. She looked at least eighty, with a scarf tied around head and was sat on a stool, peeling carrots. As we approached, I noticed her bent, arthritic fingers, each tightly clinging to the task in hand. She looked up at us, a beady face with an enigmatic smile revealing a few lost teeth.

'Geiasas,' she said.

'Geiasas,' we replied and continued walking down the hill.

Soon, we came across a supermarket, more a local shop, selling much of the island's local produce: chickpeas, cheese and wine. 'Any pasta?' asked Paul.

'We're in Greece now, not Italy' I casually reminded him. Along the aisle, I found a pack of spaghetti. 'Here, will this do?' I asked

'Thank God, yes. Any herbs?'

Scuttling off in search of herbs, I eventually retrieved small packets of basil and parsley. Lifting the basket onto the counter, I awaited to see if the shopkeeper spoke English, as I had no phrase book with me. Fortunately, he announced the price in English, albeit with a pronounced Greek accent – that was easy.

Outside the supermarket, a small gift shop caught my attention. 'This way, here,' I said.

'Do we have to?'

'Yes we do, I might find something for Andrea in here.'

Small statues, ornaments, and jewellery were displayed around the tiny shop but it was the jewellery that caught my eye. The shiny bracelets and necklaces were encrusted with gemstones. I found a purple amethyst necklace, delicately tied together and I picked it up. 'Here, help me on with this.' Paul took hold of the dainty chain. 'Yes, I'll have this one, in fact two; the other can be for Andrea. This bracelet, it's amethyst you know. The Greeks believed it was good at stopping people getting drunk.'

'You are joking?'

'No, "Amethustos" means "not to be drunk." Apparently a beautiful maiden called Amethysta attracted the attention of Bacchus, the god of wine. Then Diana, the goddess of the hunt, came along and rescued her by turning her into an amethyst. It's brilliant, isn't it?'

Looking along the shelf, I snatched up a small lighter, an ashtray embellished with gold leaf and a tiny ornamental Greek church. Paul remarked that we'd never get through customs 'with all that,' as he put it.

'But it's my heritage,' I cried, hurt at his apparent lack of understanding.

He smiled at me indulgently. 'Of course it is, I'm sorry.' I felt touched by his sudden concern.

The arduous journey back up the hill took its toll. My legs were beginning to ache. Paul reminded me that I shouldn't smoke. I told him that my mum had worked in a tobacco factory and that Greece was one of the biggest smoking nations. When he continued, talking about passive smoking and the plight of the unborn foetus, I just smiled.

Halfway up the hill our conversation was thankfully redirected by the sight of the old woman.

'God, she hasn't moved and she's still peeling those carrots,' remarked Paul.

As we approached her, we stopped. 'Geiasas, mei-leenah Sophia,' she greeted us.

Putting down his bags, Paul walked over and took her hand. 'Geiasas, mei-leenah Paul. Katarina'

'Geiasas, Paul and Katalina.' Her eyes twinkled as she looked at us. I pointed to where we were staying. She nodded repeating the word "Nai, Nai."

Back at the apartment, I collapsed on the settee. 'Geiasas, mei leenah Paul,' I mimicked. 'Yes, I've managed to pick up some Greek.'

In the kitchen, I started to unpack the food – it was Paul's turn to cook.

'Another Sophia,' I said, watching him fling strands of spaghetti against the wall. 'What's with the spaghetti?' I asked, pointing at two pieces that had glued themselves to the wall.

'Easy, it's an Italian idea. If it sticks to the wall it's cooked.'

'Oh.' I stared at the stuck spaghetti, wondering whether he was going to put them on the plate.

I continued to watch this Italian chef at work. He rinsed the spaghetti and divided it onto two plates. Olive oil and chopped basil were hastily mixed. A plate of sliced tomatoes and a bowl of bread were placed on the table.

'That's it then?' I asked.

'Yep, enjoy.' Pouring me a glass of wine, he suggested that I wear my special amethyst bracelet just in case the wine got too much. I assured him that I wouldn't need the bracelet as I didn't intend to get drunk.

The spaghetti appeared rather basic without the usual tomato sauce. Despite this, it tasted good, especially accompanied by a bottle of the island's local wine.

Next morning we were up early. 'Well, are we going to see Akrotiri beach?' Paul asked. 'I guess so and perhaps a donkey ride later. Don't forget that I arranged for us to meet Philip at 2.30.'

Santorini had a history of volcanic eruptions as well as its fair share of earthquakes. The numerous volcanic eruptions had resulted in different coloured lava being deposited all over the island. At the beach, smooth red sand lay for miles around. The orangey-red cliffs stood like giant mythical monsters waiting to engulf the waves as they came into shore. We sat on the sands.

'I wonder what he'll be like. Sebastien said he's aloof.' I hesitated for a moment, unwilling to give voice to my fears. 'Do you think he'll like me?'

Paul looked towards me and frowned. 'Why wouldn't he?'

'I don't know. Sebastien and Anna were great but if Philip's aloof, like Sebastien said, why would he want to talk to me?'

Back in the village, a man stood surrounded by donkeys and tourists.

'Come on, quick, before he starts the next ride,' I said, taking Paul's hand.

Paul, six feet tall and not too keen on the prospect of sitting on a donkey, begrudgingly complied. Only two donkeys remained. The man quickly removed a muzzle from the taller one, which had a dark mane with a white streak running throughout the centre. He indicated to Paul that this was to be his donkey. Paul frowned for a second and carefully mounted. The man then directed me towards a smaller donkey. Along with the others, we proceeded up the hill at a slow trot. To begin with, all went well and the surrounding scenery was a pleasure to see. Our ride took us along a back street and we passed whitewashed houses with the most spectacular plants displayed outside. Suddenly my donkey stopped. I talked to it nicely, and stroked it, but still nothing. Paul was a good few paces ahead of me, unaware of my predicament.

'Help!'

To my embarrassment everyone stopped and turned around.

In a quiet voice, I said, 'It won't move.'

Paul came back and caught my reins. Within a few minutes, my donkey trotted off again. Catching up with the others, I noticed a group of tourists walking towards us. As they came closer, Paul's donkey began to make strange noises. The noises became louder, until suddenly it lifted its front legs, almost butting into the closest tourist. Paul caught hold of the reins, got the donkey under control again and apologised profusely.

'Now you've got an audience,' I said. 'Perhaps that's why he had a muzzle on.'

Arriving at the end of the street the donkey slowed and came to a halt. My bottom and legs were aching and Paul also looked a bit worse for wear. Walking up the hill, we passed Sophia brushing the path outside her house.

She looked up, 'Geiasas.'

I launched in with the story of our donkey ride. She looked confused for a moment until I started making donkey noises, pointing towards the village. Her confused look gave way to laughter, 'Ah, nai, nai.'

Later that day we took a bus to the other side of the village to visit Philip. How would he react, knowing that I had spoken to Sebastien, the brother he didn't get on with? Paul nudged me; it was time to get off the bus.

A few yards down the road stood a small whitewashed building with a brightly painted yellow door. We knocked and waited. The door opened and there stood Philip, tall and slim with long, dark hair tied back in a pony-tail. 'Kalispera,' he said.

I acknowledged his greeting and smiled hesitantly. He led us into a small room with doors leading out onto a patio. The room was full of books, with papers strewn across the floor. Philip invited us to sit. He looked at me with an expressionless face that made me feel uncomfortable. A fear of rejection, coupled with the uneasy silent atmosphere, clouded my thoughts. Paul intervened, attempting to make polite conversation, and commented on the books and papers. Then he tactfully asked Philip what he was writing about.

'Oh, it's a children's book. That's what I do, write stories for children. No doubt Sebastien told you.' He gave a look of discontent at the mention of Sebastien's name. Once again, I felt the hostility that I had feared existed between the two brothers.

'Katalina works in a cafe,' said Paul, giving me a nudge in the hope that I would respond. I looked at him and told him about Mr Cotterill, Harry and Suzanne. A smile was followed by laughter as Philip's face began to open up with warm emotion.

'I'm sorry; your story reminded me of some of my characters – brilliant. Please, I'm sorry if I've been quiet; it's just that when I knew that you had been talking to Sebastien, I felt uneasy. But please, it is good to meet you, how can I help?'

I was about to reply, when laughter, shouts and screams came from outside. 'Oh, God spare us; it's that taverna two doors away. So noisy in summer, I can hardly think at times,' said Philip, pressing his hands up against his face. He walked over and shut the patio doors, insisting that I continue. I told him about my struggle to locate my family. I showed him photos of my brother and father. 'Your father had a sister called Livana. She lived and was married here and had three children, but thirty years ago she moved to Cyprus,' explained Philip.

'A sister?' I exclaimed.

'Yes, she would be in her late eighties now, if she's still alive.' said Philip. I looked at Philip who was deep in thought, contemplating his next words. 'The local Greek Orthodox Church would have records and details of your father's sister's marriage and the baptisms of her children. The church is just down the road; I could take you if you want.' Paul looked pensive, trying to anticipate my response. 'Please, I have been rude and not offered you anything to eat or drink. Perhaps … '

Paul intervened and suggested that we had something to eat at the taverna.

'Yes, that would be good. I am not a very good host I'm afraid,' Philip said with an apologetic look.

The Ariana Taverna was spacious with a large patio. We chose to sit outside. Another spectacular view of Poseidon's ancient blue sea lay before us. The reflection of the sun caught the top of a glass, its powerful light sending me into a daze. Santorini was a dreamlike island compared to the buzz of Athens. Philip appeared carrying a bottle of wine. The clink of the bottle brought me back into the real world once more. Philip started to pour out the wine.

'No, stop, I'll have water, thanks,' I said.

'Are you sure?'

'Yes really, I'm sure.' Paul looked at me surprised.

I talked about our journey, telling Philip about the archives as Paul remained quiet, looking out towards the sea. Our drinks finished, we headed towards the Church.

Philip went ahead and opened the heavy wooden door. Inside, the smell of incense was apparent. As I passed an ornate decorated icon, I froze. Memories flooded back. I was five years old standing at the back of the church with my dad. He took hold of my hand, helping me to cross myself then carried me to the icon, lifting me to kiss it.

'Something wrong?' asked Paul.

'Nothing really, it's just that it reminds me of my dad. He used to take me to a church. I didn't really understand what was going on but he would cross himself, so I'd to do the same. Then we would kiss the icon. Afterwards we'd go up for Communion – the bread was nice and the wine wasn't bad either. Then we'd go back outside and my mum would be there, waiting for me.'

Paul was just about to speak when Philip called out to us. There, on an old wooden table, lay a heavy, leather-bound book containing all of the parish records: births, deaths, marriage and baptisms. Although it was in Greek, the name was easy to spot: Livana Christine married George Paplou. Another page revealed the births of their three children, Alysia, Calista and Irena. There it was, the proof I needed. Leaving the church, Philip reminded us that it was Easter and that there would be a service the next day. He insisted that we meet up again before it was time for us to leave.

Later that evening I explained to Paul in more details, the memories that had been stirred up. 'I only knew him for a few years; my mum left him when I was young. Every so often on a Sunday he would come down from London and take us to Southampton, to visit the church. Afterwards my mum would reappear and we'd go off to a Greek restaurant for lamb chops and chips.'

'Lamb chops and chips? Are you joking? That's not very Greek,' he said laughing.

I asked him how he felt about the Easter service. He said he didn't mind going along, if it made me happy.

The next day, the streets were teeming with people as extended families, including grandparents, mothers, fathers and children, made their way to the church. 'Incredible,' exclaimed Paul, as he glanced at the icons around the church. He then looked at the gold crucifix situated at the front of the altar. The smell of incense, the candles and gleaming icons took me back to my childhood once again. I took Paul's hand, squeezing it tightly.

'Ouch, what's that for?'

'Sorry, nothing,' I said, pushing back the painful memories as best I could.

We found two empty seats near the middle of the church. The chanting of the Greek liturgy distracted my attention. More and more people gathered in the church until all the aisles were filled. Turning, I saw Philip in the distance.

The priest approached the altar, wearing black cassocks and kalimavki, carrying an ornate gold cross. Together with his deacons, he processed past the congregation. One deacon carried a casket of incense, swinging it backwards and forwards. I breathed in the pungent aroma, almost like smoke from a bonfire. Sophia sat at the end of the aisle. As the church door opened, she turned and scrutinised the latecomers.

Towards the end of the service, the worshipers lined up to receive communion. I snatched Paul's hand. 'Come on, let's go, I've had enough.'

'Go, what now?'

Pushing past the queuing communicants, we made our way to the back of the church and out into the open. The fresh air and the bright sun were a welcome release. I threw myself down on the bank and began pulling out handfuls of grass.

'Are you OK?' Paul asked then, frowning, he continued, 'I gather not.'

I was silent for a moment. 'No, I'm bloody not OK. Too much – all that communion stuff; that's what my dad used to make me do.'

Paul was about to speak when the church doors swung open.

Crowds of people tumbled out, voicing the words "Christos Anesti" to one another.

'What does that mean?' asked Paul.

'Christ has risen. Come on, let's go,' I said, pulling at his shirtsleeve.

Back at the apartment, Paul poured cups of strong coffee.

'What were you staring at in the church?' I asked.

'When do you mean?'

'Just before I squeezed your hand.'

He hesitated. 'Oh nothing, it was nothing.'

In my head I spoke to Athena:

Dear Athena	**He said it was nothing, I know it was not nothing, but more to the point that Greek Easter thing. Putting it plainly, it did my head in.**
Dear Katalina	**It did your head in? Do you mean it stirred things up for you?**
Dear Athena	**YES.**
Dear Katalina	**Do not worry; it is understandable, given your experiences. Easter time is a very special time for Greek people and although you cannot fully appreciate the full impact of it, just go with it.**
Dear Athena	**Fine, I suppose, but how about Paul?**
Dear Katalina	**Leave him to find his own way.**

I was startled by a knock on the door; it was Sophia. 'Christos Anesti,' she cried.

Not feeling very religious at that moment I endeavoured to be polite, and replied, 'Christos Anesti.' Looking down I saw that she held an oval dish containing pasta and what looked like snails. Strange, I thought France was the place for eating snails. Then I remembered reading in a local guidebook that, Santorini was famous for its snails, a dish called salingaria me makaronia. Sophia pushed a spoon into my hand, gesturing for me to try it. Taking the spoon, I scooped up a few pasta shells. Sophia then pointed, saying "Paul."

Oh God, she wants him to try it, I thought with dismay. Then my mischievous side surfaced. This was perfect – if he likes squid then he's sure to love snails.

'Paul, could you come here a minute?' Paul appeared holding his coffee in one hand. 'She wants you to try it,' I said, shoving the spoon into his hand. I watched him look down at the dish. He frowned then slowly picked up a snail, scooping the flesh out and popping it into his mouth.

Sophia gave us one of her twinkling smiles and clapped with approval.

'Oh yes, it's good, good, thank you,' said Paul.

Sophia pressed the dish into my hand. 'Efcharisto,' I said.

'Well, that's dinner sorted then, I guess,' said Paul, still looking disdainfully at the snails.

Later, I asked Paul once again what he had been staring at in church. Reluctantly, he admitted the gold cross had caught his attention. As I pushed him further, the conversation turned to the Holy Spirit. Retrieving a book, I began reading aloud Buddha's thoughts on the Holy Spirit, how it touches the highest spiritual plane in man.

'Stop, oh God don't go on, enough of that, I'm going to bed.'

He disappeared into the bedroom and I felt awkward, sensing that I had upset him. The remains of the pasta lay in the bowl. I thought of Sophia and decided that I couldn't bear to waste it, so I scooped up the last few mouthfuls. My stomach was now at bursting point. A last sip of wine and a cigarette finished off my evening with thoughts of Paul and religion in the background.

The next day I packed my sunglasses, tourist book and cigarettes into a brightly coloured canvas bag.

Paul's telephone rang. 'That's great, great news. So the statue does date back to that time period?' I heard him say. A moment later he began furiously tapping numbers into his mobile. I watched him as he waited for a reply. I heard him say something about the luminescence dating then silence. 'That was Professor Yannis from Vergina. He told me off.'

'Told you off?'

'Yes, because I contacted *The Times*, who have published an article implying that the Aphrodite statue belongs to Greece and hinting at the presence of a second statue. I apologised, trying to say that my editor kept twisting my arm to come up with something. The professor understood, but insisted that I do not mention it again. The Italians will be up in arms.'

'And?'

'Just before I rang him, the museum in LA rang to confirm that the luminescence analysis has dated the statue back to around 335 BC. He said that I must go back to Vergina – they have found a silver coin with the head of Alexander on one side and a signature on the other. He couldn't say more than that, but insisted that I go back as soon as possible.'

'What's the urgency?'

Paul explained than an American professor had heard the news and was starting to panic, worried that the Greeks would be demanding the statue back. My heart sank as I had hardly seen anything of Philip and somehow knew he had more to tell me. Paul was sorry but insisted that we could only have another two days on the island.

On the way to visit the local museum, we passed a Catholic Church. Paul stopped for a second giving it a fleeting glance. At the museum, we entered a large room. The delicately painted frescoes depicting the life of the Minoans were magnificent. The small figurines and vases caught Paul's attention. My thoughts were elsewhere as I thought about the relatives that I had found and the ones I had yet to find. Paul remained glued to the spot, examining every detail.

I tugged impatiently at his shirt-sleeve. 'Come on, I want to go now,' I said, my mind on Philip.

'Can't you wait? There's just one more room I want to see.'

'I suppose so,' I sighed.

Ignoring my comment, he hooked his right arm into mine and led the way to the next room, which contained more Minoan vases.

Leaving the museum, we walked back through the streets and the Catholic Church came into view. Paul marched ahead and turned into the main entrance of the church. Stunned, I followed him. The place was empty except for two people kneeling at the altar. Paul walked to the front row and sat down. At the altar, stood a large statue of the Madonna and child; Paul gazed towards it. Was it the gentle smile of the Madonna that captivated him, I wondered. I stopped two rows behind. As I sat down an image of my father returned. He was holding my hand pointing towards the Madonna. I felt sad and confused. Paul suddenly stood up and walked rapidly from the church. I followed behind.

It was my turn to cook that evening, so I prepared a Greek salad with pasticcio, what the English call macaroni cheese. Paul sat in the chair with a melancholy expression. The meal was accompanied by silence. I began to feel anxious. After some gentle prodding, he eventually spoke, telling me that he'd never had any time for religion and that he'd always felt in control, only dealing with observable scientific facts. I suggested that sometimes facts may not be enough; we continued our conversation into the early hours of the morning.

As we neared the end of our stay, we made one last visit to the church to check the parish records. Walking down the cobbled street, we passed Sophia, who seemed to be very excited. She waved her arms in the air, gesturing then disappeared down the street.

'What was that about?'

'Haven't a clue.'

Nearing the church, we saw crowds of people gathering. Philip appeared from around the corner. I turned to look at Paul. 'I don't think you are going to see your records today,' he said.

'No, I'm not.' I said feeling disappointed as Philip came running up to us, telling us there was a wedding.

Spiros, a friend of Philip, arrived. 'Ah, Philip, away from your writing, uh?'

'Yes, I need a break.'

Spiros turned to us. 'And who are these people?'

'This is my aunt, Katalina and her fiancé Paul, they are … ' said Philip.

A huge grin appeared on Spiros's face. With a slap on each back, he welcomed us. 'Please come to the wedding. It's my uncle; finally, he's getting married!'

Philip looked at the crowd. 'But there is no room.'

Spiros looked towards the church. 'It's true, yes, well perhaps come back in two hours, join in with the festivities. You must be my guests.'

Philip led us to the local taverna. It was almost empty as practically all the villagers were at the church. Paul told Philip about his research. Two hours later we returned to the church. Suddenly the doors opened and people spilled out, running onto the forecourt shouting and laughing, among them the brushing bride and groom. Tables of food were set out with a number of Greek women attending to the different dishes. I recognised Spiros and Sophia, Spiros holding a pile of plates, Sophia dishing out a jar of olives into bowls. She seemed to be in charge, gesturing to Spiros to hurry up. With a shrug, he turned away. Seeing us he opened his arms in welcome.

'Ah there you are, please join us,' he said, placing the plates down and walking away from the tables. With a look of exasperation, Sophia took the plates and began laying them on the table.

A band of musicians appeared and the crowd organised themselves into a circle.

Sitting on the grass, I noticed the people's smiling faces and listened to the colourful sound of Greek music filling the late spring air. Suddenly, the music stopped and two chairs were brought forward for the bride and groom. Shiny boxes, wrapping paper, ribbon and money showered them as people came forward to greet them. Just like a king and queen, they sat on their thrones receiving expensive gifts and treasures. As the music started up again, we watched the children dancing and giggling. I turned to look at Paul, seeing that he was deep in thought and looking at the children playing.

'What are you thinking?' I asked.

He remained silent for a few minutes then reminded me that he was forty-four. When he told me that he wanted children, I stared at him for a moment. 'Who with?' I stammered.

'You, of course.'

Not knowing how to react, I told him that the feeling would pass, that it was being on Greek soil that brought the breeding instinct out in people.

'I guess,' he said, looking bewildered.

Two waiters appeared, each carrying a pile of plates. The taller waiter took the first plate and threw it to the ground, shattering it into tiny pieces.

I jumped up, 'We can't miss this; come on!'

'No, go ahead. Enjoy yourself!' he snapped.

I stared at him for a second then leapt up snatching the first plate on the pile. I smashed one after another, each plate breaking into tiny pieces. The music ended and everyone piled round to the front of the church, where the food had been laid out.

Picking up what looked like a biscuit, I asked, 'What's this then?'

'Bom-bom-yara, it's candy coated with almonds,' replied Philip.

Champagne and wine flowed. Not wanting to miss out, I drank a number of glasses of the vinsanto, red and very sweet. It was time to get drunk. 'To Dionysus,' I cried.

Paul's mouth gapped open. 'Oh no, you're drunk again.'

'No, not drunk; to Dionysus,' I retorted, lifting my glass up to the sky, 'the god of blessed ecstasy, drink, wine and merriment!'

'I think you are drunk, and your amethyst bracelet hasn't worked either. Also it's time to go home,' he said observing my unsteady gait.

'I'll see you quickly tomorrow before you leave?' asked Philip.

'Yes you will,' I slurred, aware that Paul had grasped my hand and was leading me away.

It was our last day in Santorini and I stepped out onto the balcony, taking a last photo of the idyllic scenery. Arriving at Philip's later that morning, his lounge appeared tidier than before. On the table were glasses and plates of olives, bread and cheese. Paul and I looked at each other with amazement. Philip appeared, this time carrying a bottle of wine which he carefully placed on the table.

'Bit early isn't it?' suggested Paul.

'Not for Greeks!' Philip replied.

Philip picked up a brown envelope and passed it to me. Opening it carefully, I took out some old black and white photos. One was a picture of a woman of around thirty sitting in a chair with two girls and a boy at her feet.

'That's Livana when she was here in Santorini. When I was tidying up I came across them, thought you'd like them?'

'Yes, thank you,' I stammered, and tears fell. I could taste the salt as they trickled down my face. Philip poured out the wine as I continued looking through the photos.

'Here, this is a map of Cyprus. I have circled the village of Nata.' He stopped for a moment. 'It is worth a try!' he said. Picking up his glass, he cried, 'Stin-ee-ys-sas.' We both looked at him. 'Greek for, good health,'

'It has been good to meet you,' said Paul.

I had appreciated my short time with Philip. Quiet, yes, and maybe a bit aloof, but honest and sensitive. I realised that there was a part of me in London in my nephew, Father Stamitos; a part of me in America in my niece Sirena; a part of me in Greece in my nephew Sebastien, and now a part of me in Santorini in Philip.

The island had many small shops, selling unique embroidery, handicrafts, jewellery and clothes. Paul bravely agreed to some last-minute shopping. We found ourselves in a small clothes boutique, walking through to the back which opened out onto a veranda. The sun shone down onto the differently coloured dresses. Such bright colours were dazzling to the eye. Looking out from the veranda, I could see the sea surrounding a small volcanic island. My eyes darted back to the dresses; as usual, I could not make up my mind.

'Which one … this … or this?' I asked, hoping for some support.

'You decide, I'll wait outside,' Paul replied.

Typical, no help at all. Cerise, turquoise or bright jasmine yellow; there were too many colours to choose from. After long moments of staring first at the sea then back to the dresses, I made my decision: the turquoise, a blue that provided me with a tranquil feeling of calm. Having made my purchase, I walked back out onto the street. No sign of Paul. I decided to carry on wandering, browsing the shop windows, when I felt as though I was being watched. Looking up, I spotted a man wearing a black jacket. He looked familiar. Seeing me looking at him, he glared. I froze. It was the police officer from Athens. As a hand touched my shoulder; I jumped five feet in the air. Paul!

'It's that police officer again,' I said, pointing to where I had seen him. Paul turned to look – he had vanished. 'He was there, I tell you!'

Paul's smile spoke volumes. I knew he thought my overactive imagination had got the better of me once more. We walked on in silence until eventually we reached the bottom of the steep hill.

Sophia appeared, brushing the path outside her house. Geiasas,' she said to us both.

'Geiasas,' we replied.

I bent down to remove a stone from my shoe and the photos of Livana dropped out onto the ground. Sophia peered down at one of the photos. 'Livana,' she cried.

'You know her?' I asked.

Sophia nodded and, with excitement, disappeared into her house emerging moments later with a photo showing two children around eight years old. One was obviously Sophia, the other Livana.

'You grew up together?' suggested Paul.

'Nai, nai.'

I tried to explain about our trip to Cyprus, hoping that we may find Livana. Sophia looked puzzled. Taking a map of Cyprus from my bag, I pointed first to it and then to the photo of Livana imitating the sound of an aeroplane.

'Nai, nai,' said Sophia, again understanding dawning on her face.

RETURN TO VERGINA

The airport lounge was almost empty. I felt at home surrounded by Greeks, puffing away at their cigarettes, unlike Los Angeles or London, where travellers couldn't smoke just anywhere. Sitting on the plane, I looked through the window as blue-domed buildings with whitewashed walls slowly disappeared from sight. Santorini was behind us, another destination conquered. I wondered why the professor had called Paul back to Vergina.

'You know, Professor Yannis reminds me of my brother. Do you remember that photo Sirena showed us, the one taken at my nephews wedding? He looks the spitting image of him.' 'Oh, right,' Paul mumbled, taking out a copy of the Ancient Greek/ Egyptian alphabet. He thumbed through another sheet of paper, and started to explain how it worked.

Half-listening, I continued to look out the window. 'Oh yes, I see.'

'What do you see? You haven't been listening!'

'Sorry, it's this aeroplane thing.'

'You're not still nervous of flying?'

'No, I've got used to it now, I'm just tired.'

The shuffling of papers, accompanied by Paul's intermittent sighs kept me awake. Eventually, Thessaloniki came into view, the lights of the city and airport appearing to move in closer. Rummaging in my bag I pulled out the photo of Livana and wondered whether she was still alive. A screeching of wheels brought me down to earth, literally. Everyone disembarked then walked to the arrivals hall to collect their bags.

We took a taxi to the hotel, the same one as before. There in the foyer was Sophia the receptionist. 'Yassus,' she said, running up to me. I looked to see whether she had any photos – for once, she hadn't.

As we picked up our bags and began to walk to the lift, Dimitri the waiter appeared. 'Geiasas, you're back!'

Paul turned round to catch the familiar sight of the waiter. Noting the look on Paul's face, I quickly intervened. 'Geiasas, yes, just for a couple of nights.' The lift doors opened and Paul tugged at my sleeve, almost propelling me into the lift. 'Problem?' I asked.

'No, just that he was the one who said ... '

'I remember, "A body like ... "'

'Yes that was it,' said Paul, pursing his lips with indignation.

The lift doors opened and, picking up our bags, we walked along the corridor; a different room this time and somewhat smaller. I felt tired and dirty. I looked down at my right leg, to see that clumps of dark hair had grown back – yuck! Pulling out a pack of waxing strips, I headed for the bathroom. It was easy enough, as strip after strip peeled away the clumps; then to tackle the backs of the legs; that was more tricky. Again, relative success as more hair came away except for a piece that had become lodged around the back of my leg. The wax strip had obviously melted in the heat, becoming stickier than usual. Paul walked in to see me in a contorted position and asked what I was doing. I replied that I wasn't prepared to exhibit my gorilla-like legs to the world. The stubborn hair was still firmly stuck to my leg so I asked for some help. Immediately he began tugging, clueless in the art of beauty therapy.

'Christ, not like that,' I yelped.

'Don't say that,' he shouted.

'I didn't think you were religious,' I snapped then instructed him on the right way to pull the strip off, in the opposite direction of the hair growth. Success this time as the hair came away with the strip and I managed to refrain from blaspheming.

Only a few guests remained when we finally made it to the restaurant. 'Just in time,' said Dimitri, handing out the menus. 'It's squid isn't it?' he asked Paul.

'Maybe,' replied Paul 'but I might like to choose something different.'

'Maybe,' said Dimitri, 'but you do like squid,' he insisted.

I wondered where this might be going but seeing Paul's bared teeth, I could hazard a guess. Dimitri stared at Paul for a while and after taking the full order walked off. I watched as he strode away. We now had the restaurant to ourselves and the deathly silence felt unbearable. Dimitri returned and placed the dishes down on the table. A contemptuous look passed between them. I burst out, 'You two, give it a rest, please!'

'It's him and what … ' shouted Paul.

Dimitri intervened. 'Oh that! I'd forgotten all about it. Remember it was meant as a compliment. I am Greek after all,' he shrugged.

I looked at Paul, waiting for his response. 'OK, sorry, yes. I guess I can forget it too.'

'Thank you,' I said, sighing with relief.

We talked about our next meeting with Professor Yannis, whilst I enjoyed every mouthful of my dessert, Baklava, heavily laced with sweet honey and almonds.

Back in our room, my mobile rang – Andrea. I told her about Philip and Sophia the old lady who knew my Aunt Livana. Once again, Andrea brought up the subject of marriage. I swiftly asked her about her patchwork – she laughed at my diversion tactics. Paul urged me to hurry up, so I quickly told her that I had got drunk in Santorini. Although she scolded me, I could hear Mandras laughing in the background as she related the story to him. Ending the call, she wished me well and sent Paul her love.

'How long was that then? I've been waiting ages for you to finish. My cell phone has gone down – I need to use yours to ring the professor,' said Paul.

'I don't know, she sends her love anyway,' I replied, throwing him my mobile.

We were woken by the shrill sound of the alarm clock. Dimitri greeted us in the restaurant. Noticing my warning look, Paul politely said "Good morning".

Leaving the hotel, we stepped out into the humid air. The journey to Vergina seemed to take forever: straight roads, short roads and roads with sharp bends went on for miles. As we drove past the shrine, the sunlight glinted on the top of the gold cross once more. Parking the car, we headed for the excavation site. The sun beat down, piercing our skin with its heat. As we walked over the dry ground, our feet kicked up great clouds of powdery dust. In the distance were groups of young people on their hands and knees, digging at the soil. Paul walked up to them and asked what they were doing. A young woman of no more than twenty told him that they were digging for vases. Paul quickly grabbed a pair of gloves, bent down and picked up a trowel, helping the small team of archaeologists. I stood and watched, fascinated: this was the first time I had seen him at work. Trowels, spades and plastic bags were spread everywhere, an archaeologist's tool kit; white tags lay on the ground.

'I've found something, here, look!' a woman cried.

I moved closer. With Paul's help, she gently lifted out two small figurines of Aphrodite.

'Ah, you've found the last two!' The deep, but familiar voice of Professor Yannis boomed across the site. Paul stood up, towering above the short professor.

A smile, followed by a look of concern, spread across Professor Yannis' face. 'Geiasas,' he said, placing his hand on his brow. 'I'm sorry to say that last night the site was robbed. They've taken a few things but thankfully not the important pieces.'

'You are joking!' exclaimed Paul. He looked sorrowfully towards the professor.

'No. They are like ants, obsessively shovelling the earth away. They don't care what they touch. They have no respect.' He turned to me and smiled, shaking my hand. It was Poseidon again, a man with passionate beliefs and strong emotion and the face of my dead brother. Professor Yannis led us away from the site. A small table with stools and a parasol allowed us to take a welcome rest and a break from the sun. He offered me a Marlboro cigarette.

'Marlboro?' I asked looking at the professor.

He laughed. 'Yes, I know, they should be Greek. I ran out and just bought the first ones available.'

Paul looked at us with an irritated expression. 'You're happy now,' he whispered to me.

'Yes, I am now, thank you,' I whispered back, lifting my coffee cup in one hand and my cigarette in the other.

'Good news!' interrupted the professor. 'The figurines we'd uncovered just before you arrived have been dated to around 335 BC. We need to check the ones we've found today, but the evidence looks good; however, this is what I wanted to show you, this coin.' The professor carefully passed the artefact to Paul. Paul looked down at the familiar image of Alexander on the front of the coin. On the back was some unfamiliar lettering – "Alexandrou-Delphi." The professor continued. 'We found this in the tomb of a rich man just outside Vergina. These coins were made at Alexander's Amphipolis mint between 330 and 340 BC. Alexander worshipped Athena and Zeus; in fact he was a bit of a mystic.'

'Mystic?'

'Yes, he used to call into Delphi on his way home to Macedonia and visit the priestess there; she once told him that he was invincible. He frequently consulted a diviner called Aristander. In the centre of Delphi is a stone, supposedly a representation of the centre of the earth. This stone was special to Alexander. We believe that the engravings on the main statue have something to do with the Delphi oracle.'

'And?'

'Well, once a year, in ancient times, they used to hold a special ceremony, a celebration to the god Apollo. At midnight, there would be a torch parade. As they paraded around, they went to a place where there was a stone monument, that marked the mid-point of the earth, or so the legend says.' Although Paul did not interrupt him, I could see him starting to question the professor's sanity. 'When the light from a UVA torch hits this stone, it is said that special markings can be seen. These markings may hold the clue and link to the statue.' The Professor sat back, and inhaled deeply from his cigarette.

'Right, right. You did say ancient times?' asked Paul, looking at the professor with amazement.

'Yes, yes. I know what you are thinking, that I'm off my head. Seriously, even today there are a group of people known as the Dodecadians who still hold this ceremony once a year. In fact, if my diary is correct this will happen in two days. And you must go. You can get in on that night – on other nights, the place is guarded. I know it must seem mad to your logical mind but it is worth a try.'

The professor handed Paul a sheet of paper detailing the story he had just told. He continued to stare at Paul, sensing his disbelief at this preposterous story.

'Is there anything else I need to know?'

The professor paused for a moment. 'Ah yes, we found part of a stone column with the inscription "Olympias Swan Cyprus." We know Olympias was Alexander's mother, and believe that the swan refers to an image. Apelles was Alexander's official court painter at the time. We believe a mosaic, with the words "Alexandrou-Olympias was produced at the time.'

'So now I'm looking for a vase still and possibly a mosaic, which would be where?' asked Paul impatiently.

'That is your job to find out, and please, this is our history … Greek history,' urged the professor, looking towards me for some moral support. I jumped in, insisting that it was our heritage that was at stake and that if the statue was ours, it should be in Greece not Los Angeles.

'Exactly,' said the professor.

Paul gave a deep sigh and looked at the pair of us. 'I'll do it, I have no choice. If these artefacts belong to Alexander, we need to know.'

I told the professor that I was still searching for my relatives and about the possibility that I had an aunt in Cyprus. A smile as wide as a Cheshire cat's spread across his face. He came over to me and wrapped his arms around me in a strong hug. I could feel my bones almost crushed into dust. 'Yes, you're Greek. You must find your family.' He took out his packet of Marlboros and offered me another cigarette, much to Paul's dismay.

I admired this strong professor. He reminded me of my brother: the trimmed beard and moustache with those intense blue eyes. I had a fleeting image of the professor under the great Mediterranean Sea, excavating the remains of a Doric column, beside him, Poseidon using his trident to help the professor dig up this great Greek archaeological work of art. The vision disappeared as hot ash from my cigarette fell onto my leg.

Facing the professor again, Paul spoke. 'I'm sorry about the newspaper report.'

'No, it's OK, I forgive you. It's just that to publish information that has not been fully confirmed can give people the wrong idea. Like I said, you must go to Delphi. The ceremony will be in two days' time, so pack your bags.'

As we left, we passed by the group of archaeologists. Paul spoke to the young woman he had helped earlier and wished her well for the future. The heat of the sun began to recede as clouds gathered in the sky. Walking back to the car, Paul took hold of my hand. 'The professor likes you!'

'Yes, he reminds me of … ' I turned away.

'Reminds you of your brother; yes I know, it's OK.'

Back in the car, we sat and stared at each other. 'Did you see that shrine again when we drove past?' I asked.

'Yes I did, and … ?'

'Well … '

'You're not going to go all religious on me are you?' he asked cautiously.

'No, it's just … '

'Rubbish, that's what it is. Perhaps that's too harsh.'

Astonished at his answer, I fumbled for my next words. 'Rubbish – how do you mean?'

'All that religious stuff. I told you before; my mother was forever crossing herself. Crucifixions, Masses and Baptisms, it's all crazy. I was baptised. What do they say? Baptism is a way of keeping you sin-free or something!' He looked out of the car window, his finger tapping on the steering wheel.

'Perhaps it can be seen in a different light,' I suggested.

'What can?'

'Baptism – I mean, in Buddhism, it's a way of ensuring that every human being is opened to the Holy Spirit. Buddhism doesn't refer to original sin, but talks about negative seeds or ideas planted in the individual.'

'I suppose so, but now you've offended all the Christians.'

'No it's just another way of looking at things.'

His fingers stopped tapping and turned to catch my gaze once more. Look, just forget it, OK?'

He turned the key in the ignition and started the engine. The journey passed in silence. In my head I spoke to Athena:

Dear Athena **God he is so uptight about religion.**

Dear Katalina **Yes, I agree but you must stop trying to push, he has his own searching to do, and I might add so do you!**

Dear Athena **Thanks a lot!**

Back at the hotel Sophia appeared, armed with more photos. Unable to escape, I leant on the reception desk "mmming" and "ahhing" in the right places. When she finally had shown me the last photo, I thanked her and made my way back to our room. I could hear Paul talking on the phone, and noted the strong Italian expressions emanating from him.

'Yes, ciao, ciao,' he said and placed the mobile on the table.

'What was that about?'

'Professor Bettulini, you remember, the Italian who was intrigued to hear about the Delphi ceremony and asked me to ring him again when we've found out more.'

Later, in the restaurant, Dimitri handed us our menus. Paul, still cautious of this gregarious Greek waiter, kept his eyes on him as he looked towards me. 'It is good to see you again. What will it be, moussaka?'

'Oh soup I think, I feel fat today!'

'Fat, pray? No, your body ... ' he started. Paul glared at him. 'Oh I'm sorry, but really, she's not fat is she?' he continued, looking to Paul for approval.

'No she's not, I agree with you.'

'How about you, sir,' asked Dimitri, attempting to keep the atmosphere safe.

'Squid, efcharisto,' replied Paul.

'Bravo,' said Dimitri.

I looked out of the window, as Paul chatted incessantly about Delphi and how ludicrous the whole suggestion was. 'You haven't listened to a word I've said, have you?' he demanded, pushing his plate forward.

No, I had not listened to a word; he was getting on my nerves again. I could only think of Sebastien, Philip, my dad and my dead brother. It was the professor – seeing him again sliced through me like a sharp sword. 'Yes … no, no, I haven't bloody listened to a word.'

'Why?'

'Just things, stuff,' I said, turning away.

Paul shook his head and was about to speak when Dimitri reappeared. Noticing my expression, he carefully placed the coffee cups down and quickly walked away.

'Pity, I thought he was about to come out with one of his Greek expressions, like "she has the body of Athena," ' said Paul sarcastically. I slammed down my cup, stood up and left the restaurant.

Dimitri was still standing close to our table. 'Women,' he said, shrugging his shoulders.

'You ain't kidding,' said Paul.

I ran a bath and inserted a loud heavy metal CD into the player. It was my turn now to be moody. I retrieved my mobile and logged in:

> **Dear Poseidon** **I've forgotten what we discussed**
> **before, yes, oh yes, being scared**
> **about meeting my relatives**
> **and that Athena would give me**
> **courage. Yes, that is right. I'm**
> **still scared, confused and, and, I**
> **don't know any more?**

**Dear Katalina Do not be scared, just hang on,
Athena is always with you.**

Some great help that was, I thought, as I logged off and stepped into the bath.

The hotel door slammed, Paul was back. He walked into the bathroom. 'I'm not a mind reader,' he yelled.

I ignored him, looking down at a pool of bubbles that had landed on my navel. He knelt down by the side of the bath and stared at me. I turned my head away, pretending he wasn't there as I carried on listening to the music. Paul stood up and switched the player off. A heavy silence hung in the air, as he stared at me. 'As I said before, I'm not a mind reader. How can we talk with that music blaring?'

I stared back at him and took a breath then gradually revealed all my thoughts and feelings about my dead brother, Sebastien and Philip as Paul listened patiently.

The previous evening had left me exhausted. The next morning nicotine and coffee came to the rescue, accompanied by a bright orange and yellow flower.

'Lovely, but how … ?' I asked, knowing that we were in the middle of the city.

'Oh, I waited until you fell asleep, ran outside and found the nearest flowerbed.'

I thanked him and then burst out laughing at the image of a tall man trying not to appear conspicuous stealing flowers.

Bags packed, we walked into the reception area to find Sophia armed once more with photos. I stood and listened patiently as she went through each one. I then pulled out a photo of Livana. Sophia smiled and said that she reminded her of her grandmother back in Athens. Dimitri appeared, giving Paul a slap on the back and a quick wink towards me. Paul gave him a cross look that broke into a forgiving smile. Good wishes all round; we set off for the next part of our journey.

DELPHI

'Stop!'

'Not again. What now?' Paul gave me that look.

'It's the scenery. Damn! Where's the camera?' I leapt out of the car into a valley of cypress trees and bright, piercing sunshine. Photos taken, we headed further along the dusty road.

Noticing a garage up ahead, I pleaded with Paul to stop. 'Don't tell, me cigarettes?'

'Yes, thanks.'

I walked back to the car armed with a carton of cigarettes. Paul looked at me, saying nothing. For the next thirty minutes we managed to stay on the road until a small but familiar object appeared in front of us. Paul stopped the car. There on the slope stood a blue and white wayside shrine, with a gold casket inside. Stepping out of the car, Paul walked straight up to it. I couldn't believe it, was he having some kind of spiritual crisis? He stood there motionless. I waited for a while then, as curiosity got the better of me, got out of the car to join him. I stood behind him for what felt like an eternity; the place was so silent.

Paul turned to look at me. 'It's beautiful, isn't it?'

Stunned, I looked towards the casket then back at him. 'Yes it is.'

In the distance, more cypress trees came into view and then Delphi, the home of Apollo. The sun was high and the heat slowly increasing as our journey continued. All was calm, until Paul glanced into the mirror.

'I don't know whether I'm seeing things, but I think we're being followed. The same white car has been behind us for at least half an hour.' I moved my head to look in the mirror. There were two people in the white car – the driver and a passenger. 'I'll go faster, see if he speeds up.'

Feeling apprehensive, I lit a cigarette. The smoke blew across my face, temporarily blocking my view of the car. As we sped up, so did the white car. Paul increased the speed again, pressing his foot down hard on the accelerator. We suddenly swerved around a narrow right-hand bend. So did the car following us. The roads became narrower and we could see steep drops ahead. Heart racing, I looked at Paul and saw small beads of sweat on his brow. Our wheels suddenly moved closer to the edge of the road, towards a sheer drop.

'God, that was close!' For a second I shut my eyes, hoping this was a dream. Paul said nothing, just kept driving, the whites of his knuckles showing as he gripped the steering wheel. The mountain drop gradually disappeared and opened up into a straight flat road with bushes on either side. Paul quickly gained speed and turned off into a small lane. Finding some trees ahead, he stopped the car. No trace of the white car could be seen.

'Why didn't you stop?'

'We need to get to Delphi, in time for that ludicrous ceremony,' he said, wiping his brow.

'That's not until tomorrow.'

'I know, but it would be a good idea to see the place in daylight first.'

We set off again. Just a few minutes later, Paul exclaimed, 'I don't believe it!'

I looked in the mirror to see the white car again – it was gaining on us. My hands felt distinctly hot and clammy. 'I'm sure it's that Greek policeman, the one I saw in Athens and in Santorini, you know, outside the clothes shop,' I said, still feeling my nerves on edge.

In front of us, a red sports car came into view. The white car suddenly overtook, only to squeeze in just in front of us. To our amazement, the red sports car sped off with the white car in pursuit. Paul's brow was now dripping with sweat. We slowed down and eventually stopped. We looked at each other. What had all that been about? A white car with a police officer made me think about the Greek, Sokritos, who was on the run. But no, the car had not stopped for us at all. Instead, it had continued in pursuit of another car. Just ahead of us I saw a signpost – Delphi 1 Km.

The Hotel Filelion lay in front of us, a small hotel with only two floors. Car parked, we collected our bags and walked into the reception area.

'Kalispera,' said the receptionist quietly.

She was short, unsmiling, with her black hair severely tied back from her face. Strange; but hopefully this one wouldn't be armed with family photos. She handed us our room keys and we walked up the stairs and along a dark corridor. Our room was small but contained everything we needed – on the left, the bathroom; on the right, twin beds. I walked over towards the window, threw the doors open and stepped out onto a small veranda. The room may have been basic, but the view was breathtaking, overlooking the Gulf of Corinth. On either side were mountainous hills with the sea running between, the sun was gleaming down on the water. I stood there in awe.

Paul came out onto the veranda and placed his arm around me. 'Yes, I agree – magnificient!'

We ate our evening meal and returned to our room. I walked back out onto the veranda to find a crimson and gold sunset; the deep reflecting colours were magical. I stayed there, mesmerised, until the sun finally disappeared.

Next morning we were up early, ready for our trip to Delphi. I quickly pushed tourist books, pictures, and sun lotion into my bag. Over breakfast, we talked about Delphi, Professor Yannis and the improbable story he had told us. Having consumed our meal, we set off.

An expansive landscape came into view, below us was the ancient site of Delphi.

I stood in awe, listening to the silence interrupted by only the murmur of the odd tourist in the distance. Paul stopped and pointed down to the ground where the remains of the main entrance to this immortal sight once stood

"Know thyself". Those were the words inscribed on the archway all those years ago.'

'You are kidding. How do you know that?'

'I am an archaeologist.'

True, I thought, but wondered whether he had said that deliberately. Was that for me or for him? 'Let's walk up to the theatre first,' I suggested.

The semi-circular stone-stepped theatre lay before us. Many plays had been performed here in ancient times. Apollo, the god of the sun, glorified thousands of years ago. I imagined actors walking out onto the stage wearing masks, the lead actor wearing the gold mask of Apollo. I looked around nervously; nobody was in sight. Taking a deep breath I raised my arms in the air and yelled, 'Hello, Apollo!'

Paul jumped back in shock as my voice echoed around the theatre. 'What did you do that for?'

'I just had to. Come on, let's walk down to Apollo's temple.'

'Well, now you've brought attention to yourself, although luckily I can't see anybody around at the moment. I'm sure you've awakened Apollo.' I strode ahead, like the great Athena marching into battle. Paul grabbed my hand, 'Let's walk though, not run.'

The temple of Apollo with its six remaining columns stood grand and tall. This was the centre point of Delphi, the Oracle. We found a seat beneath a tree. For a moment, everything was silent, only the whisper from the leaves as a gentle breeze blew through. A magical stillness pervaded the scene. As we sat, I thought about the Apollo, a god known to be pure and cleansing. The Delphi Oracle was starting to come to life. In ancient times, the Oracle was the means by which worshippers could hear the spoken words of Apollo.

'Zeus,' I murmured.

'What?'

'Zeus, he was the one that started this.'

'Started what?'

I told him about the legend, how Zeus had released two eagles from the opposite ends of the world. When their paths crossed in the sky, which of course they did at Delphi, this marked the centre of the earth. The eagles landed on a stone, the navel of the earth. This famous stone was to be the centre point, the magical artefact that at midnight would reveal Professor Yannis's indelible markings.

'Come on, let's find this stone, this will be the one that your professor was talking about.'

Climbing a steep path, we turned a corner that led onto a straight path. There it stood, a dome-shaped stone that resembled the tip of a World War II bomb. The stone was grey and smooth housed on a block of cement.

Paul looked down at the stone. 'Is that it?'

'Yes, that's it. It's a bit plain I know. Here, look at the guide book,' I said, pointing to a page showing a picture of the stone.

He knelt down to touch the stone. His fingers kept running over the same spot. 'It's smooth, but at the back you can just feel some faint lines. Not enough for the naked eye to see.'

I knelt down beside him and felt the stone, wondering what it might reveal.

Back at the hotel, our room smelt fresh with polish. The cleaner had left the small table by the balcony gleaming. I leant over to see my reflection in the glass then opened the veranda doors and stepped out to breathe in the warm Delphi air. Taking hold of my mobile, I logged in:

Dear Apollo   **We have not spoken before, but Delphi was something else. I am filled with awe.**

Dear Katalina **Filled with awe, you say. It used to be a place where people would come for purification, a way of purging their sins, a bit like some of your people today who go to church as a way of helping them to be forgiven.**

Dear Apollo   **I see, but I suddenly see you holding two stringed instruments, a bow and lyre ...**

Dear Katalina **Yes, I would play music. Music to**

	feed the human spirit, music that would help a person to see the truth as to who they really are.
Dear Apollo	Yes, music, I like music, but perhaps not quite the thing you have in mind.
Dear Katalina	That's ok. It is about music that can send your soul soaring towards the sky. Soaring upwards, so that you can rise above a situation to see everything as it really is.

As I heard Paul shuffling through his papers, I ended my conversation with Apollo.

Paul read through the information that Professor Yannis had given him again. 'Listen to this, Alexander, a mystic, had temples built, one to Zeus, another to Athena; and as for the Diviner called Aristander, just incredible.' I noticed his furrowed brow, his expression contorted by thoughts of what lay ahead: the Delphi Oracle; the ceremony; the markings on the navel stone. Would they reveal the missing information?

The Oracle was fascinating but gave me a sense of unease. I watched Paul fiddling with what looked like a pen. 'What's that,' I asked, pointing at the object he was now placing carefully into his bag.

'It's a special ultra-violet penlight. First I rub in some of this special dye,' he said, pointing to a small pot, 'then I shine this light on it. With the help of the beacons, I should be able to see and copy down the engravings.'

For a moment, I sat deep in thought. 'But why hasn't anybody done this before?' I asked.

'Two reasons. One, nobody has questioned the origin of the Horatio statue before. Two, this excavation site is out of bounds at night, with security guards around. However, according to Professor Yannis, on this one night of the year, when the procession happens, the security guards don't bother.'

'Oh I see,' I said, struggling with a polo neck jumper, which I was attempting to pull over my head. I had read that at night-time it could get quite cold, especially in the hills. I stuffed cigarettes, sweets and a small torch into my bag. Paul watched me, shaking his head in dismay.

'What's wrong?'

'Why do you have to pack so much? The last thing you want to do is light up a cigarette.'

'I might get nervous.'

'Nervous? You won't have time for that, and why in god's name a torch?'

'I might trip up; I like to see where I'm going.'

'Well, don't switch it on without asking me first. The last thing we want is to draw attention to ourselves. Now, are you ready?'

'Yes,' I said, taking a quick swig of the gin I had found at the back of the mini bar.

We locked the door behind us, left the hotel and jumped into the car. Ten minutes later we arrived at the ancient excavation site, cautiously parking the car out of view. Finding a position close to the temple of Apollo, we crouched down and waited.

'The gods wear many faces and many fates fulfil to work their will,' I whispered.

Paul looked at me. 'What is that supposed to mean?'

'It's a quote from a Mary Renault book, all about a Greek actor and how he wears the mask of Apollo in his performances,' I said, congratulating myself that I had managed to read this intellectual right to the end.

Shooting me an exasperated expression, Paul chose not to pursue the discussion. 'Can we concentrate on these Dodecadians people now?'

'Yes OK, I just thought you'd be interested.'

In the distance, we could hear the crunching sound of gravel: the Dodecadians had finally arrived. We watched their approach from our hideaway. Twelve of them appeared and walked up the temple ramp. Eight of them then lit the beacons they were carrying. The darkness of the night disappeared as the beacons illuminated the temple floor. A couple, dressed in bridal outfits, stood holding another beacon. I had read about this ancient marital ceremony. The woman was wearing a white gown. As she moved, the light picked out glittering shards. 'They're diamonds,' I whispered.

'Diamonds?'

'Yes, they represent the tears of the gods and are supposed to reflect the flames of love.'

Paul raised his eyebrows in disbelief.

A veil of red and yellow was placed around the woman's head. 'The veil protects the bride from evil spirits.'

'Oh God, not more superstition,' he said in a loud voice.

'Ssh!'

The man wore a tunic tied at the waist with a cord. A white braided crown was placed on his head. To our amazement, the twelve moved into a circle and began chanting. It reminded me of Buddhist chanting. The meditative sound made me look up to see twinkling stars dotted across the dark night sky. I was enchanted, reminded of the time when I had been entranced by the stars at the traffic lights on the way to visit Andrea that cold December evening.

'I'm sure that's some form of Ancient Greek,' said Paul. He saw me looking up at the sky. 'Are you listening?'

'Yes … no … I'm looking at the stars, they're fantastic.'

'I said, I'm sure that's some form of ancient Greek they are speaking!'

'I thought you didn't know any Greek?'

'Well, a bit of course, but I haven't had much need to use it recently.'

'It's exciting isn't it? Very pagan,' I whispered as I looked towards the bride.

'Quiet,' he snapped.

I bit my lip and went back to think of Buddhist chanting.

The Dodecadians stopped and moved into a line. They then walked back down the ramp and along the pathway. We followed them, keeping our distance. Finally, they arrived a few yards away from the navel stone, adjacent to it. They stood at the remains of the sanctuary of the goddess Gea then formed a semi-circle. Their beacons lit up the surrounding area, reflecting down onto the navel stone. As they began chanting again, the moon appeared to shine directly onto the stone. Paul crouched down and felt the faint lines embedded in the stone. Quickly he rubbed in the dye and took out the penlight, shining it onto the lines. Heart pounding, I thought of that night at the Parthenon, the sudden light, the way that the temple came alive.

'Damn, I can't see the lines, the light isn't strong enough.'

'What do you mean, not strong enough?' I whispered.

'Not strong enough!'

I pushed my hand into my bag and pulled out the torch. 'Here, try my useless torch!'

With a look of both disdain and gratitude he took the torch. As he was about to switch it on, the chanting suddenly stopped and voices spoke. Instantly he turned off the ultra penlight and held the torch tightly. When the chanting resumed, he switched both of them on. Faint lines appeared once more. 'Oh God, it's still not enough, I can only see a few lines.'

'What do we do now?'

'Shhh, I'm thinking. Blow on it.'

'Blow on it, how do you mean?'

'Blow on the stone, where the lines are.'

'Are you mad?'

'Just do it. The heat might bring it out.' Feeling ridiculous, I took a deep breath and breathed on the stone. The lines were fully illuminated. Paul smiled. 'Quickly, copy the inscriptions!'

'Inscriptions?'

'Yes, inscriptions … markings … lines!'

I quickly took out some paper and pencil and carefully copied down the inscriptions. 'Got them,' I said quietly.

Paul nodded and then turned off both lights. The chanting stopped and this time, the Dodecadians moved back into a line and walked down the path to the temple. We followed at a distance, waiting to see what would happen next. A cast iron bowl was placed on the platform and sticks and leaves were poured in and lit from one of the beacons. Within minutes, a fire had taken hold. The bride and groom stepped forward.

'God, they're not going to make a sacrifice, are they?' asked Paul, half worried, half smiling.

'Don't be stupid.'

The bride's veil and the groom's head-piece were removed. Crowns of laurel leaves and gold-plated leaves were placed on their heads.

'Laurel leaves, a sign of fertility' I whispered.

'Oh, great!'

Gold goblets were passed around filled with liquid. Each of the Dodecadians drank a toast. More chanting followed then they then collected their belongings, packed everything away, blew out their beacons and left. We breathed a sigh of relief. The ceremony was over and we headed back to the hotel.

In the early hours of the morning, papers were spread everywhere. Paul looked at my drawings of the inscriptions. 'What's this?' he asked, pointing to one of the marks.

I leant over and stared at the piece of paper. 'Well, that's what it looked like.'

'But it doesn't make sense. I'm looking at a transcript the professor gave me and this third symbol doesn't make sense. Are you sure that the top mark went to the left?'

'I can't remember. Try drawing it to the right,' I said impatiently.

Paul scribbled away, changing the position of the markings. For a moment, he stared at the paper, expressionless then suddenly, 'Eureka! That's it, the ancient alphabet! Each mark represents one of the letters.'

'It's what?' I asked, bemused.

'"Basileus Makedonon" – King of Macedonia.'

Despite the late hour, he rang Professor Yannis to tell him the news. The professor was excited, agreeing with Paul that the inscription proved that Alexander the Great had visited Cyprus. So Cyprus was the place where we would find the vase and the mosaic. Would we also find my aunt?

We finally fell asleep only to be woken a few hours later by sunshine streaming in through a gap in the blinds. It was 7.30, time to return to Athens to catch a flight to Cyprus.

CYPRUS

Another runway, another plane, I had lost count of how many flights we had taken. It was crazy, for most of my life there had been no travelling at all. The air hostess stood in the aisle holding a tray of food. Paul peered across and commented that it was a pity there wasn't any Italian food. I tutted as the air hostess passed us each a plate of Spinoanakopita, a Greek dish comprising filo pastry filled with feta cheese. He pulled a face. 'Wow, that's cheesy!'

We continued to eat our meal in silence. Outside the window, I could see a clear blue radiant sky. It made me feel warm inside, like sitting in front of a log fire. It wasn't winter though, the sun was out and the temperature was rising. The sea below was still and calm, not a flicker of a wave, just the sun gleaming and shimmering across the surface.

'Please, do you have any black olives?' a voice asked. I turned to the woman sitting on the other side of Paul.

'Black olives? No, sorry, I don't,' replied the air hostess

'But why not?' she demanded. We have just come from Greece and now we are going to Cyprus!' She frowned at the air hostess.

My mouth opened before my head could intervene. 'I like olives as well; you would think they would have them, wouldn't you?' We struck up quite a conversation. She told me that she always had olives with her meal and had forgotten to bring her usual jar.

'A jar?' I exclaimed. Paul tried, without success, to ignore the conversation.

The woman leant forward. 'Yes, a jar. Olives are very good for you; they help to keep the skin young and supple.'

I nodded, deciding to start eating plenty of them to avoid getting wrinkly too early in life. She told me that her son lived in Paphos.

Paul put down his book. 'Would you like to sit here? Then perhaps I can get some work done.'

I looked out of the window, not really wanting to let go of my view of the bright blue sea and sky. Seeing the look of impatience on his face though, I decided that it might be a good idea. 'Oh, ok then.'

A shuffle ensued as I stood and squeezed past Paul, who slid behind me into the window seat. I plonked myself down beside the woman and we continued our conversation.

Time passed quickly and soon we landed in Paphos. Customs checks over and baggage collected, we headed towards the hotel. Arriving at the reception desk, I sorted out the booking. The receptionist handed us the keys and Paul picked up our suitcases. Turning, we saw a young couple standing at the bottom of the hotel stairs, their arms intertwined, they kissed passionately.

'Geiasas and welcome.' A loud Greek Cypriot voice came from behind. In the foyer stood a smartly dressed waiter. He had straight, brown hair and deep blue eyes with a classic Greek nose.

Paul glared at the new waiter, presumably wondering what he had in store for us. The waiter introduced himself as Theo. I gave a beaming smile, much to Paul's annoyance. 'I don't believe it, here we go again … '

'Me synchoreite,' Theo said, giving Paul a puzzled look.

'Oh yes … not another Theo. We met quite a few in Greece.'

'You got out of that quickly,' I whispered.

'Ah well, Theodore is a common Greek name. Please, let me help you with your bags.'

Paul followed reluctantly.

Our hotel room was large: along one wall were twin beds with turquoise and white covers that matched the bedside lamps. I knelt to look closer at the rug that adorned the laminated floor, bearing a beautiful woven image of Aphrodite. Paul picked up the leaflet, detailing the facilities, which included a gym and swimming pool. I decided to take a take a look at the gym whilst Paul chose to read.

I found my towel stuffed at the bottom of my suitcase, changed into shorts and a t-shirt and went downstairs to find the gym. The room was well equipped and a few people were already using the machines. I couldn't make my mind up whether to use the rowing machine, the jogging machine or the weights. Then, recalling the exhilaration of my run around the Olympic stadium in Athens, drunk and being chased by the police, I opted for the jogging machine. I pressed the start button and the machine began to make a whirring noise as the treadmill started to move. At first it was too slow, so I turned up the speed. My legs and feet took off, my mind back in the Olympic stadium. I was running for Greece, running for Zeus. Unused to the exercise, my legs quickly began to tire. I took a quick shower and walked out of the changing room.

Leaving the changing room, I spotted the door to the swimming pool. Light emanating from the water illuminated the room. I stood there for a seconds, the lights beneath the water dazzled my eyes. I was just about to turn back, when I saw Paul. I watched as he stretched his arms forward and shot like a bullet through the water. I quietly edged to the side of the pool, hoping to surprise him. I sat for a moment, gazing at the murals then suddenly found myself being yanked into the water. I looked at Paul. Water dripped from his nose and chin, his dark eyelashes glistened from the water. Our glazed expressions met.

Our final hotel restaurant; a medium-sized room dotted with plants. A large window looked out towards the sea; pictures of Greek gods and goddesses stared back at me: the immortal face of Zeus, the passionate Poseidon and the courageous Athena with her regal helmet and sword; all had their own stories to tell.

Walking to the table, I thought about Aphrodite. Her statue stood by the window, the white marble capturing her beautiful curves of beauty.

'Aha, you've been admiring our Greek gods.' Theo appeared wearing a smart white waistcoat. 'Of course, now you're looking at the famous Aphrodite, goddess of love,' he said, darting a quick look at Paul, 'and the patron goddess of Cyprus.' As Theo handed us our menus I told him that I was half Greek and was hoping to find my aunt. He smiled and left. On the other side of the room I noticed the young couple sitting at the table, their legs entwined. 'Our final hotel and now I'm surrounded by everything

Greek. Another buoyant, over-the-top Greek waiter and picture after picture of Greek gods,' groaned Paul.

'Sorry, yes, it's brilliant.'

Paul raised his eyebrows and, with a sigh, opened the menu. Theo returned and Paul pointed to the word "garithes soulaki".

'Excellent, yes; grilled prawns, with Greek olive oil and, of course, fresh Greek lemons. And for you madam?'

'The stuffed vegetables for me, parakalo,' I said, turning to look at the pictures again.

'Ah, you are still fascinated by Aphrodite,' Theo commented. 'She invokes great passion and love. She was born from the white foam produced from the severed genitals of Uranus, when he was castrated by the Titans.'

'Oh God, please, no,' interrupted Paul.

'Ssh, carry on Theo, please.'

'Where was I? Ah yes; some say she rose from the waves off the island of Kythera in the Peloponnese, but this was too rocky, so she sped away on her shell here to Cyprus. The rock, Aphrodite's rock, is her legendary birthplace. It's a magical place and romantic at sunset.'

'Have you finished now?' asked Paul grumpily.

'Yes, and may I suggest some Cypriot white wine?'

'If you insist,' said Paul.

Theo walked away, leaving me mesmerised by his story. I remained fascinated by the Aphrodite picture: another goddess had come into my life. All I needed now was to find my aunt Livana.

Theo returned with our food and wine. When he left, I stared at my glass and hesitated, choosing not to drink.

'These prawns are awesome!' said Paul, chasing a one round his plate with a fork.

Theo reappeared, 'Everything ok?'

'Perfect,' I replied.

'Ah,' he said, looking at my wine glass. 'I was about to say, when in Cyprus, never drink a glass dry, it's not considered polite, but I see you haven't drunk any?'

'Sorry Theo, I must drink water,' I said with conviction.

'Water?' he exclaimed. 'But you are Greek!'

'Yes I know, well half Greek, I want to keep a clear head in case I find my aunt Livana. I don't want her to think I'm an alcoholic.'

Paul stared at me, dumbfounded. 'Are you wearing that amethyst bracelet?'

I giggled. 'Yes I am, actually.'

'Good, I'm not superstitious, but keep that thing on!'

Next morning I put on a pair of shiny flip-flops. Paul suggested that the flecks of sand would get in between my toes. I decided to keep them on anyway. After breakfast, we headed towards the Tomb of the Kings, located on the outskirts of Paphos in the direction of Coral Bay. I picked up my guidebook and lit a Greek cigarette, a karelia slim. Smoke obscured my vision as I read aloud. 'The tombs did not hold kings or royalty, just Ptolemaic aristocracy.' Silence. I waited for his answer. 'Yes, I know,' he said, eventually.

'So what's the connection? What's your reason for going there?'

'This used to be a burial ground, just as you've said, so that's why we're going there.'

'Oh,' I replied, throwing my cigarette out of the window.

'It's interesting. The Macedonians used to bury their royalty and nobility in elaborate tombs. They didn't just bury things in the same place; they would spread the stuff around. The Tomb of Kings was famous at the time. Professor Yannis suggested that there may be a link between the aristocracy in Macedonia and Alexander the Great.'

'What like a family link? A bit like what I'm trying to do, tracing my family all over Greece?'

We parked the car and took a walk onto the beach. I began to feel the grit between my toes. Removing a flip-flop off, I shook the sand out. A few moments later the same thing happened with the other foot. 'Oh God, this sand!'

'I told you, you wouldn't listen.' Ignoring his comments, I took both flip-flops off and proceeded to walk bare-footed. 'Come on, we haven't got all day. Oh that's really sensible,' he remarked, staring at my bare feet.

Childishly, I stuck my tongue out and marched forward. Carved steps led down to the burial chambers, the steps worn away by previous tourists. 'This is like descending into the underworld of Hades himself,' I remarked.

The tombs were carved from reddish rock and the cold, dark atmosphere made me feel claustrophobic. I felt a tug on my left arm and was relieved to be pulled away.

'These would have been ornately decorated tombs, fascinating, but not exactly helpful,' Paul said.

'Can we go now? I just don't like it here,' I said, clinging to him, wondering what else he wanted to explore.

'I just can't make you out at times. Let's just try one more tomb.'

The next tomb appeared rather dark and small but this time I felt intrigued. The doorway curved around the rock face. Inside there were small scratch marks on the wall. 'Here, how about this? It's a bit small and poky,' I called out.

'That small and poky area is a burial chamber, and the marks don't reveal anything.'

I scrutinised the marks. They looked like the letters M and E.

'I think it's a love note. You know – the ones you used to do at school, "Mandy loves Edward," that sort of thing.'

Paul frowned. 'Yes maybe, but there's nothing here.'

We spent the rest of the day walking around Paphos. Back at the hotel, I collapsed onto the bed and fell asleep. Paul woke me from a dream where I was stuck in the underworld with Hades and Persephone. Retrieving my mobile, I sat on the veranda and logged in. Paul suddenly appeared behind me. 'Oh there you are. What's that you've logged onto? Aphrodite ... ' he said.

'Umm … yes … ' I replied, placing my hand over the screen.

'Don't worry; I'll let you carry on in private.' As he walked away, I breathed a sigh of relief:

Dear Poseidon I dreamt about Hades, it was terrible, then Paul just turning up like that. Anyway, Hades, Hades means death, doesn't it?

Dear Katalina Yes maybe, but like most things, it has a metaphorical, symbolic meaning. In your case, death means loss; loss of relatives. However, my advice is that your journey has probably not ended yet.

Dear Poseidon I guess, but …

Dear Katalina No buts, just go down to the gym and get some exercise and if need be go and think more about it then.

EXCAVATIONS

Back in the gym I stepped onto the jogging machine. The belt moved too slowly so I pressed the keypad to select a faster pace. As the speed increased, my legs flew. Next, tried the weights but it proved to be too heavy, so I settled for a couple of dumb bells instead. In my mind, the Tomb of Kings, Hades and the underworld returned. They hovered in the background as I thought about my dead father and brother.

Back in the restaurant, Theo stood at our table. 'You have been to the gym, eh?' he asked, glancing at the tops of my arms. Surely they weren't that big?

'Yes I have, thank you, Theo.' I said looking at the tops of my arms again.

'Ah, make you have strong muscles like Hercules himself.'

Paul shot an indignant glare towards him. 'Excuse me?' he enquired.

'Hercules, the great Greek warrior,' Theo repeated.

'Yes, I know who Hercules was, thank you,' countered Paul. 'Well, she has been to the gym. Was that meant to be a compliment?' he demanded.

'Yes, I think so. Here are your menus,' Theo replied, then quickly left.

'God, another one. Why do you have to wear that vest? It shows everything.'

'It's too warm for anything else, and anyway, what's wrong with it?'

Paul considered me for a moment. 'Nothing, in fact I quite like it.'

'Thank you,' I said. 'Now, let's look at the menu.'

I turned to see the young couple sitting opposite us, engrossed in each other, the man stroking his partner's hair. I noticed Paul, also watching the couple.

Theo appeared, ready to take our orders. I found myself staring at the picture of Aphrodite again. The curves of the body, her delicate smile caught my imagination. If she were alive today, what would she think of modern woman? Paul carried on talking about the problems he had come across in his research and how he was going to search for the mosaics.

Theo carefully placed our dishes down on the table. 'I couldn't help but overhear your conversation regarding your trip and your struggles,' he said. 'It reminded me of the great Greek traveller Odysseus who faced many perils on his way home to Ithaca; women that would turn you to stone; the ravaging one-eyed Cyclops ... '

'Please, get to the point,' insisted Paul.

'Well, he got there, in the end,' he said and smiled as he left us to our meal.

Tomato sauce with pasta and red wine absorbed our taste buds for the next few minutes. The red wine was especially good at this point as I mused over Theo's story.

Paul pondered for a second then looked up. 'He's incredible, totally mad, but he does have a point, not to give up.'

'Yes, not so mad, in fact I'd say intuitive. This red wine is good; it's making me feel sleepy.' Yawning, I suggested an early night, to sleep.

Next day, we visited the mosaics of Paphos. Taking out my guidebook and read about the pagan mythology surrounding the house of Dionysus, a journey through pagan mythology. Dionysus, god of wine and pleasure, I was reminded of the Cypriot wine the night before that made me feel sleepy and dreamy ... Returning to the present, I felt a sharp tug on my arm as Paul ushered me to the next mosaic: the House of Orpheus and a mosaic of Hercules, fighting the lion of Nemea. Here was the great warrior, the one that Theo had spoken about.

'It reminds me of Alexander the Great.' Paul commented. 'The first time we met, Professor Yannis showed me a fresco depicting Alexander on horseback. The fresco was found on the front of the main tomb. Alexander's horse, Bucephalus, was a spiritual horse.' I wondered if this held any spiritual significance.

As we turned to leave the House of Orpheus, I noticed a perfect mosaic of a peacock. The colours had faded but the intricate detail of this magnificent bird remained. The House of Aion depicting Leda being approached by Zeus in the shape of a swan was the last main mosaic.

'I just don't believe it, nothing! Professor Yannis said to try the house of mosaics, but there is nothing.'

'I would have thought that if you wanted to find such a mosaic, this would be too much of an obvious place to find it,' I suggested.

Paul slumped down against a wall. I squealed as a tiny lizard ran in between the stones of the wall. 'What was that for?'

'A lizard just ran in between where you were sitting,' I squeaked, pointing between his legs.

'You haven't seen one before then?'

'Well no, only on the TV,' I replied.

We continued to look around before returning to the hotel. 'Did you ring him then?'

' 'Yes. I explained that we saw nothing at the mosaics. He is going to get in contact with an old retired friend, Professor Vasilis. He's retired now, but he may be able to help us.'

'Good. I'm off to the gym.'

'I'll come too.'

The gym was empty, the equipment free for us to use. Paul had not used the gym before and I waited to see what he would choose. Seating himself at the rowing machine, he swiftly took hold of the paddles and began to row like fury. I was amazed by his energy. The treadmill felt heavy that morning and my feet did not want to move. I stepped off, choosing to watch Paul instead. His long legs seemed to fold up like a concertina, backwards and forwards. After twenty minutes he stopped. Only slightly out of breath, he got up and glanced at me. 'I'll see you back upstairs then.'

I returned to the changing room and took a shower. Back in our room, there he was, calm, relaxed and reading a book. 'You never cease to amaze me, you're so fit,' I said.

'Unlike you!' His mobile phone rang. It was Professor Vasilis arranging to meet Paul, the next day at the sanctuary at Kouklia.

That evening, I persuaded Paul to visit a local Cypriot tavern. Poulos Taverna was situated in the middle of Paphos. The Greek flag was flying and numerous plants lay around the edge of the establishment.

The waiter took our order, "meze", a variety of Greek dishes to be shared. Paul remarked he didn't mind what it was, just as long as it had squid in it.

I looked around to see another statue of Aphrodite situated in the corner, beautiful, serene, and so delicate, fashioned in cool, white marble.

The waiter appeared bearing dishes of olives in lemon dressing; tahini; taramosalata, octopus in red wine, *zalatina* brawn pickles of capers; *loukanita* smoked Cyprus sausage and *kohlrab*i greens and carrots tossed in oil and bound with egg. Paul looked down at the different platters, searching for the squid. I ate creamy taramosalata with kohlrabi.

A group of Greek musicians walked towards the small platform situated in the middle of the taverna. The enlivening spark of Greek music filled the room. They played the datsia, a local dance frequently heard in many of the Cypriot tavernas. A Greek-Cypriot man in authentic dress stood in the middle of the floor. As the pace of the music increased, he placed a tray topped by a glass tumbler on his head. His arms moved out to the side, as his hands made a circular movement. Then the infamous finger clicking started. Bending at the knees like a Russian Cossack, his movements became faster and faster. Then as he slowed down, somebody passed another glass tumbler and placing, it on top of the previous one, the dancer started again clicking his fingers, bending his knees and kicking his feet in the air. The last two tumblers were placed on top as the music changed to a familiar tune. The dancer stopped and all the tumblers came crashing to the ground. I felt my adrenalin rush. The unmistakable tune of the Zorba dance followed. This was my last chance to go for it. I ran into the semi-circle of people and joined in, kicking my heels.

I could feel my brother and father dancing to this. The dance continued for another ten minutes. Breaking away, I ran back to the table, exhausted, to find Paul still stuffing his face with squid.

The next morning I groaned. 'God, my legs ache.' I was pleased that I had experienced the Zorba dance, but still something was missing.

'At least you didn't dance on the tables,' a distant voice replied from the bathroom.

Washed, dressed and prepared with sunglasses, maps and books, we were ready to visit Kouklia. A quick breakfast in the restaurant of black coffee and bread and marmalade sufficed. I pulled a face, taking a sip of the strong black coffee.

Theo appeared. 'What a face. Please, you need to drink water with black coffee, that's what Greeks do here,' he said, passing me a glass. I thanked him pulling out the guide book from my bag.

'So, what's this Kouklia place then?'

'Well it used to be the old town of Paphos. That is where we're to meet Professor Vasilis at 10,' Paul said, looking at his watch. 'We need to go.'

We arrived at the Sanctuary of Aphrodite and met Professor Vasilis, a small man in a cream jacket and trousers, wearing a trilby sun hat. He introduced himself.

We followed him into the museum where the remains of the sanctuary were to be found. The professor explained to us that part of the building dated back to the Bronze Age, whilst other parts dated back to the Roman period. 'Here,' he said, pointing to a number of gouged-out holes in the wall. 'Unfortunately it's suspected that robbers were searching for the Treasure of Aphrodite.'

Walking into another large room, we saw a wall displaying a large mosaic of Aphrodite. All three of us gazed at the mosaic. 'But this isn't the one with the swan, you know the one Professor Yannis was on about,' I asked.

Paul jumped in. 'What about the vase? Did the professor explain that to you?'

'Yes, he did. If you go to the museum in Paphos, there is a

vase of the type that you are talking about that was excavated three years ago. I haven't been there for years. Being retired now, my legs aren't what they used to be!'

'But how did the vase get here, if that is the one?' I asked.

'Ah, good question,' replied the professor.

'I was just about to ask that question myself,' added Paul.

' Well, by sea. People travelled a lot by sea you know, trading pots, olive oil … any local produce at the time, it wasn't unusual.'

I interrupted. 'Yes, but the mosaic, and what about the second statue?' Paul gave me a nudge.

'A second statue? I have not heard about that, and as for the mosaic, keep looking,' replied the professor.

Paul sighed. 'Thank you for your help.'

'It's my pleasure, it has been good to meet you both, but I must go now. Please give my regards to Professor Yannis when you next speak to him.'

Paul went back to look at the mosaic. I walked just outside the entrance and plonked myself down on a stone. As the sun shone down, I felt the warmth pierce the side of my arm. Suddenly, I saw the image of my father again, he appeared a lot older now. He seemed glad, telling me that happy days would soon be here. I sat there flummoxed.

Paul appeared. 'God you look deep in thought?'

I hesitated. 'I keep, well, have had images, you know, thoughts, dreams about my father on this journey,' I said

'Your father?'

'Yes, I didn't want to say anything up until now. You wouldn't believe me. You'd think I was mad … '

'Go on,' Paul urged, as he crouched down beside me.

'Images of my father, holding my hand when I was little. Just now, he told me that happy days would soon be here – it's bizarre and upsetting. I know I never really knew him, but it's like a part of me that's gone.'

'I'm sorry, I had no idea, but at least you've found some of your relatives, haven't you?'

GETTING CLOSER

It was hot that morning as the sun shone through. I wound the window down and asked Paul if we could go to Limassol first, even though it was in the opposite direction. Limassol was a big, brash and bustling place. The guidebook described it as a cosmopolitan place with great nightlife, plus shopping and drinking venues. We entered the town centre which was filled with numerous market stalls, laden with exotic goods.

My eyes scanned the rows of stalls until a gleaming rail with black leather jackets caught my attention. 'Come on, this way,' I said, taking his hand.

'Remember, an hour … '

'Yes, yes, I know!'

There were dark brown, tan and black leather jackets and bags, as well as other accessories. I scanned the rail. 'Yes, this is the one,' I said, taking hold of a black jacket with large v-shaped lapels. 'Here, try this on.'

He looked taken aback for a second. 'What, me?'

'Yes, you.'

Taking off his denim jacket, he slid the leather one on.

'Perfect fit!' I said, admiring the stylish jacket. 'Do you want it?'

'Well, if you like … ' He replied.

Not giving him a chance to change his mind, I found the sales assistant and pushed the jacket into her hands.

'Thanks,' he smiled.

'Oh, it's nothing. It really suits you.'

The next stall contained fruit and vegetables, sweet biscuits and cakes. I spotted loukoumi, a local Cypriot dish that was jelly-like in appearance and based on fruit like a Turkish delight. I bought a bag and dipped my finger in, tasting the sweet, rose-scented sugar. 'Good with coffee I guess,' I said, passing the bag towards him.

'God, that is sweet, yes. It needs coffee, I agree.'

Another stall, this time selling embroidered lace – the kind of lace that had survived since the Venetians. Picking up a square place mat, I looked at the intricate shapes and designs, painstakingly sewn together. I thought of Andrea – she would appreciate this. Heading back to the museum, I sighed with a sense of satisfaction; I had acquired some Cyprus leather goods, without considering the vegetarian angle.

Driving out of Limassol, the eternal backdrop of bright blue sky and piercing hot sunshine continued to follow us. We passed a sign – "Boat trip to Aphrodite's Rock."

'Look, there it is; a boat trip to Aphrodite's Rock. We have to go there before we leave this island.'

'Maybe,' was the reply.

The rock – the centre of the story of Aphrodite, just as Theo had told us. Paphos appeared in the distance. I got out a map and tried to work out the location of the museum. Just round the corner, it appeared. Paul parked the car. As we walked up to the entrance I took a sweet from my bag. The Paphos Arch museum was a small, flat, white building, with a brightly painted blue seat outside. The first hall contained discoveries from the Neolithic period and the Bronze Age. Gold jewellery caught my attention, just like the gold artefacts found in Vergina. The second hall contained Cypriot vessels, paintings and sculptures. Paul was busy looking closely at every display. I continued to stare at a piece of delicate gold jewellery, four slender chains wound round each other. Then I thought about Livana.

Paul called out to me, 'Look at this!' I walked over unenthusiastically. 'I thought you were interested in this stuff?' "Stuff?" I looked at him. "Stuff?" This archaeologist's language had now turned primitive. 'Yes, these are your Greek vases and statues,' he said, looking at me surprised.

'Oh yes.' I said indifferently.

A bust of Socrates looked back at me. Of course I was interested, but distracted; distracted by thoughts of Livana. Would I find her?

He walked over to another cabinet. I continued to stare at Socrates.

'Over here!' Paul called out. Pulling myself away from Socrates, I walked over and stood beside him. 'There's the vase, and there's the image of Athena and the thunderbolt, just like Professor Yannis said.' He stood back and gazed at the vase, while I stepped in closer and read the information. It dated back to the same period, and had been found in Cyprus.

'Well, that's it then?' I said.

'No, I need to see the bottom of the vase. I can't see it in this position on the shelf, can I?'

'How are you going to get over that then?'

'The museum attendant … I'll have to ring Professor Yannis and get him to speak to the attendant. He's not likely to open the cabinet just for me. I have my credentials on me but I don't think that will be enough.'

Paul found the attendant and began explaining the situation to him in slow, careful English. The attendant rang the professor. A few minutes of raised noisy Greek, then he put the phone down. He stared at Paul, gave him a quick nod and then took out a bunch of keys from underneath the counter. We followed him over to the cabinet. He unlocked it, carefully took hold of the vase, turning it over and peered at the base.

Paul looked carefully at the inscription. '"Megas Alexandro,"' he exclaimed. 'This is definitely the vase,' he said smiling.

I started to squeal, shouting, 'We've found it, that's it then?'

'Not quite, where's the mosaic? We need the mosaic.'

I sighed. 'Oh no! Well, I'm going downstairs,' I said as Paul continued to scrutinise every cabinet.

Downstairs was a small lobby, with rooms leading off in all directions. My eyes passed glass panel after glass panel as I searched. Up ahead a mosaic lay across the floor like the ones in Paphos. Moving closer, I could make out a picture of a woman and a swan. There, in the right hand corner I saw the words "Alexandrou-Olympias." That's it! I ran up the steps nearly tripping in my haste. Catching my breath, I looked round to find Paul, who by this time was sitting on a bench reading a book. 'I've found it, quick!' He looked at me in disbelief, presumably thinking that my active imagination had got the better of me once again.

He followed me down the steps in great anticipation. 'There, see?' I said, pointing to the words.

Paul pulled the glasses down from his head and moved in closer. 'Yes,' he said slowly, 'this is the one … '

Jumping up and down, I kept repeating the words 'It is the one!'

An attendant looked round, wondering what all the commotion was about.

'Just calm down!'

'No I can't, I think it's fantastic!'

'Why not go outside for a cigarette,' he said, hesitating for a second at the idea he had suggested.

'Yes ok, fine.'

We walked out together and sat on the wall. So that was it, the statue did belong to Alexander the Great; all four figurines had been found, along with the vase and finally the mosaic.

'Wouldn't it be good to find the other statue though,' I asked.

'Yes I know, but you can't have everything,' said Paul, a slight tone of disappointment in his voice.

Back in our hotel room, Paul sat in the chair and surveyed all the information. Then he picked up his phone and rang Professor Yannis. I left him to it and went to the gym. Jogging on the treadmill, I thought about my Aunt Livana. Her village, Nata, was our next destination. Stepping off the machine, I took a quick shower then headed back upstairs.

In the restaurant I found my favourite table and stared at the Aphrodite statue.

'What are you going to have?' Paul asked, noticing me gazing at the statue.

'Souvlaki me lakhanika.'

'Which is?'

'Vegetable kebabs.'

'Beef a la Paphos, I think would be good.'

Theo appeared. 'You've chosen then?'

'Nai, parakalo,' I replied.

'How about wine? You haven't tried the famous Cypriot Commandria red – it's a honey red wine, a red wine, deep with passion that runs through your veins.' I looked at Theo shocked; then looked at Paul.

'She could do with that!' said Paul, grinning.

'Yes, it's time to celebrate, we've found a … ' I burst in then stopped, sending an quizzical look towards Paul.

Theo looked at me. 'You've found a … ?'

'Yes, we've found a marvellous museum with wonderful ancient Cypriot artefacts.'

'Yes. Oh I see. Well anyway … ' Presumably, Theo wondered why finding a museum could prompt such a celebration. 'Commandria has a story. It was your Richard the Lionheart who, when he came to this island, exported it to many European countries. Much of course went to England.'

'Fascinating.' said Paul, pointing to the bottle. 'In that case we'll have some of that.'

When Theo had poured our wine and returned to the kitchen, Paul exclaimed, 'Deep passion through your veins! God, what will he come out with next?'

'Never mind that, how about "she could do with that." What was that supposed to mean?' I asked.

'Well, look at that couple over there.'

The young couple were spooning ice-cream to each other. The man stopped to give his partner a kiss on the lips. I gazed intently at Paul, then stood up and leant over the table. 'What like this?' I stretched forward landing my lips on his. He responded, holding tight for another few seconds before I drew away.

'Yes, like that,' he replied.

Theo appeared just at that moment and placed our dishes on the table. I took a sip of the red wine; it tickled the back of my throat. The sweet taste was irresistible and I found myself taking a large mouthful. My vision was starting to blur, and I saw two Aphrodite statues merging before my eyes. A quick chat with Dionysus was needed:

Dear Dionysus Theo, the waiter is fantastic, telling us a story all about red wine and Richard the Lionheart.

Dear Katalina Yes it is true, but what is your question? Remember, I am the god of merriment.

Dear Dionysus Should life be lived to the full, and if so how?

Dear Katalina Yes, of course it should be lived to the full. In fact life should be lived for the moment, and you are starting to do this. It's what Greeks do best, sometimes with the help of alcohol and dancing. I might add the alcohol needs to be taken in moderation, at which you don't appear to have been too successful.

Dear Dionysus I take your point, perhaps more dancing and less alcohol would be better. However, for today I don't think I've achieved that very well.

Dear Katalina I would agree with you; never mind, there is always tomorrow.

On our journey to Nata, the Cypriot countryside appeared different from that in England. No lush green grass, instead a pale sunburnt landscape, an abundance of wild flowers and olive groves. Up ahead a signpost indicated "Nata 4 Km." We were nearly there and my heart started beating faster. I glanced at the map Philip had given me. Looking up at my reflection in the mirror, I spotted a white car. As it drew nearer, I could see the driver.

'I don't believe it, it's that … ' my voice slowed, ' … policeman.'

'What, the one you thought was following you?'

'Yes, that one.'

The car increased in speed and a siren began to wail. The car drew up beside us and the driver beckoned us to stop. Paul pulled over to the side of the road and switched off the engine. . My hands felt very clammy and my heart beat like a pair of jogging feet that couldn't get away. We stepped out. The police officer spoke English. 'Are you Katalina Sokritos?' he asked in a strong Greek accent.

'Nai,' I replied, starting to giggle nervously.

'Please don't try to be clever,' he replied.

Paul gave me a nudge in the ribs. 'Yes I am, why?'

'Do you have a passport on you?'

'Yes, I do.'

Paul asked, 'Please can I ask what this is all about?'

'I'm afraid we cannot discuss this here, you will need to follow me to the police station at Paphos.'

'Oh God, I'll never get to see whether Livana's alive.'

Paul jabbed me in the ribs again. 'Ssh, just keep calm; I'm sure there's a simple explanation.'

We followed the police officer's car back to Paphos. Silence; no words, just a dark black menacing cloud pervaded my thoughts. A last cigarette seemed the only good thing left at that moment. My mind went back to the newspaper article I had seen in Athens: "Greek Sokritos shot a Turk." Of course, that must be what this was all about. I was just about to say something to Paul when the car stopped; we had arrived. The police officer stepped out and waited for us to follow. I looked up to see a red-topped building with small windows. The police officer led us into the building and then into a small dark room: a table and two chairs, a small skylight window giving the only light. The place reminded me of my father, all those years spent in Jail in Cairo, tortured by the Arab police; my heart sank.

The police officer slapped a newspaper down on the table, the same newspaper that I had just recalled. There it was in black and white: "Greek Sokritos shot a Turk."

Suddenly, with nervous laughter, I blurted out, 'Bloody Turks, you never know where they're going to be next!'

Paul's hand flew round and smacked me on the arm. 'Are you crazy? You'll get us arrested at this rate.'

'Please Madame, this is no laughing matter. Nowadays, we try to keep the peace as much as possible here in Cyprus. Those on both sides of the Green Line try to avoid trouble if they can.' He stared at me for a few moments, letting his words sink in. 'How long have you been on the island?' he continued.

'A few days, I'm carrying out some research, this is my fiancée Katalina and she's trying to find her Greek Cypriot relatives,' Paul replied.

The police officer nodded with approval. 'Can you show me your passports?' I took the passports out of my bag. He examined them thoroughly, nodding again.

'Please can you tell us what the connection then is between this event, and, I can only presume, Katalina's name?'

The policeman flicked his pen. 'The Greek Sokritos shot this Turk, some say by accident. We believe a sudden argument broke out, and unbeknown to the Turk, the Greek had a gun. Things got heated and very quickly out of control, and well, the rest is history. The Greek obviously ran in a panic. We have been trying to trace his relatives to locate his whereabouts. We thought he had relatives in Athens.'

I interrupted him. 'That was the first time I saw you, in the archive library, wasn't it?'

'Yes it was, we had to suspect anybody with this name and so that is why you have been followed.'

'Well I can assure you I know of no Sokritos family member I've met so far that could be involved in a murder.'

'You've shown me your passports, but is there anything else that can prove to us who you are?'

I showed him some family photos and then came up with the idea of telephoning Andrea. The police officer agreed to this. I dialled the number. Everybody waited patiently. Eventually

Andrea answered and, breathlessly, I explained what had happened. I passed the phone to the police officer. Finally, after a heated discussion, the police officer said 'Efcharisto,' and replaced the receiver.

'Your friend, hmm ... Yes, she is obviously Greek, and she has confirmed fully who you are. You are free to go. I hope that you find your relatives.'

CELEBRATIONS

'Double ouzo and tonic, double port and double everything,' I said, raising my hands in the air towards Theo.

Paul stepped in front of me. 'Cancel all of that. You need food first.' He gestured to Theo to put the bottle back on the shelf.

'Yes but I'm … I'm stressed after that … '

'Aren't we all,' he said. Taking my hand, he led me upstairs. I sat in the armchair, and started tapping my fingers on the armrest. 'What did happen to my father in Cairo?'

Paul looked at me. 'What do you mean what happened?'

'Why was he tortured?' I asked feeling confused.

'Oh yes, I remember, the story your niece told us. I don't know Katalina, I don't know,' he said in a helpless tone. 'Here, drink this coffee, you should rest now. We can go to the village tomorrow.'

I took his advice and slept for a while. Later, refreshed, I announced that I would like to go to the taverna. Paul conceded, with the agreement that we would be back by midnight. Arriving at the taverna, we found a table and ordered our drinks. A group of musicians appeared. As they began to play, people rose from their seats to dance. The sounds of laughter and clapping filled the taverna. I fiddled one of the straps on my red satin top.

'You are not going to join in, that top will come down!'

'No it won't, there is some elastic here somewhere,' I replied, fiddling with the other strap. Ignoring Paul I leapt from my seat to join the dancers. Two waiters cleared some tables and pushed the tables towards the dance floor. Suddenly, one of the dancers leapt up onto a table and started kicking his heels, his arms waving in the air. He beckoned to the others to join him, but no one responded. Spotting my chance, I ran up to the table. He grabbed my arm and pulled me up to join him, then held me tightly, one arm around my shoulder. We began kicking our legs in time with the music. I quickly adjusted my strap that had slipped down towards my elbow. Paul's face was a picture as he stared at me with his mouth open. I felt fantastic, like a true Greek. Soon, two other people joined us on. Paul stood up and promptly walked towards me. Urgently, he tugged at my leg. Taking my hand, he helped me down from the table then, to my surprise, linked arms with the others on the floor and started dancing, kicking his legs.

Later, walking back to the hotel, we found another gift shop still open. 'I'll stay outside,' said Paul. 'Little knickknacks aren't really my thing!'

Entering the shop, I immediately spotted a shelf containing small white statues. There in the middle was a model of Aphrodite with Athena at her side. I just knew I had to buy it. Marching out of the shop, I presented my treasure to Paul.

'Aphrodite, of course,' said Paul, smiling.

'Or Athena,' I replied.

Next day, we were on the road again, heading towards Nata. I hoped that this time, there would be no diversions. The roads were rough and bumpy, as we drove closer to our destination. I looked ahead to see an expanse of bush, olive groves and the traditional flat roof-tops of houses. 'We're here!' I exclaimed with excitement. The village was very small, with only a few houses and a café, bearing a sign, showing the Greek word "Nata." 'Let's go in there,' I said, seeking a distraction. 'We can get a coffee or something.'

Inside, we found a group of elderly Greek men, some playing backgammon. The strong smell of cigarettes and coffee filled the air. As I walked to the counter, the men stopped talking and turned round to look at me. Nervously I spoke. 'Kalimera.'

Suddenly I remembered reading that some old villages still only allowed men into their cafes. I looked at Paul. 'Come here, I feel really uncomfortable, they obviously don't like women in there.' We walked back outside and I pulled out a photo of Livana. 'Here, perhaps you could go back in and show them this photo to see if any of them recognise her.'

'Are you nuts,' asked Paul

'Oh please, you saw the look they gave me.'

Paul took the photo and walked back into the café. I stood

back from the door, wondering what their reaction would be. Outside on the wall, a goat's skull was hung beside some orange lanterns. The sound of raised voices came from inside. I could only make out the word "ochi". Paul joined me outside. 'Well, did you have any luck? I heard the word no.'

'I'm, sorry,' he replied, 'none of them recognised the woman from the photo.'

'Come on, let's walk up here. I can see some buildings up ahead.'

Continuing into the village, we came across a small school with two children in the playground. One boy had a patch over his eye, the other had grabbed hold of a large black tyre and was rolling it along a gravelled surface. A tall woman then appeared. 'Kalimera.'

I returned the greeting and asked whether she spoke English. When she nodded, I told her of my reason for my visit. The woman invited me into the school, asking if I would like to look around. 'Nai parakalo,' I replied.

'I'll stay here,' said Paul.

I followed the woman into the school building. The main classroom was of average size. Sitting at one of the tables was a little girl diligently attending to a jigsaw puzzle. The woman told me a little about the Greek education system. Half-listening, I turned to look at the girl: such dark curly hair and deep brown eyes; and busily intent on finishing a jigsaw puzzle.

We walked out into the bright warm sun. 'If you carry on up the hill, there are some more houses. You may have some luck there,' she instructed me.

I thanked her and joined Paul, who was standing by a tree trying to shade himself from the sun. Continuing up the hill, we found a deserted white church, with a shrine surrounded by the remains of old buildings left over from the island's earthquake.

Outside one house sat an elderly man, enjoying the sun. I walked up to him and took the photo out of my bag. 'Kalimera,' I said.

'Kalimera.'

I held the photo in front of him. At first, he was totally expressionless as he looked at the picture then, screwing up his eyes, a slow smile appeared. 'Nai, nai.' God, I thought, he recognises her. The old man stood up and pointed further up the road. 'Nai, nai,' he repeated.

I thanked him and turned to Paul. 'Great but which house does he mean?' he asked.

'Well there aren't exactly millions of them. I guess we'll just have to try each one,' I said, trying to contain my excitement.

I knocked at the first house – nobody home. The second house drew the same response. I knocked on the third door, waited and was just about to walk away when the door opened. An elderly woman with white hair, dressed in black and wearing a white apron looked up at me. 'Kalimera,' I said. Taking the photo out of my bag, I passed it to her, wondering how she would respond.

She looked at it and smiled. 'Nai,' she said, and pointed to herself.

I stared at her and smiled. My God, I've found her. Tears started to roll down my face. Paul stood next to me and took a tissue from his pocket. 'Thanks.' The woman led us into her kitchen and invited us to sit down.

I sat speechless and tearful, so Paul spoke. 'It's Livana, isn't it? This is Katalina, we've come from England.'

'Nai, yes I must be, Katalina's aunt, her father's sister.' Livana was amazed, overwhelmed that a niece had come all this way in search of her.

Without thinking, I leapt up and hugged her. She responded with a massive Greek hug back. I told her about our journey, about how I had found Philip on Santorini and Sebastien in Athens. Livana smiled. I then gave her a small package. 'I believe it's traditional to give a gift,' I said.

Livana opened it. 'A photo of you and your father in a beautiful silver frame,' she exclaimed, and smiled.

I then asked her how she came to live in Cyprus. She explained that she and her husband had moved from Santorini to northern

Cyprus in the late 1960s. During the 1970s, the Turks had invaded, separating the north from the south so they were forced to flee. Livana became quiet for a while then gradually revealed that her husband had been killed. He had forgotten something from their house and had insisted on going back when he was shot by a Turkish solder. He died later in hospital. 'So I brought my children here and set up a home,' she finished.

Livana stood and began to prepare snacks and drinks. The front door opened and a young woman appeared. 'This is my daughter, Aysia' said Livana.

Still overwhelmed, I summoned enough energy to stand and shake her hand.

Paul shook her hand too. 'God, you look just like my brother's daughter in Sicily, doesn't she,' he said, turning to me.

'Yes she does.'

'Please you must all sit down and eat, we have lots to catch up on. Tomorrow there will be a wedding in the village. You must come back and join us.'

Finally, we returned to our hotel just in time for an evening meal. Theo served our drinks, this time Palamino, a fresh fruity Cypriot white. 'The wine of the gods,' he announced, bowing towards me.

'Oh God, we're off again,' muttered Paul under his breath.

'Dionysus himself, the god of dance and merriment would approve. A time to celebrate,' said Theo.

'Well, you're right there,' I said.

'You have a reason to celebrate then?' asked Theo.

'Yes, I found my aunt in the village of Nata.'

'Bravo, you must try this wine; it's certainly a time to celebrate!'

Paul frowned then smiled.

In the bathroom that evening, I picked up a hairbrush, trying to brush out the knots from my wet hair. Paul rushed in. 'Where are my glasses? I had them a minute ago.'

'Careful,' I cried out as he nearly bumped into me.

His glasses were there on the shelf. He picked them up, then looked in the mirror and saw my face. Placing the glasses down again, he gently took the brush from my hand. I sent him a fleeting glance, giving him the signal to continue. He stroked the back of my hair. Without thinking, I blurted out the word "Trowel."

Paul stood back. 'What?' he asked, bemused.

'Trowel; it's a word association game. You say the next word that comes into your mind, that sort of thing.'

He looked confused for a moment then understanding dawned. 'OK. "professor",' he said.

'"Greek",' I replied.

He looked me in the eyes. '"Athena",' he said, taking both my hands.

I felt elated next morning as I stood in the bathroom and logged onto the website:

Dear Athena	**I've found my aunt Livana, I cannot believe it, thank you.**
Dear Katalina	**Brilliant, I thought you might find her. I told you that my courage would take you along this journey.**
Dear Athena	**Thank you, yes, you have given me courage, but now I need to speak to Aphrodite.**
Dear Aphrodite	**That time at the Parthenon, I said there was something more.**
Dear Katalina	**Yes, you did.**
Dear Aphrodite	**I now know what it is!**
Dear Katalina	**What is it then?**
Dear Aphrodite	**Easy, I love Paul, that's what it is!**
Dear Katalina	**Excellent, I'm pleased for you. PS – look after your mobile.**

As I stepped out of the shower thoughts of finding Livana dominated so that I didn't hear the bathroom door open. I turned the water off and heard Paul exclaim, 'Oh my God. "Dear Aphrodite, easy I love Paul … "' Curiosity had the better of Paul and I peeked out from the shower to see him scrutinising the message I had just typed in. My body dripping with water, I stared at him. He stared back at me and smiled.

'You must think I'm mad,' I said.

'No, not at all, I think it's quite different … yes, different.' He turned to leave then paused. 'Anyway, why the interest in these Greek gods?'

I told him about a teacher at school, Mrs Fryer, an American who had taught classical studies. I had been fascinated by all the Greek myths and legends and my interest in the Greek gods remained. I still felt embarrassed by what he had seen, but it didn't seem to matter anymore.

We headed back towards the village, for another Greek wedding. I wondered if it would be like the one on Santorini. Livana and Alysia came out to greet us and together, we walked down to the church. Stone steps led up to the main door and a large Greek flag flew from the rooftop. We arrived early and Livana insisted that I go into the church before the service. She handed me a candle, beckoning me to follow her. Candle lit, I crossed myself and leant towards the icon, kissing the saint's picture. Paul stood back, watching us. The church soon filled up and we just managed to squeeze into the back. The ceremony was of course all in Greek, but I was used to this now. The air soon filled with incense and the smell of burning candles. After the marriage service, the bride and groom walked outside to be sprayed with a fountain of confetti. Around the back of the church, long tables of food had been served and in the small forecourt, musicians were preparing their instruments, including the violin, laouto, and a set of four double strings. They played the sickle dance, a traditional dance often performed at social occasions. A man dressed in black leather boots, trousers, white shirt and black waistcoat, holding a sickle, walked onto the stage. As the music quickened in pace, he made great swiping movements in the air. The music increased in pace as each movement became faster and faster, accompanied by somersaults around the swift movements of the sickle. Finally, as he plunged to the ground, everyone applauded. Next, the Antikristos: a graceful dance with men and women standing in rows opposite each other. Alysia took my hand and took me to join the women, whilst another villager took Paul's hand and led him to join the men. Paul faced me nervously and we looked intently at the others. It seemed easy enough to follow, until I found myself confused by the complicated steps, much to Paul's amusement. A few moments later, we dropped out from the dance, bursting with laughter and collapsing onto the ground. Finally the bridal dance: the couple joined hands, and much to my amazement, everyone dived into their pockets and bags, pulling out banknotes, then rushing up to the bride and groom to pin them on to their clothes.

Eventually, everyone stopped to rest and found ourselves being led towards a large table laden with food. Livana and Alysia joined us telling us about the different dishes. There was *loukanika*, Cypriot sausage soaked in red wine; *kleftis*, grilled lamb; *seftalia,* grilled meatballs; and so the list went on. The rich desserts included *keik me bana*, or banana cake, and a variety of Greek pastries. At the end of the table a plate contained something that looked like meringues.

'What are these?' I asked.

'Rose tartlets; in memory of Aphrodite, if you like.'

'Aphrodite?'

'Yes, the rose is a symbol of love, and Aphrodite is the goddess of love. Rose petals are collected, washed, sorted and crystallised. Daktila, bouzekia and baklava are all flavoured with rose water. The rose tartlets are made of ground almonds, egg whites, sugar, rose water and puff pastry,' Alysia explained.

I took a bite. 'You can taste the roses.'

Aunt Livana spoke. 'You know your dad hated eating chicken.'

I noticed Paul taking a bite of chicken. 'Why was that?'

' His father, a farmer, made him kill them … you know, wring their necks.'

'Oh God!' I exclaimed with disgust.

'Yes precisely, ever since then, he refused to eat chicken,' she said, placing a bowl down. 'Please, before I forget, you must come back to the house. I have something to show you both.'

After the festivities, we followed Livana and Alysia back to the house. Seated in the kitchen, I noticed a photo on the dresser. I walked over to pick it up. It was a picture of me when I was little holding my dad's hand. Was it my dad or Livana that had brought me here, I wondered? I turned away from the photo as Livana walked into the kitchen. 'You brought me here, didn't you?'

She touched me on the shoulder and smiled, then placed a rectangular wooden box on the table. Slowly, she removed the lid and lifted out a tiny statue of Aphrodite.

Paul was stunned. 'You have the second statue! How?' he asked.

'This statue has been passed down generation after generation. I believe Alexander had it made in memory of his childhood sweetheart. During the Second World War it had to be hidden from the Germans. In fact over the centuries it has been hidden from many invaders,' explained Livana.

Paul took the statue and carefully turned it upside down. He put on his glasses and peered at the base. 'It has the markings, just like the ones on the statue in Los Angeles,' he said, showing me.

'I don't believe it. Why was a second statue made?' I asked.

Paul cleared his throat. 'Well, I read that when Alexander came to Cyprus he discovered that his teenage sweetheart, Cassandra, had been killed by the Persians and so he had a smaller statue made in her memory. I was suspicious at first, but hey!'

Livana walked back into the lounge, returning with a small envelope, and gave it to Paul. Looking surprised, he asked, 'What's this?'

'Open it, please,' said Livana. Putting his hand into the envelope, he pulled out a small gold cross. 'For you, it was my husband's, you should have it.'

'But how can I … ?'

'I insist, please.'

'I wouldn't argue with her, she's Greek!' I exclaimed. Paul fell silent. 'Here, let me put it on for you,' I said, taking hold of the chain and clipping it around his neck.

As we left, Livana called out, 'Keep in touch.'

'Yes we will,' we answered.

Stepping into the car, Paul retrieved his mobile and rang Professor Yannis, putting the phone on speaker mode so that I could hear both sides of the conversation. 'Yes, it's true, Katalina's aunt had the second statue all this time, I saw it with my own eyes.'

'Bravo, Bravo, you have done well. A victory for all Greeks!' exclaimed the professor.

Driving out of the village, my mind buzzed. I didn't know what to think about first: Livana, the villagers, the wedding, the food, or the dancing. She was the final missing piece to both Paul's search and my own. I took out a book on Buddhism and turned the page, taking a drag from my cigarette. 'Just before we get back, let me read you this,' I said. *'Night designates the contemplation of invisible things after the manner of Moses, who entered into the darkness where God was, this God who makes of darkness his hiding place. Surrounded by the living night the soul seeks him who is hidden in darkness.'*

I was about to continue when he placed his hand on the book. 'Very nice and very deep, but now it's your turn to listen to me.'

'Listen to you?'

'Yes, I want you to close your eyes now.'

'Why?'

'Don't argue, just do it, it won't be for long.'

I closed my eyes and wondered what would happen next, as the car continued over bumps in the road, swerving round corners.

It was strange that when you closed your eyes you could feel all of these things. A few minutes later I felt the car stop. I opened my eyes. There in the foreground stood Aphrodite's Rock.

'Oh my, I thought you had forgotten.'

'No I hadn't.'

We crossed the road and walked over a wooden bridge looking at a magnificent angular piece of rock that dominated the sunset horizon. In my head, I spoke to Aphrodite:

Dear Aphrodite **I've found Cyprus, I've found Livana and another statue and I've found Paul. I still have a long way to go but thank you.**

Dear Katalina **Excellent. Cyprus is beautiful, Livana is lovely and you've found Paul. Yes, you still have a long way to go but that is the same for all of us. Well done!**

I stood and contemplated the rock – Aphrodite, my goddess of love. Once a year, the people of Paphos assembled at an ancient shrine to commemorate her existence and her gift of love.

The sea was calm, and the waves made gentle splashing sounds against the sides of the boat. Aphrodite loomed closer, and the sea and sky seemed to disappear as we approached the great rock. Stepping onto its surface we stood together.

'Here, I have something for you,' Paul said.

He pulled out a red velvet box. Opening it, I gasped at the beautiful silver cross encrusted with diamonds that shone like stars in the night sky. I stood on tiptoes and reached up to kiss him.

This was both the beginning and the end: a struggle; a journey across the sea, a desperate search and a desire to find one's true roots linked with the origins of a statue. I thought back to our adventures: archaeological ruins, mysterious policemen and dynamic Greek waiters. The Green Line to Aphrodite was now complete.

Turning towards each other, the rock surrounded us like a deep white cloak of snow.

'Where to next?' I asked.

'That's easy, Cairo,' Paul replied.

'Oh, that's where my dad and brother grew up.'

I smiled at him, wondering what the future might hold.

EPILOGUE

A small girl clad in white appeared offering me a gold box. I opened it and gasped: inside lay a familiar gold watch. Gently, I reached in to the box, took out the watch and held it up to the sun. Turning it, I read the Inscription – *Stavros Sokritos, Cairo 1948.*

BIBLIOGRAPHY

Cartledge, Paul. *Alexander The Great, The hunt for a new past.* Macmillan. 2004
Hann, Thich Nhat. *Living Buddha, Living Christ*. Rider. 1995

For further reading
Souli, Sofia. *Greek Mythology*. Toubis. 1995